W9-BJM-634

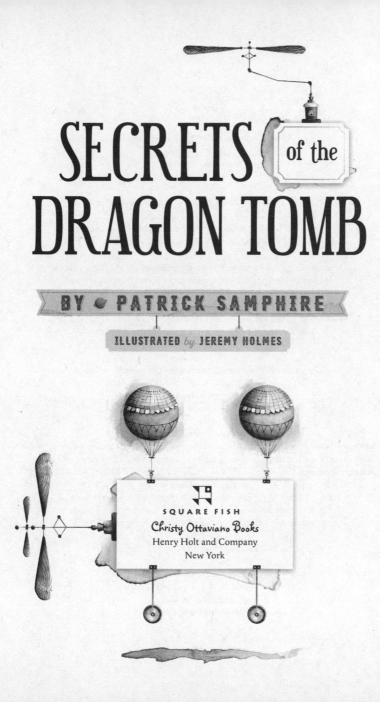

SECRETS of the DRAGON TOMB

BY PATRICK SAMPHIRE

ILLUSTRATED by JEREMY HOLMES

SQUARE FISH

Christy Ottaviano Books

Henry Holt and Company

New York

SQUARE
FISH

An imprint of Macmillan Publishing Group, LLC
175 Fifth Avenue
New York, NY 10010
mackids.com

Our books may be purchased in bulk for promotional, educational, or business use.
Please contact your local bookseller or the Macmillan Corporate and Premium
Sales Department at (800) 221-7945 ext. 5442 or by e-mail at
MacmillanSpecialMarkets@macmillan.com.

Library of Congress Cataloging-in-Publication Data

Samphire, Patrick.
Secrets of the dragon tomb / Patrick Samphire.
pages ; cm
"Christy Ottaviano Books."
Summary: While dreaming of being a spy like those in his favorite magazine, twelve-year-old
Edward has been stuck holding his eccentric family together but when his parents are kidnapped,
he leads his sisters and cousin in an effort to rescue them across the danger-filled landscape of
nineteenth-century Mars.
ISBN 978-1-250-10415-1 (paperback)   ISBN 978-0-8050-9907-2 (ebook)
[1. Eccentrics and eccentricities—Fiction.   2. Family life—Fiction.
3. Kidnapping—Fiction.   4. Mars—Fiction.   5. Science fiction.]
I. Title.
PZ7.1.S255Sec 2016   Fic—dc23   2015004517

Originally published in the United States by Christy
Ottaviano Books/Henry Holt and Company
First Square Fish Edition: 2017
Square Fish logo designed by Filomena Tuosto

1 3 5 7 9 10 8 6 4 2

For Stephanie—
Without you, this book would never have been.

And for Ben—
I think you would have liked this one.
Sorry you never got to see it.

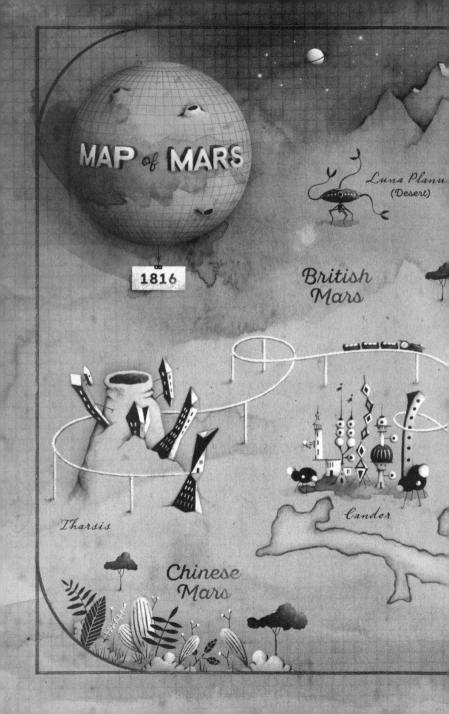

Lunae

Wilderness

Ophir

Sullivan
House

SECRETS of the
DRAGON TOMB

PART ONE

Uninvited Guests

A Complete Disaster

Mars, 1816

I was dangling from a rope, fifty feet up the side of a great pillar of red Martian rock, with my arms buried in a sopping curtain of tanglemoss and bury-beetles trying to build a hill over my head, when I finally realized I had chosen the wrong summer vacation.

My friend Matthew, Viscount Harrison's son, had invited me to spend the summer with him. But no. I'd decided to come home instead.

What an idiot.

Right about now, Matthew's family would be settling down for their tea or going for a quiet stroll in the warm afternoon air. In the evening, when the glitterswarms rose from the depths of the Valles Marineris to spread like a cloth of gold across the sky, they would raise a toast to King George, like any normal family on British Mars.

What they would absolutely, definitely not be doing was swaying dangerously halfway up a giant stack of rock, hunting for an angry bushbear.

This hadn't exactly been my plan when I got up this morning.

What I *had* planned was to get my latest copy of *Thrilling Martian Tales*, lock my bedroom door, and be left alone until lunchtime. I'd finished my chores and even made a great big "Do Not Disturb" sign for my door—to keep my little sister, Putty, out.

In the last issue of *Thrilling Martian Tales*, Captain W. A. Masters, British-Martian spy, had been left hanging by one hand from a mountain temple while the tyrant's dragon swooped down upon him.

I'd hardly been able to sit still all month, waiting to find out what would happen in the next issue. If *I* had been Captain Masters, I would have waited until the dragon was almost upon me, then launched myself onto its neck, clambered onto its back, and battled the tyrant riding it. But Captain Masters always did something unexpected.

Today, I would find out what.

Or I would have, if our malfunctioning ro-butler hadn't wandered off, taking the mail with him.

I caught up with the ro-butler just in time to see him coming down the attic ladder carrying three parasols and a wig stand, but no mail. So, with a sigh, I climbed up into the horrific chaos of our attic to see where he might have put it.

I didn't find my *Thrilling Martian Tales*, but what I did find was an infestation of crannybugs. The tiny creatures had snuck in during the night and built their little glass palaces under the rafters. Now they were hanging out their miniature silk flags. Soon, they would be multiplying.

I put my head into my hands and groaned.

Matthew had every issue of *Thrilling Martian Tales*, back to the rare issue no. 1 with the free clockwork death spinner that Captain Masters had used to destroy the Emerald Tyrant's flying palace.

I'd never even read that issue. And there wouldn't have been any crannybugs in Viscount Harrison's house. If there had been, I wouldn't have had to deal with them. Viscount Harrison's valet would have sent out to Isaac's Xenological Emporium for a consignment of catbirds to chase the crannybugs right back out of the attic. Or, if Isaac's was out of catbirds, he might have sent the automatic servants up to the attic, armed with dusters and drills, to clear away the crannybugs' palaces, and hope the creatures would leave in a huff.

But no. Here I was instead, while my family tootled about in their own little worlds, leaving it all to me.

Any *normal* family would do something that would actually get rid of the crannybugs, before they ate completely through the rafters and collapsed the roof down on top of us all.

Not my family.

My family is not good at that kind of thing. They wouldn't notice the crannybugs until the house collapsed and they were sitting there in the dust and rubble, wondering what had happened.

Which left it to me to save us all from complete disaster, as always.

That was why, an hour later, Putty and I found ourselves on top of one of those pillars of rock, searching through the thick curtains of tanglemoss for the only thing—other than a catbird—that could clear out an infestation of crannybugs: a bushbear.

The bushbear is an evil-looking creature, all spikes and tongues and damp, moldy fur. It lives deep in the wet, slimy folds of tanglemoss, only peeking out at sundown with tiny, bloodshot eyes. If you can drag it into the daylight, it curls up tighter than a hedgehog and you can take it back with you to deal with the crannybugs.

Bushbears try to eat crannybugs, but that's not what bothers the crannybugs. What they really don't like is the bushbear's horrible appearance and general bad temper. Put a bushbear nearby, and the crannybugs get so offended they move out.

Of course, first I had to find one, and that was turning out to be harder than I'd hoped.

From up here on the pillar of rock, I could see the whole of Papa's estate. The house itself was a great, sprawling mess of a building on the shores of the Valles Marineris. To either side, thick stands of fern-trees whispered and chattered to each other whenever the wind blew, but in front of the house, the lawns stretched down to the water, and good English oaks lined the drive.

Right now, the lawns were being covered by stalls and trestle tables for Mama's long-planned garden party, which was due to take place tomorrow afternoon. Ridiculous, fake native Martian hovels were being erected on the edge of the fern-trees, and workmen were arguing over the half-finished, towering dragon tomb that Mama was having built beside the water's edge just for the party. Beside it, a steam lifter stood motionless, its enormous arms spread wide, puffing steam from its mouth into the clear sky.

The dozens of pillars of Martian rock behind the house formed a maze of gullies and dead ends. Mama had wanted them flattened so she could have a proper, carefully designed wilderness like the one on her father's estate, but Papa wouldn't hear of it.

Which was a good thing, because without the pillars, the blankets of tanglemoss wouldn't grow, there would be no bushbears, and we wouldn't be able to do a thing about the crannybugs that would soon collapse the house around our ears.

So, as I said, Putty and I were on top of a pillar of rock. Although, when I said "on top," I meant Putty was on top, looking after the rope, while I swung halfway down with the rope around my waist, clawing through the thick moss.

I tried to imagine myself as Captain W. A. Masters, battling my way to the lair of a tyrant of Ancient Mars. Except Captain W. A. Masters would have a helichute or sharp-clawed grip-gloves and would swing easily down the precarious rock face. He certainly wouldn't have to rely on Putty keeping him safe.

There's something you should know about Putty. First, her name isn't Putty. She's my little sister, and her name is Parthenia, but "Putty" fits her far better. Putty is nine years old, three years younger than me. She is incredibly enthusiastic and as impressionable as wet putty. Show her a new idea, and she'll throw herself into it like a diver from the top of a cliff.

A month ago, for instance, she met a photonic mechanician and spent the next few weeks poring over books about photonic capture and emission devices. Before that, she read an article by the celebrated xenologist Frank Herbert Kynes and decided to dedicate her life to the study of sandfish. She even got halfway through building a sandfish containment tank in the corner of her bedroom before she encountered the photonic mechanician. And before that . . . Well, you get the idea. Right now, Putty had decided she was going to be Papa. This was one of her more common obsessions. At least once a year, she turned herself into a little doppelgänger of Papa, complete with tweed jacket, disheveled hair, and eyeglasses she didn't need, to Mama's complete despair.

The other thing you need to know about Putty—and this

one is much more important—is that she's very easily distracted. Which might make it seem odd that I would be hanging fifty feet up in the air, suspended only by a rope that Putty was looking after. Well, it was odd. But the chances of me being able to persuade either of my older sisters, Olivia and Jane, to do anything so improper and unladylike were slightly less than zero.

Which left me with Putty, who was at least enthusiastic.

"I say, Edward."

I shoved my way free of a fold of tanglemoss and shook the damp from my face. Putty was looking down at me.

"Are you holding that rope?" I shouted.

A guilty look crossed Putty's face, and her head disappeared. A moment later, she reappeared. "Yes," she called.

"What is it?" I said. I dug one hand deep into the tanglemoss, just in case.

"Is that a pterodactyl, do you think?"

I twisted around and squinted in the direction she was pointing. High above the house, coming toward us from over the glittering water of the Valles Marineris, was a tiny but growing black speck.

You don't often see wild pterodactyls these days, but from time to time you can glimpse one flapping past, far out over the water. I'd heard there were several breeding colonies on the Chinese side of the Valles Marineris, and a hundred miles or so down the coast from us, well away from civilization, there was a pterodactyl reserve. Even so, it would be rare for one to fly so close to where humans lived.

The brightness of the sun and the glare from the water made it impossible for me to see the shape clearly, but it didn't look quite right. It was bobbing and slipping from side to side in an unpredictable, jerky manner, quite unlike the usual smooth glide of a pterodactyl. A strange whirring sound accompanied it, too, growing quickly louder.

It sagged down briefly, almost catching on a chimney.

"Oh, no," I said as I realized what it was. "Oh, no."

It was a cycle-copter, but its balloon had almost deflated and was dragging behind it. From what I could see, its springs were completely wound down. Its rider was pedaling as fast as humanly possible, but it was hardly enough to keep the device up. The blades spun manically above his head.

The cycle-copter brushed the tops of the fern-trees, then tipped to one side and stuttered its way up again, heading right toward the pillars of red rock.

The rider wrenched one of his steering levers. His cycle-copter lurched around the first of the pillars, slipping sideways and down. The rider gave a shout of alarm and tugged the other steering lever. The cycle-copter straightened. Now it was aiming directly at me.

"Down, you idiot!" I shouted. "Go down!"

The rider's legs spun even faster, and the cycle-copter surged up.

But not far enough. The pillars were at least a hundred

feet tall. No amount of pedaling was going to lift a damaged cycle-copter and rider that high.

"No!" I yelled, waving my free arm wildly.

A grimace of horror crossed the rider's face, and he did absolutely the worst thing possible. He let go of both steering levers and covered his face with his hands. The cycle-copter spun, completely out of control. It crunched into the pillar, not six feet above me, and buried itself in the tanglemoss.

The rope holding me parted, sliced neatly through by the copter blades, and dropped down.

Parts of cycle-copter clattered past me. A spring broke free with a twang. I hid my face in the tanglemoss. A shower of brass cogs spun by, bouncing off my shoulders and back.

"Edward!" Putty shouted.

I pulled my face free to shout back that I was unhurt, but before I could, a great tearing sound came from above.

The whole blanket of tanglemoss ripped free of the rock, and I was falling.

— 2 —

A Wet Landing

If you're going to fall fifty feet with the remains of a cycle-copter right behind you, it's a good idea to do it in a blanket of tanglemoss. Tanglemoss is softer than a pillow—although a whole lot wetter—and can be several feet thick.

I hit the ground with a squelch and a thump that knocked the breath from my chest. Pieces of metal thudded around me, embedding themselves in the moss. A heavy copter blade speared the ground a couple of yards away. With a yelp, the rider hit the moss beside me.

What on Mars had he been thinking? He could have killed me. A couple of yards lower and he might have skewered me.

The rider groaned. His brass goggles were covered in dirty water from the tanglemoss. He peered at me through his obscured lenses.

"Good Lord," he said. "Are we dead?"

I recognized that voice.

"Yes," I snapped.

"What? What?"

I leaned forward and pulled his goggles up. He blinked at me.

"Cousin Freddie," I said. And I'd thought this day couldn't get any worse.

"Ah," he said. "Cousin Edward. Ah-ha-ha. Well."

Freddie wasn't actually my cousin. He was the son of my dad's oldest friend, Charles Winchester. When he'd been younger, he'd spent so much time at our house that we'd started calling him our cousin. Now I wished we hadn't. I mean, I knew he was an idiot, but this was too much even for him.

I clambered to my feet and glared at him. "Haven't you ever ridden a cycle-copter before?"

Cousin Freddie rubbed his eyes, smearing the muck from his sleeve across the only clean part of his face. "Ah. Not as such. But how hard can it be?"

I looked at the wreckage around us and raised an eyebrow.

"Right, right," Cousin Freddie said. "I see what you mean. Not all my fault, though. See, no one told me the springs would run out when I was halfway across the Valles Marineris. Then some pesky bird mistook my balloon for its dinner.

Had to make the rest of the way by pedal power alone. Bit of an exertion, to tell you the truth." He poked around in the wreckage and came up with a polished walking stick, topped by a silver handle. "Ah. Almost thought I'd lost it." He swung it happily around.

I boggled at him.

It was hard to believe, but when he'd been younger, everyone had thought Freddie was brilliant. They had been sure he was going to be a stunning success. Then, when he'd turned sixteen, something had changed and he'd suddenly become an amiable idiot. I was sure he must have fallen on his head. My uncle Henry had even taken to referring to him as "The Idiot Freddie" after the unfortunate incident with the stalking-grass and my aunt Amelia's new evening gown. But I didn't think I'd ever heard of him doing something quite this stupid.

"What on Mars possessed you to try to cross the Valles Marineris on a cycle-copter?"

"Ah," Cousin Freddie said. "Well. Bit of a story there, as it happens. You see, there was this rather pretty girl in Chinese Mars, who *I* thought—"

The sound of scrambling footsteps interrupted us. Putty leaped the last few feet to the ground and came racing toward us. She stopped a couple of paces away.

"Cousin Freddie," she said. "We weren't expecting you."

Freddie brightened. "Cousin Parthenia? My. You've grown.

And what an—er—interesting outfit." Putty was wearing a miniature version of Papa's rather dated frock coat and breeches.

Putty peered closer at Freddie. "What's that on your face?"

Freddie touched his upper lip somewhat self-consciously. "This? You noticed? Ha-ha. My mustache. Don't you think it rather dashing?"

"It looks like a dead caterpillar. Why are you wearing a mustache?"

"Ah. Well," Freddie said. "There's a bit of a story there. It's all part of a disguise. You see, I was—"

"It's not a very good disguise," Putty said. "I recognized you straightaway."

Freddie looked aggrieved. "It's still growing. I think it looks quite Prussian."

"Hang on a moment," I broke in. "What are you doing here? I thought you were supposed to be away at Oxford. On Earth," I added, just in case it hadn't really sunk in. "At university." As far as I knew, he should have been studying right now. He wasn't due home for months.

Freddie grimaced. "Ah. Yes. Well. You see, there's a bit of a story there, too." He let out an awkward laugh. "There was this little matter of a disagreement about a boxing match, and, well, what happened was—" He cleared his throat. "Anyway, I'm sure you don't want to hear the details." He swept out a wet hand, spraying dirty water everywhere.

"Why are we standing out here dripping like a pair of bath sponges? I'm starving. I haven't had a bite to eat since yesterday." He leaned closer to Putty. "If you're ever in Chinese Mars, keep away from those little skewers of meat they sell. Didn't agree with me at all. Rather unfortunate effects over the Valles Marineris. I wouldn't have wanted to be those fishes, I can tell you!" He took Putty's arm. "Come, Cousin Parthenia. Dinner awaits!"

I narrowed my eyes as I watched them go. Freddie had avoided my question. He was hiding something. It didn't take a genius to figure out that Freddie was in trouble again, and trouble followed him around like a beaver-hound chasing a landfish.

Not that my family, some of whom actually *were* geniuses, would notice. Mama was completely absorbed in planning her grand garden party to impress the other ladies of the neighborhood, and Papa was so obsessed with his inventions that it would have taken being shot out of a steam cannon to get his attention. In the meantime, my oldest sister, Jane, would be far too busy falling in love with whichever eligible young man happened to be floating by, and Olivia was far too proper to even acknowledge the existence of trouble. As for Putty, well, there would be nothing she would love more than to dive right in. So that just left me.

I might be only twelve years old, but it was up to me to

find out what trouble Freddie had gotten himself into, and whether he'd brought it with him.

Captain W. A. Masters would have to hang on a little bit longer.

◆

Freddie emerged from his bedroom half an hour later, just as the dinner bell sounded. He had changed out of his battered, moss-stained pantaloons, torn cravat, and leather flying-coat, washed the mud from his face and hands, and shaved off his mustache, and now he cut a rather striking figure.

In many ways, Mars was similar to Earth. The day was only half an hour longer, and you could breathe the air on Mars just as easily as on Earth. Even the seasons were the same, although the year on Mars lasted almost twice as long, which meant that winter sometimes seemed to go on forever. But the gravity on Mars was less than half that on Earth. Those of us who grew up on Mars tended to be slimmer and lighter.

Freddie's two years on Earth had changed him. His muscles had bulked out, making him look solid and tough. He seemed to have learned a new, fashionable, and very complicated way of tying his cravat, too, so that it stretched high up his neck, lifting his chin to what looked like an uncomfortable angle. He was even wearing two waistcoats, one on top of the other. All in all, Freddie had adapted far too well to the role of Oxford student.

"Perfect timing!" Freddie exclaimed as the bell rang.

"Wasn't it?" I said.

If he'd been trying to avoid talking to me, he couldn't have timed it better.

Putty had been loitering around with me outside Freddie's room, and her eyes narrowed in contemplation as she took in his outfit.

"Wait here!" she said, and darted back to her room.

"I need to talk to you," I said to Freddie.

He blinked. "Nothing I'd like more, old chap, but we can't possibly be late for dinner. It would be terribly rude. My mother would never forgive me if I offended Aunt Caroline." With a twirl of his walking stick, he swept downstairs, toward the dining room.

The rest of the family was already seated at the dinner table when we hurried in. Papa sat at the head of the table, surrounded by scraps of paper on which he'd scribbled indecipherable designs. The wide windows that looked over the lawns and down to the shores of the Valles Marineris were covered with curtains to shut out the sight of the workmen still laboring away at Mama's garden party. An elaborate candelabrum stood in the middle of the table, casting flickering light. Gas lamps burned along the walls.

Mama rose to her feet in a rustle of green and gold fabrics as we entered.

"Frederick! We are delighted you were able to come visit with us."

I frowned. Had Mama known Freddie was coming? Surely she would have said?

"Bit of a surprise for everyone, eh?" Freddie said. "One minute here I wasn't, and, well, the next here I was." He gave a wide, vacant smile.

"But a delightful one," Jane said, rising elegantly to join Mama.

Jane was my oldest sister. She was nineteen years old and probably the sweetest person on Mars. She also had the power to make young gentlemen fall in love with her from a hundred paces. We hadn't seen Freddie for almost two years, while he'd been away at university, and it would be an interesting scientific experiment to see if he still had any immunity to Jane.

"Couldn't stop myself dropping in when I, ah, found myself in the area. Or should I say *over* the area."

My next oldest sister, Olivia, looked as stiff-backed as a new book as she inclined her head. "Mr. Winchester. You are most welcome." For some reason, her cheeks had turned pink. A wisp of brown hair had escaped from the tight bun at the back of her head.

"Hugo!" Mama said. "Frederick is here."

Papa blinked over his dirty eyeglasses. He'd been scribbling notes on a pad of paper. His bushy eyebrows rose.

"Ah. There you are, my boy. I'd wondered where you'd gotten to."

For a moment, I thought he must be talking to me. Had Papa actually been looking for me?

"Frederick has been on Earth, attending Oxford University," Mama said, and I thought, *Of course, he meant Freddie. Why would Papa be looking for me?* He never seemed to notice whether I was there or not.

Sighing, I slid into the chair next to Olivia. She was still sitting as stiffly as an automatic servant whose springs had run down.

"What's wrong with you?" I whispered.

Olivia shook her head minutely, her cheeks still flushed.

The door burst open, and Putty hurried in. She had taken off her old frock coat and replaced it with a pair of waistcoats just like Freddie's.

"What is the meaning of this?" Mama snapped.

"Er . . . Of what?" I said cautiously, as the ro-butler trundled in carrying a dish of plesiosaur steak flavored with cracked pepper and rosemary, and fire-beans.

"Parthenia!" Mama exclaimed, flinging a hand out in such a dramatic gesture that it almost sent her glass flying across the table.

"We've all been wondering that for a long time," Olivia murmured to me.

I leaned back as the ro-butler splatted food down onto my plate.

"What have I done?" Putty said.

"That *outfit*," Mama sniffed. "You are supposed to be a young lady. What must Frederick think?"

"Well—" Freddie tried.

"Frederick has been to Earth! To England! He must think we are savages here!"

"Oh, I don't—"

"I almost traveled to England myself, you know," Mama said, turning to Freddie. "I was invited. England is so much more civilized than Mars. I am not too proud to admit that the experience did much to refine me. I would not be the lady I am today without it."

"Er . . . experience?" Freddie asked, but Mama wasn't listening. She turned back to Putty.

"It is bad enough that you are late—"

"My fault," Freddie said. "Awfully sorry. Delayed everyone. Couldn't quite remember where I'd put my spare cravat. A gentleman can never be seen without a properly tied cravat."

Papa, whose own attempts at tying a proper cravat rarely lasted more than a few seconds, raised his eyebrows at that.

"It is remarkably handsome," Jane said. "Is that the latest London style, Cousin Freddie?"

Jane might be as sweet as a syrupberry, but as far as I could tell, she'd never had a single thought that wasn't about fashion or young men.

Freddie reached for his ridiculous cravat. "Ah, now, well, that is to say, it is a style I am *debuting* myself. I call it the

Winchester Cascade. Do you think it might catch on, Cousin Jane?"

"Oh, I'm sure it will!" Jane gushed.

"You know," I said, "I'd have thought you'd want to *debut* your new fashion in London, Freddie. What exactly made you come back to Mars before your university term ended?"

"Ah!" Freddie's eyes lit up. "As I started saying before, what happened was that old Podgy—er, that is, Viscount Podwood—got rather merry one night and he had this fantastic idea that we should all bet on him in, well, it was a boxing match . . ." He trailed off as Mama, Jane, and Olivia all stared at him.

"Right," Freddie said. "Not suitable for mixed company. Apologies." His eyes flicked toward me. I stared back. Had he done that deliberately? He must have known he couldn't talk about that kind of stuff in front of Mama, Jane, and Olivia. I knew he was an idiot, but even he must have known better.

Freddie cleared his throat. "Uncle Hugo. Father said you were working on some new invention. Couldn't make head nor tail of what he was talking about, but it sounded thrilling."

Putty bounced in her seat, almost overturning her plate. "The water abacus."

"A water abacus, eh? Is that to help fish count? Ha-ha."

Papa was a mechanician. Like the hundreds of other mechanicians on Mars, Papa took the fantastic mechanical devices found in the dragon tombs of Lunae Planum and turned them into the inventions that had changed the face of both Mars and Earth. But none of the other mechanicians even came close to Papa's genius.

Papa's first great success had been the clockwork automatic servant. Before Papa, automatic servants had been steam-powered, bulky, simplistic machines that were useful only for carrying and lifting. They lumbered around, belching smoke, leaking steam, and horrifying good society. Then Papa invented an automatic servant that was entirely spring driven, completely clean, and totally silent, and he'd turned their brains into delicate things of beauty, capable of carrying out thousands of tasks. He'd set up a manufactory to build the things, and when he brought out his first ro-butler, it was a tremendous hit. Every good family on Mars had wanted one, and Papa had made a fortune. The *Tharsis Times* had described Papa as "the greatest success story of British Mars."

Until a couple of years ago, when he'd started work on his latest invention, the water abacus. He'd left his business to run itself, and the only place it was running itself was into ruin.

As far as I could tell, the water abacus was just a room full of machinery that added up and subtracted enormous numbers. While I could see the appeal of avoiding arithmetic lessons, I couldn't quite understand why Papa wanted to spend every free minute poking away at it.

"It is a calculating machine," Papa said. "With it, one might solve problems a thousand times faster than if one was forced to carry them out by hand."

"Wouldn't be hard to be faster than me," Freddie said. "Never could quite get the hang of my abacus. Beads all over the place. Still, dashed clever of those Greeks to come up with it. Or was it the Romans? Always get them mixed up. Drives my Greek master mad. Or maybe my Latin master."

"In fact," Papa said, ignoring Freddie's blithering and rooting through the papers around his plate, "I received a letter only today from my old colleague Professor Lane."

"Good heavens, Hugo," Mama cried. "No one cares about your blessed letter. Jane was talking to Frederick."

How had Papa received his mail? My *Thrilling Martian Tales* was still missing. Putty shifted nervously on the other side of the table, and I narrowed my eyes suspiciously.

"You must remember Professor Lane," Papa said, entirely missing Mama's quelling look. "We worked together on the dynamics of dragon paths."

"I can hardly be expected to remember your friends, Hugo!" Mama said. "They do not exactly"—she sniffed—"move in good society."

"In any case," Papa sailed on, "Professor Lane wondered if my water abacus might help in deciphering the functions of the artifacts from the dragon tombs. There is quite a lot of higher-order mathematics in understanding them, you see."

"Hugo!" Mama snapped. "This is not a proper topic for conversation."

"But, my dear, imagine the great leaps of science that might be made if he is right."

"I shall not! Dragon tombs, indeed! I will not have *people*"—she shot a glance at Freddie—"think this family so poorly mannered."

"Oh, Freddie's not people," Putty said cheerfully.

"Parthenia!" Olivia said, her gaze flicking across to Freddie. "Don't be so rude!"

"It's true enough," Freddie said. "Most days I'm barely *person*. Ha-ha."

"Cousin Frederick," Olivia said, her gaze fixed resolutely on her plate, "you have traveled the dragon paths. What is your opinion as to their origin? Are they a natural phenomenon or a creation of the Ancient Martian civilization?"

"Olivia!" Mama squawked, sounding half strangled.

The dragon paths stretched through the void between Mars and Earth. Although I'd never ridden one, I'd read plenty about them. Great currents of wind rushed up from the surface of Mars through the void all the way to Earth, then twisted back to Mars again in an unending double spiral. Carefully constructed ships could ride the dragon path winds, swept along by their great sails, carrying people and cargo between the planets.

So far, only half a dozen dragon paths had been found.

The one that connected Oxford, England, to the slopes of Tharsis Mons on Mars had first been discovered in 1602. Within a couple of years, Britain had established its first trading post with the native Martians who lived near the ruins of the Ancient Martian city of Tharsis, and the British colonization of Mars had begun. It was only years later that they discovered that both the Chinese and the Mapuche Indians from Patagonia had already established colonies on Mars.

Admittedly, most of what I knew about how dragon paths worked I'd picked up in the pages of *Thrilling Martian Tales*. In one particularly exciting adventure, Captain W. A. Masters had battled the tyrant's minions as they were swept along a dragon path, exchanging fire.

Freddie's gaze darted back and forth between Olivia and Mama. "My opinion . . . ?"

"I believe they must be natural," Olivia said. Unusually for her, she was ignoring Mama's furious glare. "Surely no technology, no matter how advanced, could create such miracles."

"Oh, for heaven's sake, be quiet, Olivia!" Mama exploded. "No one wants to hear your opinion."

Olivia hunched over her plate. I opened my mouth, but before I could think what to say, Freddie interrupted.

"Oh, I say! I would hardly say that."

This defense only made Olivia huddle closer to her plate.

Mama reached over the table and patted Freddie's hand. "You are very gallant, Frederick, but it is not necessary. We have all quite come to terms with the knowledge that Jane has inherited all the beauty and grace in this family. In fact, Jane is quite the most beautiful young lady on Mars, as I am sure you must admit."

Freddie cleared his throat awkwardly. "Ah. Well."

Next to me, Olivia's cheeks reddened again.

Mama smiled like a hungry serpent-shark. "Now, Jane. Tell Frederick about the ball at Hardhaven Court last season. That gown you wore was the envy of the other ladies." She glanced at Freddie. "I chose the silk myself. I have impeccable taste. In fact, Jane reminds me of myself at that age. They called me the Crystal Rose of Tharsis, you know. Every young gentleman admired me." She sighed. "I was to travel to all the great cities of Earth and Mars. I would have set fashions and presided over the most elegant of salons." She sighed again.

I met Olivia's glance. We all knew how the story ended. Mama's father had gambled away everything. Mama had been left with nothing, and her admirers had slipped away as quickly as mist over the desert.

I cleared my throat. For the first time since the meal had begun, there was a break in the conversation, and Freddie couldn't escape my question.

"Freddie—" I started, but too late.

Mama's eyes flashed. "And as for you, Edward!"

"Me?" What had I done?

"Why didn't you invite your friends to stay for the summer? When Frederick was a boy, he frequently visited families of higher social standing. I remember Arabella boasting about it." She sniffed. "Why can't you be more like your cousin? How can you expect Parthenia to marry well if you don't bring your friends home to meet her?"

That wasn't fair! I'd been invited to stay with Viscount Harrison. Mama would have swooned if she'd known. And I'd wanted to! I'd come back because this family would fall to pieces without me.

Across the table, Putty choked on a spoonful of firebeans. "I'm nine years old," she spluttered. "And I'm not going to marry anyone!"

Mama ignored her. "She can hardly be expected to attract a husband by herself, running around like a street urchin. Attend, Edward! Frederick is the perfect image of a young gentleman. You would never catch your cousin having a career or"—she shuddered—"doing anything *useful*."

"Good Lord, no!" Freddie said.

With a sigh, I turned back to my dinner.

"Now," Mama said, "we will have no more talk of dragon paths, dragon tombs, or Hugo's wretched inventions at this table. We shall confine our discussion to the weather, fashion, and the social calendar."

I slumped down. That was that. There was no way I could ask Freddie again at dinner. But when the meal was over, the ladies would retire, and Mama would expect Papa, Freddie, and me to remain. I would get another chance, and Freddie would have nowhere to run.

— 3 —

The Perils of Stickleberry Juice

Finally, Mama stood, and my sisters followed her out of the room. Papa wiped his forehead with a napkin and looked awkwardly around.

"Well," he said, to no one in particular, and picked up his pen to start sketching on another sheet of paper.

If he'd had his way, Papa would have had his meals in his workshop, eaten them with greasy hands while he poked about machinery, and emerged into the sunlight only when some particularly interesting visitor turned up. Hanging around after meals with guests was not exactly his strong point.

At least that meant I would have the floor to myself. Freddie could only dodge my questions for so long. I fixed him with a piercing look.

"I say, Edward," Freddie said. "You should try this." He

pulled a small bottle from inside his jacket. "It's called stickleberry juice. It's all the rage over in Chinese Mars, apparently. Delicious stuff. Absolutely full of bubbles!"

He pulled over a glass and sloshed a purple liquid in. I sniffed at it suspiciously. It smelled sweet. Bubbles were rising to the surface.

"Go on!" Freddie said. "It's even taking off in Tharsis City, I've heard."

I picked up the glass and took a sip. He wasn't having me on. It was nice. It tasted like gold might have if you could have grown it on a bush and made juice out of it. And it was bubbly. Really bubbly. Freddie nodded enthusiastically, and I took another big gulp. Wow. The bubbles felt like a sandstorm bouncing around inside my mouth.

Freddie topped up my glass.

I took one last mouthful, then shook my head. He wasn't going to divert me this easily. Even if the stickleberry juice was really, *really* nice.

I opened my mouth to say, *Freddie, why are you really here?* But all that came out was, *"Murrgrrphsthm."*

I stared down at my mouth and tried again.

"Gurrflbnurrrrr!"

My tongue had gone completely numb!

Freddie raised his eyebrows at me, then turned to Papa. He'd done this on purpose!

"So," Freddie said. "This water abacus. A jolly clever thing, eh? What might one use it for? Could you, for example, use it to help you design new structures or machines?"

"Quite, quite!" Papa said, finally diverted from his sketching. "The water abacus could perform all the calculations one must now perform by hand. What might otherwise take weeks could be done in hours on the water abacus, and I fully expect that, when it is completed, it will be able to perform calculations no man could hope to manage."

I grabbed for a glass of water to clear the numbness from my tongue. It didn't help. I bulged my eyes at Papa, but he didn't notice. I wondered if I should bang on the table.

"How about for travel?" Freddie asked. "Might a man with such a device in his ship be able to navigate away from the dragon paths and fly through the void between the worlds without becoming lost?"

Papa frowned. "Perhaps. I hadn't thought of that. Of course, such a man would need sufficient power to escape the planet's gravity well, and a means of sealing his craft such that the air did not escape. And, of course, the distance between the worlds would be far greater if one did not use a dragon path. Still, it might be possible. It might be possible indeed."

I squeezed my eyes open and shut a few times. Why was Freddie so interested in the water abacus? A few minutes ago, he'd claimed he couldn't operate an ordinary abacus and didn't know the difference between Latin and Greek.

Now he was discussing engineering and flying through the void with Papa.

"And codes?" Freddie asked. "I read in *The Times* that the Emperor Napoleon has begun to send his orders in code so that they can't be read if they're intercepted. Could your device decode these?"

I'd thought Freddie had just been running away from trouble, but maybe it was more than that. Maybe he'd come here because of Papa's water abacus. By *why* would he want it?

Papa frowned. "I see no reason why not. But Mars is not at war with France, and I will not allow my device to be used in the pursuit of violence."

"Even so," Freddie persisted, "could it break such a code?"

"With ease. Napoleon's codes will not be complex. My water abacus could break much more difficult codes."

"Ah." Freddie sat back in his chair, a slight smile on his lips. "Well, well. It does sound fascinating. I wonder . . . might I have a demonstration of the device? I'm sure I could never understand it, but I would love to be able to say I've seen the work of a genius."

Papa's eyes lit up. "Of course! Of course!" He and Freddie rose. "You know, none of my family, except Parthenia, have shown the slightest interest in the device. I had once hoped that Edward might follow me, but . . ." He shot me a slightly disappointed smile. "Well. But I am pleased to find *you* so inquisitive, Frederick. It says good things about you. Yes, it does. You were such a promising child, but we all thought . . . Well, never mind that! Come!"

Wait, I tried to croak. But my tongue still wasn't working, and Freddie was guiding Papa toward the door, one firm hand on his back.

I tried to stand, but my legs didn't want to obey. Suddenly, I felt awfully, horribly tired. My eyes drooped, and I slumped in my chair, furious and helpless. Freddie gave me an apologetic shrug, and then he and Papa were gone.

I couldn't even get out of my seat to stop him.

⧫

I woke with my head pounding and my mouth dry and sticky. My brain felt like it had shrunk and was trying to pull away from the inside of my skull.

It was dark. The starlight through the curtains was too dim for me to make out anything. I didn't even remember coming upstairs.

Freddie! He'd tricked me. Something in that juice had knocked me out completely.

I groaned, and a hand clamped my mouth shut.

"Don't struggle!"

I pulled free. "Putty? What are you doing? It's the middle of the night."

"No, it's not. It's three in the morning. And I'm trying to keep you quiet."

"I was being quiet," I said, each word feeling like a hammer whacking away inside my head. "I was asleep." I'd been asleep for over eight hours, but I still felt exhausted. "Now, I'm tired, and I have a headache. Leave me alone."

"Don't be ridiculous." She grabbed the pillow. "Who else am I supposed to wake? Mama? Jane? Or would you prefer I went and woke Cousin Freddie?"

"God, no," I said. "Why do you have to wake anyone?"

"Because someone's trying to break into the house."

I shot up. "What?"

"Someone. Breaking into the house."

I rolled out of bed. My head spun. I rested my feet on the bare floorboards until the dizziness in my head subsided and I was able to peer out the window.

The Martian grass glowed soft red under the night sky, outlining two figures crouched near the shrubbery. They seemed to be in the middle of a whispered argument. One of them jabbed his finger at the conservatory, but the other shook his head and a moment later they scurried away toward the back of the house.

"I bet they're trying to steal Papa's water abacus!" Putty said, at my shoulder.

"Well, good luck to them," I said. "It's the size of the drawing room. They'd need a hundred steam-mules to drag it out."

"I'm going to get a big stick so I can hit them."

"We're not going to tackle two grown men," I said.

Putty looked rebellious. "I thought you wanted to be a spy."

I reddened. I'd thought I'd kept that secret. Trust Putty to figure it out. Ever since I'd started reading *Thrilling Martian Tales*, I'd been determined that I would be a spy when I grew up.

"Spies don't just go leaping in," I said. "They're not idiots."

"You're scared," she said.

"No, I'm not. I just don't want you to get killed."

She rolled her eyes. "I never get killed."

"We should wake Papa," I said.

Putty blinked at me. "Are you mad? What's Papa going to do?"

She had a point. Papa would try to stop them, and he'd be hurt. I was going to have to do this the smart way.

Back in issue 42 of *Thrilling Martian Tales* (part two of "The Army of the Dead"), Captain W. A. Masters had been trapped in the tyrant's temple by a thousand mad priests. He had raised the ancient clay warriors of Mars to fight for him and escaped. I didn't believe in sorcery, and there wasn't going to be any fighting if I had my way, but I knew exactly where I could get an army of my own.

"Come on," I said.

"What are we going to do?" Putty said, eyes wide.

"Magic," I said.

While Putty tiptoed toward the drawing room at the front of the house, I snuck down the narrow servants' staircase, heading for the basement. My plan was for Putty to turn on the gas lamps in the drawing room so the intruders would think someone was awake and stay away from the front of the house. The rest would be up to me.

When Papa had built the house, he'd split the basement in two. The larger part held his workshop, while the other section contained the house's winding room. What I wanted should be waiting there.

In the dim red glow of the winding room, the automatic servants had lined up against the wall, facing outward, the panels on their backs open. Their expressionless metal faces were unmoving. The room was full of heat and escaped steam from the furnace and boiler. The slow grind of the steam engine vibrated through the floor.

The automatic servants had backed themselves onto the spindles that protruded from the wall and clamped hold of supporting rungs with their metal hands. The steam engine turned the spindles, winding the automatic servants' powerful springs to drive them during the day.

I dried the sweat from my hands, then disengaged the spindles. With a *clunk*, they stopped turning. The servants lurched forward.

What I needed wasn't in any of the automatic servants' standard instructions. I crossed to the elaborate brass speaking tube on the far side of the room. It was similar to the auto-scribe that most gentlemen had in their studies, but when you talked into it, it didn't write the words down. It produced small cards with patterns of holes punched into them that could be fed into the automatic servants. The patterns of holes told the servants exactly what to do.

"The back of the house needs cleaning," I said into the speaking tube. "Carry candles. Don't turn on the gas lamps. Twelve copies."

With a whir, the machine spat out the neatly punched cards. I snatched them up and placed them in the automatic servants' command slots.

The servants jerked into motion. One after another, they trundled out of the room, pausing only to pick up candles, mops, brooms, and dusters, then clattered up the narrow stairs. I followed my mechanical army. In the dark, the intruders would see only the gleam of candles and the approaching figures.

The first automatic servant pushed its way into the corridor, whacking the door back on its hinges. I heard whispers, then sudden silence from further down the corridor. I slipped past the remaining automatic servants and poked my head around the doorway. Nothing.

A second servant, then a third, thumped out into the corridor. Still no movement from the intruders. This wasn't working.

"Who's there?" I called, in as deep a voice as I could manage. "Show yourselves!"

Another moment of stillness, then something swished above me and thudded into wood. I looked up to see a clockwork Martian starblade vibrating above my head.

They had tried to kill me!

"Get them!" I said, and the servants juddered into motion. Buckets and mops crashed. Metal feet thundered on the floorboards. They sounded like a whole army charging.

Someone cursed up ahead, and I heard the sound of running footsteps. My bluff had worked.

Putty slipped past me. "Don't let them get away!"

"Stop!" I hissed. She was supposed to be staying in the dining room. But it was too late.

I ducked below a broom and took off after her. Behind us, the automatic servants started to clean.

The back door slammed open, and the red glow of the Martian grass briefly silhouetted the two men as they raced away across the lawn.

Putty reached the door a couple of steps ahead of me. I lunged and caught the back of her nightgown. She stumbled against the doorpost.

"Let go!" she said.

"Do you want to get skewered?" I said. "The moment you step out, they'll be able to see you. They'll know you're just a child and you're not armed. You think they'll keep running?"

"Well, they should," Putty said crossly.

"Well, they won't."

I peered through the doorway. The men had nearly reached the snaggle of gullies and rock pillars behind the house.

"This way," Putty said, nipping back into the house. "If they came by steam carriage, they'll have parked on the road. They'll need to cut through the fern-trees. There's really only one way through. We can get there before them."

"No," I said. "If they see us, they'll kill us."

"Well, I'm going after them," Putty said. "Unless you want to stand here and hang on to me all night, you can't stop me."

Gah! Putty was the most frustrating sister *ever*.

"Fine!" I said. "But if it gets too dangerous, we're coming back. No arguing."

"Of course not!" Putty said unconvincingly. "Now come on. We can go through the conservatory. I've got a key."

We padded quickly along the darkened corridor to the lit drawing room, then through the garden room to Papa's conservatory beyond.

With only the glow of the Martian grass outside and the sparks of tiny, darting firebugs, the conservatory was a dark and shadowed place. Papa had always kept it unfashionably overgrown and tangled, and at night, the shadows could have concealed a dozen men.

Putty dodged between two rows of trees, neatly avoiding

a snapping serpent oak that lunged out of the darkness. I caught up with her as she slipped the key out of some hidden pocket in her nightgown.

I put a hand on her shoulder. "I'm going first. Don't argue."

If anyone was going to have starblades thrown at them, it was me.

I pulled the outer door gently open. The only sounds I could hear were the occasional sleepy muttering of the fern-trees, the creak of crickets, and the quick *snap-snap* of dueling-beetles. I let out a relieved breath. Whatever Putty might say, the men were long gone.

Putty darted past. "Follow me!" she said, and leaped into the shrubberies. I rolled my eyes and let her go. If I didn't let her run around wildly for a while, we'd never get back to bed.

Clouds of night-bees rose around us, their enormous pale eyes staring like mad moons. My nightshirt flapped awkwardly around my legs. Putty was a clear white shape a dozen yards ahead of me. The grass was wet and the air was chilly.

"Be careful!" I hissed. The fern-tree forest was dangerous at night. Deadly razor-saw weeds sprouted like snares beneath bushes, and dagger-thorn bats swooped low over patches of stain-moss, hunting for warm-blooded prey.

"Don't be ridiculous, Edward," Putty said. "I'm hardly

going to get caught by anything. I've done this a thousand times."

"You've—" I bit back the comment. Now was not the time.

"Just watch where you're going," I said as I pushed my way into the grumbling fern-trees. "If we get eaten by bear-cats, Mama will never forgive us."

Five minutes later, Putty came to a stop.

"They have to come through here," she said. "It's the only safe way."

She wriggled into a snarl of bushes and vines. I got down on my hands and knees and followed her. We peered through the leaves into a clearing. There was no one there.

"See!" I whispered. "They didn't come this way. Now can we go home?"

Putty gave me a look of contempt. "Don't be a dunder-head, Edward. They had an awful lot further to come than we did. They'd have to find their way out of the rocks, then through the trees."

I settled myself as comfortably as I could on the damp ground. All of a sudden, I was horribly tired again. The effects of the stickleberry juice still hadn't worn off completely. All I wanted to do was fall back asleep. At least Putty was easily bored. When the men didn't turn up, she would lose interest. I let my eyelids droop shut and rested my forehead on my arms. Maybe just a few moments of sleep. That would do me. Then we could go on home.

Putty elbowed me in the side. I glared at her. She nodded toward the clearing.

Blast it! One of the intruders had come out of the fern-trees. I'd been sure they'd be gone. The man peered around angrily. His dirty shirt was torn down one side. He was squat and short, as though he'd been sat upon by an elephant. His face was so squashed he looked like a frog. Frog-face sat heavily on a log and dropped his head into his hands.

What now? I hadn't planned on us actually catching the intruders. This was bad.

A sudden crack was the only warning I got. A hand grabbed me by the back of the neck.

"Well, well," a voice said. "What have we got here?"

— 4 —

Caught!

Fingers squeezed my neck so hard I thought my spine might break. Our captor wrenched us up through the undergrowth. A clump of snatch-thorns bit into my leg. I gasped.

"Spies," the man breathed into my ear. He squeezed tighter.

I twisted around and caught a glimpse of our captor. He was a native Martian. If all you've ever read about native Martians is the mean-hearted nonsense in newspapers like *The Martian Chronicle*, you might not realize that they are as human as the rest of us. No one knew exactly when the first humans had come to Mars, but it had been thousands of years ago. Over those millennia, under the influence of the low Martian gravity, they had evolved into a tall people with long, thin limbs and elongated faces. Just like people on

Earth, native Martian skin color varied from light to dark, although I'd never seen a native Martian with very pale skin, and every native Martian had rich brown eyes.

Native Martian civilization had reached its peak back in the second century BC, eighteen hundred years before the first British explorers discovered Mars. Back then, dragons flew through the skies of Mars and crossed the void between the worlds, and the Martian civilization was greater than that of the Egyptians or the Romans.

Once, there must have been wild dragons on Mars, but by the time the Ancient Martian Empire had reached its peak, all those that remained had been kept as pets of the Martian emperors, to be entombed with them when they died. With the collapse of the empire in the first century AD, the last of the dragons were buried.

Dragons were now extinct and the Ancient Martian Empire had fallen long ago, but the native Martians remained.

The Martian's dark eyes stared away from us, as though we were of no interest to him.

A native Martian will never look you in the eyes. I'd read that somewhere. I'd thought it was a rumor, some stupid, cruel gossip as ridiculous as Mama's idea of native hovels. Now I wasn't so sure.

"Let go!" I shouted, and kicked out at the native Martian. He kept his eyes turned away as he shook us. My neck creaked and for a moment my vision went dark.

With his thin, stretched limbs, the native Martian should

have been frail and weak, but this man was far stronger than me. He heaved us out of the bushes, then dumped us into the clearing. Putty's elbow caught me on the ear as she fell on top of me. My face thumped into the ground. I saw grass and dark shadows, and the legs of the Martian's frog-faced companion coming toward us.

I rolled away, but Frog-face was already on me. He kicked me, and I collapsed again, losing my breath. Through streaming eyes, I peered up at our captors. They were standing over us, just out of reach, so I couldn't even kick at them.

"You know what I think?" the Martian said, still not looking directly at us. "I think that with these two little fish, we can get whatever we want from that inventor. We don't need to break in. He'll just hand it over and say thank you."

Frog-face shook his head. "That's not our orders. We're not to be seen."

"We've been seen," the Martian said. "Unless you want me to cut their throats, that's not going to change."

I put a protective arm around Putty. If they tried anything, I would throw myself at them. Putty was fast and slippery. If I gave her a couple of seconds, she'd be away. She'd raise the alarm.

"Don't be stupid," the other man said. "We'll take them back with us. Get new orders. See what *he* wants to do with them. If he says he doesn't want them, then you can cut their throats." He turned to us. "Get up."

He aimed a kick, and I scuttled back.

The Martian's strong hand closed on the back of my neck again and pushed me across the clearing. From what I remembered about the fern-tree forest, we weren't far from the road. I glanced at Putty. She was walking bent over, as though every step was painful. There was no way she could run like that.

She turned her face toward me and winked. I hid a grin. She was faking it. I should have realized. Now all we had to do was overpower our captors, knock them out, and get away.

Easy . . .

Frog-face walked a couple of steps ahead of us. His broad, muscular shoulders looked as solid as the Great Wall of Cyclopia. The Martian hadn't loosened his grip an inch. He was marching us like a pair of geese on the way to market.

Up ahead, the fern-trees thinned, and I caught the first glimpse of the road and the hulking steam carriage beside it. We were out of time.

I stepped across a fallen branch and pretended to stumble. The Martian's hand instinctively tightened as I fell, and my momentum dragged him forward a pace. He lost his balance, and I kicked out, slamming my bare foot into his knee. I heard a crack, and the man shouted in pain. His hands let go. Putty slipped free, and I threw myself at Frog-face.

I caught the back of his shirt and let my weight drag him down.

With a roar, the Martian was on me, gripping me by the

arm and pulling me up. His hand came toward me in an open-handed slap. I jerked away, but the blow still snapped my head back. I squinted through the tears to make sure Putty had gotten away.

She hadn't. She was standing behind us, a branch in her hands. As I staggered away, she cracked it against the back of the Martian's head. He collapsed to the ground, unconscious.

"No!" I shouted. "Get away!"

She shook her head and stepped toward Frog-face, her branch coming up and around again. This time, she didn't have surprise on her side. The man caught the branch in his left hand. He curled his right hand into a fist and jabbed at Putty's face.

My legs felt like they were made of paper, and my knees didn't want to hold me up. I half lunged, half fell in front of Putty. Frog-face's fist caught me on my shoulder. He leaped over me, right for Putty.

I grabbed his legs and hung on. He crashed down. His knees thumped into my chest. Air shot from my lungs. I couldn't see. My arms loosened even as I tried to hold on.

Then there was a sharp crack, and something fell across me.

Everything swirled into darkness. I subsided on the grass.

◄─◆─►

I awoke to find someone patting my face. In fact, they were patting it quite hard. More like slapping it.

"Come on, Edward! Get up!"

I forced my eyes open. Putty stood above me, holding her branch in one hand while bringing the other up to slap me again.

"All right, all right," I mumbled. My whole body was battered, bruised, and throbbing.

Both men were lying knocked out on the ground. Putty must have hit Frog-face across the back of his head while I was hanging on to his legs.

"Should I tie them up?" Putty said. "I don't have any rope, but we could use their clothes."

I struggled up. I felt like a landfish that had been trampled by a pack of hungry buffalo-wolves.

"No," I said. "They might wake up. Let's just get out of here."

Putty put her shoulder under my arm to help me upright.

"You're not very good at fighting, are you?" she said. "You were lucky I was there."

I glared at her, and she grinned back.

After a few minutes, the house came into sight through the drooping fern-trees. Lights glowed from the dining room and filtered faintly through the conservatory from the drawing room beyond, but otherwise the house was in darkness.

"At least we know one thing," Putty said.

I stared at her through exhausted eyes. "Huh?" I said, showing my usual instinctive grasp of what Putty was talking about.

"We know where those men were from."

"We do?"

"Honestly, Edward. Don't you listen?"

I frowned and tried to pull my battered brain cells together.

"Their accents," Putty said. "They were both from Lunae Planum. Anyone could have told."

Anyone except me, it appeared. The Lunae Planum was an enormous desert far to the north, made up mostly of red rocks and sand. It would have been stunningly boring if it hadn't been for the river valley that cut through its heart.

Not that river valleys were particularly exciting in general. I mean, you have a river, and a valley, and, well, there's only so much of that kind of thing you can be expected to take.

But this one was different. The river had once been one of the centers of Ancient Martian civilization. It was lined with ancient, ruined temples, and in the desert around it were the dragon tombs. When Sir Stanley Robinson, the British explorer, had first discovered the river in 1648, he had named it the Martian Nile. But as it turned out, there was a lot more to the Martian Nile than a bunch of old ruins. The dragon tombs were stuffed full of incredible inventions and devices that had been preserved through the centuries by the dry, hot desert air. Nobody on Earth had ever dreamed of such technology. It had changed everything.

Even when the Ancient Martian Empire disappeared, the

native Martian people had remained, in small towns and villages beside the ruins. I supposed there must be an accent native to the area, but I had never thought about it.

"How do you know what a Lunae Planum accent sounds like?" I said.

"Really, Edward," Putty said, managing to look superior even though she was shorter than me and wearing a sodden, grass-stained nightgown. "The foreman of Mama's workers is from Lunae Planum. Didn't you notice how similar they sounded to him?"

I wasn't sure I had ever heard the man speak, and I couldn't have pointed him out if you'd asked me to.

"Mama told you not to bother the workers," I said as we approached the house.

"I didn't! I just overheard. That's all."

"Well, don't overhear again. They've got work to do." I sighed. "You know we're going to have to tell Papa?"

Putty perked up. "I could do it, if you like. I've had lots of practice at waking people up. It's one of my specialties."

"Actually," I said, "I've got something else for you to do."

"You do?"

"Yes. Because I've been thinking and I figured something out."

Her eyes widened. "You have?"

"Yes. I figured out that *you* took my *Thrilling Martian Tales*. Now you're going to get it and give it back."

Putty's jaw dropped. "But I haven't even read it yet!"

"Exactly. I want it back before you spoil it for me."

We slipped in through the conservatory door, locking it firmly behind us, and doused the gas lamps in the drawing room.

I was about to turn to the stairs when a faint glow down the corridor caught my eye. Maybe it was the automatic servants still cleaning. Except it didn't look like candlelight, and it was coming from Papa's laboratory. I touched Putty's arm and stilled her.

"Wait here," I whispered.

She followed me as I made my way down the corridor.

What if those men hadn't been alone? What if while we'd been chasing them through the forest, their accomplices had been continuing their work? They could be in there right now.

The heavy blood-oak door was fastened with four solid padlocks. The first had been levered free by brute force, but the other three were unlocked and hanging loose.

Maybe it was Papa. If he'd heard the noise, the first thing he would have done was check on his water abacus.

I eased the door open and crept down the stairs. Halfway down, where the stairs switched back, I crouched to peer into Papa's workshop.

If you're anything like me, you'll have seen pictures of mechanicians' workshops. All right, you probably won't have had a clue what you were looking at. Most mechanicians' workshops looked like something just exploded. They're full of weird brass contraptions, glass funnels, pipes, gauges, and steam engines perched on benches or standing against walls. I mean, you know they're supposed to be *something*, but for all you know, all those cogs, tubes, levers, chains, and springs might just be a device for hanging up socks. Or they might be a machine to shoot people at high speed down tunnels. Papa tried that one once, but only once. All I can say is, it's lucky I managed to stop Putty having the first go.

But if you thought those workshops were confusing, you haven't seen Papa's.

At first glance, Papa's workshop looked like what would be left if the workshops of half a dozen other mechanicians had been dropped into a single room and stirred madly. There were bits of machinery everywhere. There were contraptions held together by wire and set into polished mahogany, as well as discarded dials and pendulums, glass tubes bent in strange angles, shaped brass, cast-iron shafts, valves, and heaps of the finest cogs, springs, gears, and hinges.

Permeating it all was the bitter smell of hot oil and raw metal.

If you looked more closely, though, you'd realize that all those bits were actually part of dozens of incomprehensible devices that were just waiting for steam or spring power to set them whizzing into motion.

At the back of the workshop stood Papa's pride, the water abacus.

I didn't understand exactly how the water abacus worked. Much to Papa's disappointment, me and machines never really understood each other, but I'd picked up a little. It all started with a tank full of water that was pumped down through a series of pipes. These pipes were joined to all sorts of valves, switches, and miniature reservoirs. When Papa set the dials at the top, the water squirted through different pipes at different pressures. The switches would switch, changing the direction the water flowed, things would gurgle, water would rise and fall, and somehow, from all of this, the answer to some calculation would emerge.

Yeah, I didn't understand how, either.

Papa had invented the water abacus two years ago, and ever since, he had been hard at work, automating the input of the calculations and speeding up the flow of water, to increase the number of calculations that could be performed each second.

The gas lamps in the workshop were lit. Water flowed from the tank, through the pipes. And instead of Papa standing before the water abacus, there was Cousin Freddie.

"What on Mars are you doing?" I demanded, stomping down the last of the stairs, into the workshop.

Cousin Freddie jumped. "Ah-ha-ha. Cousin Edward. And Cousin Parthenia. Well, you see, there's a funny story there." He looked around guiltily. "You see, I was sleeping upstairs and having this rather peculiar dream about . . . well . . . I'd best not say what it was about, when I awoke and heard

noises downstairs. So I thought I'd better come down and have a look at what was going on." He scratched his nose. "Didn't want to miss breakfast, and you do all have it so unfashionably early on Mars. A man who starts the day without a kipper is a man who will feel like a smoked fish until bedtime! So says Plato, or, er, someone. Anyway, when I got down, it was dark, and the automatic servants were all busy cleaning—dashed funny time to be doing it, if you ask me . . ."

"Freddie . . ." I warned.

"Yes. Right. Right. Well, the door to your papa's work-shop was open. 'Funny thing,' I thought. 'I wonder if old Uncle Hugo is still up,' and seeing as I was awake, I thought I'd see if he wanted company. Anyway, when I got down here, it was quite empty and this confounded machine was gurgling away. I've been trying to get it to stop ever since."

"Oh, honestly," Putty said, pushing past me. "It really is quite easy, Cousin Freddie."

"Wait!" I said, but as always, Putty ignored me. She nipped around the piles of half-finished inventions and tugged a lever at the side of the water abacus. With a last gurgle, it shut down and the dials clicked back into place.

"Ah. Good gracious," Freddie said. "Well, well."

I swore silently. Now we would never know what the water abacus had been set to do, and that was something I very much wanted to find out. Because I knew as sure as I knew my own name that the intruders hadn't opened the door to Papa's workshop.

Freddie had opened it. Freddie had set the machine running. And one way or another, I was going to find out why.

— 5 —

The Great Sir Titus Dane

It took me nearly half an hour to wake Papa and explain what had happened. By the time he'd stopped patting me on the head and vaguely calling me a "good fellow" and I'd persuaded him to send an automatic servant with a message to the local magistrate, I could have sworn the first glow of morning was seeping into the sky. I hadn't even had the chance to get my *Thrilling Martian Tales* back off Putty. I went to bed anyway. It didn't last long.

Before I realized it, Mama was calling through my door. "Edward! Where are you, child? It's almost dawn!"

"But not quite," I mumbled into my pillow.

If I could have asked for one thing above all else, it would have been an extra hour or two of sleep to make up for what I'd lost. Well, that and another uninterrupted hour in bed with my copy of *Thrilling Martian Tales*, finally, *finally* finding out what had happened to poor old Captain Masters since I'd left him hanging there on the mountainside.

And a cup of really strong tea.

Some hope.

Today was Mama's garden party. It might not start until midday, but Mama wasn't leaving anything to chance. Even with hired laborers and the automatic servants hard at work, no one was staying in bed.

During the night, my muscles had seized up. I felt my face with my fingertips. My jaw was sore and so was one of my cheeks, but I couldn't feel any swelling. With luck, the bruises wouldn't show. I rolled out of bed with a whimper and pulled on my clothes. The worst part was my ribs. They were tender to the touch, and when I fastened my waistcoat, I had to grit my teeth against the pain.

I wiped my face with a wet flannel, tried to untangle my hair, then gave up.

The automatic servants were already preparing breakfast and carrying trays of food out to the lawn when I got downstairs. Maybe it was just me, but I thought the sun looked tired this morning.

The entrance hall was filled with flowers from Jane's hopeful suitors, as usual. The smell was overbearing. I covered my nose and mouth and hurried toward the breakfast room.

"Edward!"

Papa was approaching from the back of the house, his face creased in worry. He didn't look like he'd slept since I'd woken him. Maybe I shouldn't have told him about the intruders after all.

"What if they come back?" He ran his hands through his thick gray hair. "They are after my water abacus. I knew this would happen!"

"That's why you called for the magistrate," I said. "I'm sure he's sending guards."

It had been the only way to protect the family. Putty and I wouldn't be so lucky against the intruders again.

"Guards? Yes, of course. But there's something even more important."

"There is?" I eyed him suspiciously. This wasn't good.

"We shall have to cancel the garden party."

I blinked. That bang on the head last night must have scrambled my brains, because I was sure he'd said we should cancel the party. I peered at him. "Did you say cancel it?"

He nodded. "We can't possibly allow strangers on the grounds. Not now."

"Cancel it," I said again. Mama had been planning it all year. She had almost bankrupted us with it. Olivia had been in tears over the household accounts, trying to make it all add up.

Papa looked shifty. "Yes. So, perhaps you'd be good enough to inform your mother, while I, er, inspect the workshop." He backed away. "There's a good lad."

I stared after him. Break the news to Mama? Did he think I was mad?

Perhaps I could persuade Putty to tell her for me.

I had just started up the stairs to look for Putty when the door knocker sounded, twice. The sound echoed through the house. I froze with my foot in the air. On the landing above, the noise of Mama and my sisters abruptly ceased. The sun had hardly risen, and someone was knocking on the front door. No respectable visitor would dream of calling this early.

The ro-butler trundled past me.

I heard the door open, and saw the spill of light down the corridor from the entrance hall, and the long shadows cast across the floor by the ro-butler and the visitor. Footsteps sounded as the ro-butler showed the visitor into the drawing room. A second later, the ro-butler emerged.

"Sir Titus Dane," he announced in his echoey voice.

There was a gasp from the landing above, and everything erupted into chaos. Feet rushed about, Mama issued commands, and then all three of my sisters cascaded down the stairs, drawn into Mama's wake. Mama looked flushed and wild-eyed, and Jane was almost swaying with excitement. Putty trailed behind. There was no sign of Cousin Freddie.

The whole torrent of excitement washed around me, and I was caught up by them.

Mama cast me a glance. "Straighten your cravat, Edward," she commanded. "And my goodness, what has happened to your hair? Oh dear, this is a disaster! Why could he not have let us know he was coming? We are all in such a state."

As far as I could tell, we were all dressed much as normal—except Putty, of course, and Putty was never dressed normally. What else could any visitor expect this early? He was lucky we weren't all in our nightclothes.

Papa had vanished into his workshop—sometimes Papa was far cleverer than me—but Mama didn't seem to notice. She swept toward the drawing room, only pausing to pinch her cheeks, to add an unnecessary hint of color to her skin.

The visitor was much taller than Papa or Freddie. He had great, broad shoulders, big hands, and wavy hair that was starting to turn gray. He'd been sitting by the fireplace, but he stood as we entered, and bowed smoothly. Mama, Jane, and Olivia curtseyed in response. Putty bowed, just as I did, and I tried not to roll my eyes.

"Sir Titus," Mama said. "You do us an immense honor. It's been such a long time."

Sir Titus smiled. "Far too long, madam." His voice was deep.

Mama looked on the point of fainting. "May I introduce my children, Sir Titus? Jane, my oldest, Olivia, Edward, and"—she threw a despairing glance at Putty—"Parthenia."

"Delighted," Sir Titus said, and swept us all with his gaze. There was something I didn't like about his look. He seemed to be laughing at us. Jane and Mama didn't seem to share my opinion, though. Both almost swooned.

Mama, Jane, and Olivia seated themselves on a chaise longue opposite Sir Titus. Sir Titus lowered himself elegantly onto his chair, and Putty and I sat together.

"I had hoped," Sir Titus said, "to make the acquaintance of your husband, madam. Mr. Sullivan's fame has spread across all of Mars, and Earth besides. His inventions have changed the face of our worlds. Is he at home?"

"At work," Mama lied smoothly. "His business has detained him, I fear. He is a very busy man."

Well, he was certainly busy, but I couldn't imagine he'd be thinking about the part of the business that actually made him any money. Right now, he'd be in the depths of his water abacus, oblivious to anything except its pipes and switches and dials.

"A shame," Sir Titus said with a quick smile. "It would have been an honor to tell people that I had met the famous Mr. Sullivan."

"Oh, but not so famous as the legendary Sir Titus Dane!" Jane blurted, then blushed.

"I've never even heard of Sir Titus Dane," Putty muttered beside me. I hushed her, although I had never heard of him, either.

Sir Titus's eyes tightened.

"It's been such a long time since we had word of you, Sir Titus," Mama said. "Ten years, at least, although it feels longer."

Sir Titus bowed his head slightly. "My business has

been most unremarkable, and I have not been on Mars in that time, I fear. I have had tedious matters on Earth to occupy my time. My father's business too often takes me away from where I would most like to be, as you must know, Mrs. Sullivan."

"Oh, yes," Mama sighed. She turned to the rest of us. "I knew Sir Titus as a girl in Tharsis City, you see. He once promised to take me to Paris and Vienna. He was a very ardent admirer of mine, were you not, Sir Titus?"

"And still am, madam."

Mama blushed. "Sadly, Sir Titus was forced to travel away from Tharsis on his father's business, and we did not see each other again after that time. If he had not been so forced, I dare to think . . . Well." She let out a breathless laugh, as brittle as crystal. "That was a long time ago."

"And a source of many regrets, also," Sir Titus said.

Olivia lifted her handkerchief and gave a little cough. Olivia was the most proper person I'd ever met, and this was her equivalent of laughing out loud and pointing a finger at him. I agreed with her. Sir Titus was one of *those* admirers, the ones who'd fled the moment they found out Mama's father had gambled away his fortune and her dowry with it. Sir Titus's father's business sounded like a convenient excuse.

"Well." Mama cleared her throat. "You are returned to us now. I trust you will stay for our garden party this afternoon? It wouldn't be the same without you. The famous Sir Titus

Dane. What an honor that would be. We would be the envy of the neighborhood."

"Oh, do stay," Jane cooed, and turned her wide falling-in-love eyes upon him, even though Sir Titus must have been as old as Papa. "I would adore hearing of your adventures, sir."

"I fear not," Sir Titus said, "although it is with many regrets. I have already intruded enough, arriving like this without word. But my business carries me to Mars so infrequently that, when I found myself in the area, I could not resist the temptation of taking a slight diversion to pay my respects to one of my dearest friends—"

"Sir Titus!" Mama giggled, sounding like Jane at her most infatuated.

"However, I have appointments to keep tomorrow, to the north of here, that may detain me for several weeks, and I cannot honorably postpone them. It is enough that I have been able to . . . satisfy my curiosity, renew a dear acquaintance, and"—here he looked directly at Jane—"make new, equally delightful, acquaintances." He paused and raised a finger to his lips, his brow furrowing. "Although." He smiled. "It does now occur to me. It may be that I can charter a private airship to carry me north. If so, I may be able to attend at least part of your party."

"Oh, yes!" Mama and Jane fluttered together.

"Sir Titus, you do us a great honor," Mama added. "A great, great honor."

"Then I shall see what I can do." He stood, and the rest of

us stood with him. "I have trespassed upon your time long enough. If I am able, I shall return at noon. If not, I can but hope that my business in the north will soon be completed and that I may impose upon your hospitality again before I return to Earth."

—◆—

As soon as Sir Titus had taken his leave, Mama said, "Mrs. Adolpho and Mrs. Cartwright must be told that Sir Titus Dane called upon us. As must Lady Ashville. If he is not able to return this afternoon, it will be of the greatest importance. But how to let them know without seeming boastful?"

A frown creased her forehead. Then she noticed the rest of us standing there. "What on Mars are you all standing about for? We have a garden party to prepare, and we have lost too much time. Olivia! See to the automatic servants, then check the tables. They must be suitably positioned in the shade, but not so far that they cannot observe the goings-on and be observed in turn. Oh dear, one just cannot expect the laborers to get it right. And tell the automatic servants to take away breakfast. We have no time for it this morning."

I stared at her as my stomach growled angrily. Mama ignored me.

"Jane," she said. "You must get dressed. Together, we shall shine over this party like twin stars in the heavens."

"Papa has canceled the garden party," I said.

"Edward! Please do not talk such nonsense. We are too busy."

I shrugged. Papa couldn't say I hadn't tried. If he wanted to attempt to persuade Mama himself, he was more than welcome. If he succeeded, it would be a first.

"What do you want me to do?" I asked.

Mama looked at me like I was covered in bugs. "*Do?* You are a young gentleman, Edward! You are not supposed to *do* anything. Just . . . try to stay out of everyone's way."

Olivia reached out a hand as I pushed my way out of the room. "Edward . . ."

"I'll find Freddie," I said, not meeting her eyes. "We'll help you with the tables." I headed for the stairs.

Freddie was in his room, standing at the window, looking onto the front lawn and the drive with his back to the room. I rapped on the door and entered.

"Cousin Freddie," I said. "There you are. You've missed the famous Sir Titus Dane."

Freddie turned. "So it would appear. What a shame."

"You saw him leave?" I said.

"What did you think of him?"

It was a peculiar question. "Why?"

"I'm just interested, having missed the great man my-self." He flashed a grin.

I frowned. This didn't sound like the idiot Freddie I was used to.

"I didn't like him," I said. "I didn't trust him." I met Freddie's eyes with a challenge.

He gave a half smile of acknowledgment. "Not many would share your opinion."

"Mama and Jane certainly didn't," I muttered, then wondered if I'd said too much. Cousin Freddie wasn't actually family. Some things weren't meant to be shared.

"The question," Freddie said, "is what did he want?"

"To renew his acquaintance with Mama," I said. I wasn't going to pass on any more gossip. "That's all. It's not unusual, you know."

Freddie laughed. "No one has seen nor heard of the great Sir Titus Dane for ten years. This is the man who discovered three dragon tombs in the sands of Lunae Planum. The man who then disappeared in a cloud of rumors that said he had stolen the maps showing the locations of the tombs from other Martian archaeologists. Now, after all this time, he turns up here to visit someone he hasn't seen for twenty years or more. I don't think so."

"Yet you don't sound surprised to see him," I said. "In fact, you seem to know rather a lot about him, bearing in mind that you can't have been more than, what?—ten?—when he disappeared. And why did you work so hard to avoid meeting him?"

Freddie gave a tight smile. "You don't miss much, do you, Edward? Let's just say that the great Sir Titus Dane may not have been seen in ten years, but I have seen that man who has just left very recently indeed. He was not calling himself Sir Titus Dane. He was calling himself Professor Westfield." He leaned back against the window. "He is my tutor at Oxford."

— 6 —

The Worst Party Ever

Half an hour later, I stood watching Freddie from the far side of the lawn as he checked the tables. People had suddenly become very interested in Papa's water abacus. I didn't know what, if anything, Freddie had to do with last night's intruders, nor how Sir Titus Dane fitted in. Maybe they all had algebra homework they were trying to avoid. But if I'd been Freddie, the garden party would have been the perfect chance for me to get to the abacus again. The house would be empty, and Papa would have to be at the party. For now, though, Freddie seemed content to dawdle his way around the tables, twirling his walking stick and humming away to himself.

This was my chance to find out exactly what he was up to.

Putty, of course, wanted to come with me.

"Then who's going to keep an eye on Freddie while I'm

searching his bedroom?" I said. "And who's going to warn me if he comes back?"

Putty pouted. "I'd be much better at searching his bedroom. I always manage to find Jane's secret diary, no matter where she hides it."

I closed my eyes for a second. "You can't read Jane's secret diary."

"Yes, I can. Although it's full of horrible love poetry and soppiness. Did you know that she thinks Cousin Freddie is 'ever so handsome, witty, and exceedingly charming, and all other gentlemen are quite inconsequential when compared'? Which is exactly what she wrote about Nicholas Wetherby last month."

"If Jane knew you were reading her diary . . ." I started. Then I stopped and took a deep breath. "Putty," I said. "If you don't keep an eye on Freddie for me, I'll tell Jane you've been reading her diary. Now go bother Freddie, and if he comes back to the house, whistle. Loudly."

Putty fixed me with a narrow-eyed stare. I didn't waver. She sighed and, with a last, loud huff, flounced off across the lawn.

I waited until she reached Freddie and started pestering him. Then I strolled casually to the house. Mama was engaged in a debate with Jane about the vast, looming wood-and-canvas dragon tomb that had been constructed at the end of the lawn. From the snatches of conversation that I heard, Mama was worrying that there wasn't enough gold on the tomb. The Ancient Martian tyrants from *Thrilling Martian Tales* would have been proud of her. When she and Jane were looking the other way, I slipped through the front door.

Our ro-butler was standing in the entrance foyer, as still as a piece of furniture. For a moment, I worried his springs had run down, but he bowed his head jerkily as I hurried past. I patted him on his metal shoulder. He might have been old and out of date, but after so many years, he was almost part of the family.

Freddie's bedroom was on the second floor, next door to Putty's. The automatic maids had finished turning the sheets and laying the fires, and were now out on the lawn, assisting with the preparations. I paused outside Putty's room, wondering if I should dart inside and reclaim my magazine. But Putty's room was always a mess, and I didn't know how much time I had.

Freddie's door was unlocked. I slipped inside.

The bed curtains had been tied back and the bed made. There was a washstand; a small, empty bedside table; a narrow wardrobe; and a secretaire to one side of the window. Writing paper and a quill pen had been laid out on the secretaire next to the auto-scribe, as though Freddie had meant to start a letter by hand. But he'd just scribbled a collection of letters and symbols, then scratched them out, as though he had been absentmindedly doodling as he thought of something else. They didn't mean a thing to me.

The secretaire's drawers were empty, other than a supply of writing paper and a spare quill. Nothing hidden there. The problem was, I didn't even know what I was looking for.

I dropped to my knees, peered under the bed, and saw a dark shape shadowing the light from the far side. I lay flat and reached under, my fingers stretching toward it, my shoulder pressed up hard against the edge of the bed.

My fingers closed on a hard china bowl. I let go quickly. *The automatic chamber pot.* Yuck. I screwed up my face. Thank heavens it had already emptied and cleaned itself. I pushed myself back up again, resisting the urge to wipe my fingers somewhere.

Freddie had arrived with little more than a change of clothes. The ones he'd been wearing when he crashed his cycle-copter had been cleaned, patched, and hung up in the wardrobe. I ran my hands over the jacket. There was a stiff piece of paper in one of the pockets. I slipped my hand inside.

It was the stub of a Mars-ship ticket. Departure was stamped a month previously, from the dragon path terminus outside Oxford, on Earth, and the arrival time was just four days ago, in Tharsis City. So he'd been telling the truth about that at least. He could easily have caught a Clockwork Express from Tharsis City to the Chinese Martian territories on the far side of the Valles Marineris. What it didn't tell me was *why* he'd come. I put the ticket stub back in his pocket and continued searching through his clothes.

A floorboard creaked just beyond the door. I froze for a fraction of a second. Then I did the only thing I could. I jumped into the wardrobe and pulled the door shut behind me.

I heard the handle turn and the bedroom door open. Light footsteps padded in. I crouched down to the keyhole and peered through.

A shape swished past the wardrobe. I caught a glimpse of a woman's dress.

It couldn't be Mama. Mama never went anywhere quietly. Jane, then? Had she snuck in to moon over Freddie's bedroom and fall in love with his spare cravats? Except that Jane had been wearing an elegant green affair this morning, to set off the jewels in her hair.

I pushed open the wardrobe door.

"Olivia?" I demanded. "What are you doing here?"

She jumped as though I'd pricked her with a needle. Freddie's papers fell from her fingers.

"Um . . . I . . . thought I should check to see if the automatic maid had tidied Cousin Frederick's room properly," she said, blushing. "You know how poorly they're working these days. It wouldn't do to let a guest's room go unserviced."

It was the most pathetic excuse I'd ever heard.

"And you were worried they hadn't cleaned his secretaire?" I asked.

"Well . . ." She blinked. Irritatingly, Olivia was quite a bit taller than me. She peered down at me. "What were *you* doing in Frederick's *wardrobe*?"

Ah.

I glanced back at the open wardrobe door and caught sight of a piece of paper folded and slipped into the join between two planks of wood. That was what I was after! That was my clue.

A piercing whistle sounded.

Putty was warning me. Freddie was on his way back. Outside, footsteps took the stairs, two at a time.

There was no time to get the paper. I grabbed Olivia's arm and dragged her toward the window. There was nowhere in the room big enough to hide both of us.

The gardens were empty. The laborers had been banished at daybreak, and the family must have come in to prepare themselves for the party. I unlatched the window and pulled it up.

"Are you mad?" Olivia whispered. "We'll kill ourselves. And what if someone sees us? What would they think? We should just tell Cousin Frederick why we were here."

"Oh, yes?" I said. "And why exactly were you here?"

Olivia blushed again.

"That's what I thought," I said.

I stepped out onto the window ledge. It was wide enough to stand on, but not much more. At the end of the lawn, the sun glinted from the waters of the Valles Marineris, which stretched all the way to the horizon. Far to the west, the great smear of lava-lit smoke from the Arsia Mons volcano spread like sunset across the sky.

Olivia climbed up beside me. Her thin slippers slid on the ledge, and she wobbled. I shot out an arm to steady her. Then we both heard the sound of the door handle.

Olivia let go of my arm and lurched to the right. I stepped in the other direction.

There was no time to close the window. All I could do was press my back against the wall and hope I couldn't be seen from inside. Olivia's fingers tightened like claws on the brickwork. Her lips pressed together and her eyes screwed shut. Her light brown hair had come free from its pins and straggled down the back of her neck. Her long, loose dress flapped in the breeze.

I heard Freddie enter. His footsteps halted. I fought the urge to twist my head and try to see inside. Then his footsteps resumed, marching resolutely toward the window.

He was going to see us. He would tell Mama, and we would be in complete disgrace. Even Papa might have to become involved.

"Must have left the dratted window open this morning," Freddie muttered loudly, and I closed my eyes in relief. "Dashed ridiculous thing, ha-ha. Lose my own head next."

He pulled the window back down with a bang, and a second later, the latch locked into place. We were trapped, with no way to get back in.

"What are we going to do?" Olivia said.

"Jump?" I suggested.

She stared at me. "We're two floors up."

"It was a joke," I said.

If the ground had been softer, I might have tried. As it was, we would have a better-than-even chance of twisting an ankle, even in the low Martian gravity.

"We'll have to shout for help," Olivia said.

"Wonderful idea," I said sarcastically. "Then not only will we have to explain to Freddie what we were doing in his room, but we'll have to tell everyone else, too."

I peered into the bedroom. Freddie had shut the wardrobe. He must have gotten whatever he'd come for. Putty's room was the next one over. If I could jump across to the window ledge, I would be able to let Olivia safely back in. All I had to do was jump from one windowsill to another without killing myself. I steadied myself, bit my lip, and crouched.

There was no way this wasn't going to hurt.

Directly below us, the front door opened. Mama, Jane, Papa, and Putty came out to stand in a receiving line at the front of the house, almost below our feet. *Botheration!* I wobbled dangerously as I tried to regain my balance.

Papa darted his head nervously from side to side, like a bird searching for predators, but his shoulders were slumped. If he had tried to persuade Mama to abandon the party, he had been thoroughly squashed.

"Look!" Olivia hissed. She was pointing with her chin. At

the far end of the drive, above the shielding line of oaks, a trail of steam traced smoke signals into the sky. The first carriage was on its way. The garden party was beginning.

"Edward," Olivia whispered. "It'll be a terrible insult to all the guests if we are not in the receiving line. You know how important it is to Mama."

"Stay still!" I said. "I'm trying to think."

The steam carriage was drawing closer, pulling out of the line of trees, its heavy iron wheels crunching over the packed gravel.

"Mama is going to kill us," Olivia moaned. "If we're not there when Lady Ashville arrives, it'll be a disaster."

A second carriage pulled through the gates of the estate, out of sight, and steamed up the drive. Within minutes, dozens of guests would be arriving. All it would take would be for one of them to look up, and we'd be caught, pinned as neatly as bugs in a display case.

I reached into the pocket of my waistcoat and pulled out a small coin. I held it between my thumb and finger and squinted down, lining up my hand with Putty's head.

The first carriage drew to a halt below us.

The ro-butler limped forward and swung open the carriage door. Mama took a step to greet her guests, and I threw the coin.

It curved through the air . . .

. . . And caught Jane full on the shoulder.

She jerked, then spun on Putty. "Behave," she said.

"I didn't do anything," Putty protested, too loud. Mama glowered at her. I remained motionless, praying no one would look up.

"Mrs. Sullivan!" Mama's friend Mrs. Adolpho said, climbing out of the carriage. "What a wonderful way of arranging the tables. Mrs. Cartwright and I could not help but admire them as we drove past. Most ingenious. Reminiscent of my own garden party last year, I could not help but think."

Mama's voice was icily sweet. "Although, of course, we have several dozen more tables than your own little event. Quite a different scale, I might say."

Steadying my arm, I threw another coin. It hit Putty full on the top of her head, bouncing off the hat Mama had forced her to wear.

"Ouch!" she said, and glared around.

Why wasn't she looking up? How hard was it to realize that if something hit you on top of your head, it must have come from above? Putty was supposed to be clever.

She rubbed her head.

I pulled out my last coin. This was it. The rest of my allowance for the week. She'd better notice this time. I aimed it carefully and threw. It smacked into the back of Putty's head.

At last she looked up. Her eyes widened and her jaw dropped. Then she reached out a hand and tugged Jane's sleeve. I gaped. Why on Mars had she done that? I screwed up my eyes, waiting for the inevitable shriek from Mama.

It didn't come. Jane pulled her sleeve free from Putty's grip and stepped forward to greet the guests. Putty was still staring up at us. In a moment, she was going to draw attention.

"What are you doing?" Putty mouthed.

"Help us!" I mouthed back.

Putty put her head on one side. "What?"

"The window." I made wild gestures at the closed window. I doubted she could see it was closed, but surely she'd realize we needed help. After all, it wasn't every day you saw Olivia out on a window ledge, her long dress flapping in the breeze, exposing her petticoat and drawers to everyone. Even Putty must think that was a bit strange.

"Parthenia!" Mama said, loud enough for everyone to hear. "Pay attention." She turned to her guests. "You must excuse my daughter. She is overexcited."

The second carriage drew up behind the first, and a couple of gentlemen I didn't recognize climbed out, one obviously the father of the other, both with prominent noses and unfortunate, weak chins.

"Mr. Allendale! Master Allendale!" Mama cried. "Welcome to my party! You know Mrs. Adolpho and Mrs. Cartwright? They were just complimenting me on my table arrangements."

Putty glanced back up at me.

"Go on!" I mouthed.

"Mama," Putty said, "I must be excused."

Mama blinked, as though she didn't recognize Putty for a moment. "Excused? Don't talk nonsense, girl." She turned back to the gentlemen. "This is my husband, Mr. Sullivan, and my eldest daughter, Miss Jane Sullivan. I have been told that she takes after me. Certainly she has a fine complexion, would you not agree, Master Allendale?"

"Mama," Putty said. "I really must be excused. Please."

Mama fanned herself, her cheeks turning pink with embarrassment. "Quickly, girl! If you have not returned by the time Lady Ashville arrives . . ." She trailed off, realizing her guests were still listening. "That is to say, we have been singularly honored by Lady Ashville, who will be attending our garden party. But that is not all." She leaned closer. "The great Sir Titus Dane himself has promised to pay us a visit. The first time in ten years that he has attended an event on Mars . . ."

Putty didn't have to be told twice. She turned tail and darted back into the house. I let out a sigh of relief. Mama would keep her guests enthralled with gossip about the great Sir Titus Dane, and Putty would be up here in a minute or two. We were going to be saved. As long as I could persuade Putty to keep quiet, we might even get away with this.

The window shot up behind me. A hand reached out and clamped hold of Olivia's arm.

And just in time. The sound of the window opening had set her wobbling again. Her foot slipped from the window ledge. Her arms spun helplessly, and she toppled forward. Then the hand pulled her around and in. I shuffled along the window ledge, then ducked back inside.

And stopped.

"Sir Titus?" I said.

The famous archaeologist smiled down at me. He hadn't let go of Olivia's arm.

"I came back, as I promised your mother," Sir Titus said, "and I saw you up here. I thought you might need saving."

"I didn't see you arrive," I said.

Sir Titus's grin widened. "I came a different way. And now, to show your gratitude for being rescued . . ." He shrugged his long coat aside, revealing a sharp sword, which he swung up to point at me. "I have a few questions."

I stumbled back, almost spilling myself over the window ledge.

"What are you doing?" I demanded.

The sword followed me.

"Doing?" He frowned. "I'd have thought that was obvious. I'm threatening you. Crude, perhaps, but usually effective. Now step away from the window. I'd hate for you to make the mistake of calling for help."

Carefully, I inched away, never letting my eyes stray from Sir Titus's sword. What on Mars had happened? This morning, he'd been charming Mama and Jane, and now here he was threatening us with something you could use to hack down a knight. I didn't get it. I didn't know what we could possibly have done. I wondered if he was mad. Sweat stuck my shirt to my back.

"What do you want?" I managed.

"That's more like it," Sir Titus said. "If you do as I say, you won't be harmed. If not . . ." He shrugged. "It would be such a shame if you were killed. I'd be sure to offer my most sincere condolences to your poor mother and father. I might even offer to hunt down the scoundrels who had done the deed. Sadly, I don't think I'd succeed. Now, this is Mr. Winchester's room, isn't it?"

I didn't answer.

"Come, come," Sir Titus said. "We all know it is. There's no point lying. You see, Mr. Winchester has something that belongs to me. A piece of paper, with a map on it. It's of little value, and no doubt he took it as a drunken prank, as students are wont to do. However, I must have it back. It has . . . sentimental value."

"I am sure Mr. Winchester has many pieces of paper," Olivia said primly. "We would not be so improper as to look through them."

"Hmm." Sir Titus smiled. "And yet there you were, perched outside his window like a couple of birds. Hardly the height of propriety, some might say." He made a cutting gesture with the sword, dismissing the matter. "Be that as it may, here is what we're going to do. You"—he pointed the sword at me—"will go and find young Mr. Winchester. You'll persuade him to come to this room. When he's here, he'll give me the paper. Otherwise, I will put my sword through your sister's chest." He gestured with the weapon. "Now—"

The door burst open. Putty raced in, her face red.

I scarcely had time to shout "No!" before Sir Titus's blade came around, swinging for Putty.

I threw myself at him. My shoulder caught him full in his stomach. He staggered back. The sword shot from his hand and thumped into the ceiling. Sir Titus twisted, spinning me, but he was off balance and I kept shoving. The back of his legs hit the windowsill. He tipped over, flailing for support. I gave him one last push, and he fell backward, out the window.

I hurried forward, in time to see him thump onto the ground below.

Right in front of Lady Ashville as she stepped out of her carriage.

Half a dozen faces turned up to see me peering out of the window.

— 7 —

Sneaking About

Mama's garden party was a disaster. I didn't get to take part—Mama banished me to my room—but I watched it from my window. Most people stayed. Maybe they hoped I'd push someone else out the window. But they spent the whole time gossiping about what I'd done to the great Sir Titus Dane.

Unfortunately, Sir Titus had survived the fall unscathed. Sometimes the low Martian gravity is a real curse. It was great that I could jump almost five feet high, but it also meant that Sir Titus hadn't been knocked silly like he deserved. I'd tried to explain what had happened, and Olivia and Putty had backed me up, but Mama wouldn't listen.

"No more!" she commanded. "It's bad enough that you shame our family in front of Lady Ashville"—she looked ready to faint—"but to continue to lie . . ."

To make matters worse, when I led Mama and Papa up to Freddie's room, the sword had disappeared.

"You can still see the hole in the ceiling," Putty said, but that only made Mama have another fit of hysterics.

Finally, the carriages began to pull away, carrying the party-goers home. Mama and Papa stood by the door, seeing them off. Poor Mama looked like she might swoon at any moment. She leaned heavily on Papa's arm. Out on the lawn, Jane was walking with a young man. I couldn't see his face—he was wearing a wide-brimmed hat and he held his head dipped, as though he were listening to her—but there was something familiar about the way he walked. He was probably one of Jane's suitors. I'd met most of them, but they never seemed worth remembering. They were basically all the same: young, rich, handsome, and as dumb as a brick wall.

The door clicked open behind me. I turned away from the window just in time to see Freddie slip in.

"Sir Titus Dane was here," he said.

It wasn't really a question, but I nodded anyway.

"What did he want?" Freddie asked.

"He said you'd stolen a map from him," I said. "He wanted it back."

Freddie peered out the window at the disappearing guests. "Perhaps I *should* have stolen it." He looked back at me. "That's not what happened. I found the map on his desk when I went for a tutorial. I didn't steal it. I copied it. I thought he wouldn't realize, but he must have been watching me. Obviously, he became suspicious and followed me when I returned to Mars."

"Obviously," I said.

Freddie raised an eyebrow.

"Why would you want to copy his map?" I said.

He sighed. "I can't tell you that, Edward. I really wish I could, but I can't."

The last of the carriages disappeared. Mama sagged back against Papa. Jane and her admirer had disappeared.

"How convenient," I said. "Why would Sir Titus want your copy if he's got his own?"

"So I won't have it, of course."

Freddie glanced out the window as Papa helped Mama up the steps, into the house. "At least he's gone now. I followed him into town. He had chartered an airship, and I watched him board it. After you pushed him out the window, he must have decided it wasn't safe to stay around, in case someone believed your story."

"You'd better be telling me the truth," I said. Something occurred to me. "Sir Titus was carrying a sword when he attacked us, but when we came back up, it wasn't there."

Freddie gave a lopsided grin. "Ah. That was me, I'm afraid. I disposed of it."

"You did *what*?" I said. "Why would you do that? You made me look like a liar. Everyone would have believed me if you'd just left it alone."

"And then what?" Freddie said. "People would have started asking questions."

I shook my head, so disgusted I could barely look at him. I'd thought he was an idiot, but he was something much worse. "That's all you're worried about, isn't it? That people would work out what you're up to."

"No!" Freddie said. "You're wrong. Sir Titus is a dangerous man. He wouldn't hesitate to kill anyone who got in his way. Your family would be in danger. Do you want to involve them in this?"

"You've already involved them!" I shouted. "They're already in danger. You brought all this to our house."

"I know." Freddie's head drooped. "Forgive me. I never intended to."

I swung away to gaze out the window. Below me, the gardens were quiet and empty.

When I managed to calm myself, I said, "What is this map? Can you tell me that much? And why did you need Papa's water abacus?"

"Figured that out, did you?" Freddie said. "The map shows the location of an undiscovered dragon tomb. If Sir Titus can find it, he'll be able to restore his reputation and make a fortune from the technology hidden within. But the map is indecipherable. All I can tell is that the tomb is somewhere in the Lunae Planum." He shrugged. "It's a big desert. If your father's water abacus could decipher the ideograms, we'd know exactly where the tomb was."

"And then what?" I said. "You want to excavate it yourself? Make your own fortune from a stolen map, just like Sir Titus? I don't mean to be rude, Freddie, but you haven't got it in you."

He smiled ruefully. "No. It's not that." Then he stopped, frowning.

"What's wrong?" I said.

He held up his hand, tipping his head to one side, listening. "It's too quiet. Your parents and your sisters have come in from the lawn, but I can't hear them."

He was right. There wasn't a sound from downstairs. My family is not the quietest family on Mars. Between Putty, Mama, and Jane, the house was normally in an uproar. After the disaster of the garden party, Mama should have been causing a scene. There should have been shrieks and swoons. Instead, there was silence.

"You said Sir Titus had gone," I said.

"You think Sir Titus works alone?" Freddie shook his head. "I don't like this. Stay here. Lock the door."

"No chance. I'm coming with you."

He looked at me for a moment. "Your choice. But keep quiet."

He cracked the bedroom door open. I still couldn't hear anything. I peered down the corridor. No one was in sight. Maybe that was why it was quiet. Maybe they were in a different part of the house, like the scullery or the basement.

Yeah, because Mama *loved* hanging out there.

"Follow me," Freddie whispered. Gripping his walking stick, he led the way down the corridor. He held up his hand as he reached the balustrade above the main stairs. A moment later, he was back, shaking his head. He raised a finger for silence.

"What is it?" I hissed as soon as we were away from the stairs.

"Someone's down there," Freddie said. "We'll take the servants' stairs."

"Don't we want there to be someone down there?" I said. "I mean, we were worried when we couldn't hear anyone. Now you're worried that you can?"

"The voice I heard wasn't anyone in your family. Trust me. I'd recognize them. This was someone else."

I remembered Jane walking with a man on the lawn. "Maybe it was one of Jane's suitors."

"Maybe," Freddie said.

The servants' staircase was narrow and poorly lit. We paused at the top, letting our eyes adjust, then Freddie started down, holding his walking stick before him like a sword.

My heart thumped loudly in my chest. My hands were getting sweaty. I wiped them nervously on my waistcoat. I'd always wanted to be a spy. But spies didn't react like this. Not in their own houses. I clenched my hands to stop them from shaking. Freddie threw me a glance, but he didn't say anything.

The door at the bottom was ajar. Light from the corridor filtered through the crack. I peeked through, but I couldn't see anyone. The hinges were well oiled, and the door opened without noise. Freddie leaned down until his lips were next to my ear.

"The voice came from the drawing room. Do you think you can get around the outside and come in through the conservatory?"

"I don't have a key," I replied. "It'll be locked."

Freddie pressed a metal key into my hand.

"Does everyone else have one of these?" I said.

"I borrowed it," Freddie said. "When you get around, I want you to open the door to the drawing room as loudly as you can. That'll distract whoever is in there. That's when I'll make my move."

I looked at him skeptically. "What if there's more than one of them?"

He winked, then without another word, slipped out. I glowered after him.

The back door was unlocked. Beyond Mama's herb garden, the Martian wilderness tangled around the columns of red rock. I could just make out the pillar Freddie had crashed his cycle-copter into yesterday. No one seemed to be watching.

I eased myself out.

The conservatory ran the length of the house. Its high, curved glass roof, supported by steel arches, reached to the second floor of the house. Vines and thick leaves pressed against the inside of the glass, forming an impenetrable wall of green and red. The key screeched horribly in the lock.

I slipped out of the warm sun into the humid shade of the conservatory. Tall Martian trees arched over me. Hover flowers from the slopes of Olympus Mons drifted between branches. A pair of wrestler-palms grunted and creaked as they attempted to throw each other to the ground. Thick wig-trees cast deep shadows. Papa's mechanical spiders scurried around, trimming back the fast-growing plants and pulling away fallen leaves. The constant ticking of their legs on glass and over leaves was enough of a background noise to cover the sounds I was making.

I crept through the conservatory, ducking automatically to avoid the lunging serpent oak.

The conservatory opened into the garden room. A few wicker-seated chairs leaned against one wall, and a small table stood in front of the fireplace. All I had to do was sneak across the room, making sure the floorboards didn't creak, then fling the door open.

I rolled my shoulders and dried my hands on my waist-coat again.

Captain W. A. Masters wouldn't delay.

I could do this. It was time to save my family. It was time to be a hero.

I stepped into the doorway.

And something sharp pricked the back of my neck.

— 8 —

Destroyed

"D on't make a sound," a voice whispered in my ear. "Don't even breathe."

I stopped dead. The point of a knife scraped across my skin. A trickle of warm blood mingled with my drying sweat.

From the corner of my eye, I saw the tall native Martian we'd chased last night.

"Good," he breathed. "Now, slowly, let's go." With his free hand, he pushed me.

My mind whirred like a spinning cog. The native Martian must have been waiting in the conservatory, and I'd walked right past him. How could I have been so stupid?

Now there would be no one to cause a distraction, no one to give Freddie the moment he needed to try to set everyone free. The man's knife followed me as I took a reluctant step. He shoved my shoulder again.

Each time he pushed, there was a split second when the knife left my neck.

"Don't even think it," the Martian whispered.

I stiffened.

"I can read your mind, boy," the Martian said.

"No, you can't!" I said. He couldn't, could he? I'd never heard of native Martians reading minds.

He chuckled softly. "I won't hesitate to kill you if you try anything. You think you're fast? I'm faster. Ask yourself, boy, do you want to die?"

I shivered. I didn't want to die. Not here. Not now. Not so uselessly. Feeling like I was betraying Freddie and my family, I let the man push me into the drawing room.

Most of my family was seated on a couple of chaise longues, but Jane was standing near one wall. Frog-face was next to her, holding a knife to her neck. There was a purple bruise on the side of his head where Putty had hit him with a branch last night. All the color had gone out of Jane's face, and she was swaying, as though she might faint at any moment. Putty looked rebellious and angry. Papa looked lost.

Frog-face and the Martian weren't alone anymore. A third man was with them. I looked across at him and blinked. Was he wearing a mask?

No. He wasn't *wearing* it. It was *part* of him. It was made of metal and fastened into his face with clamps like claws or insect legs. They dug deep into his flesh, stretching his face as tightly as if someone had grabbed it in a fist and pulled. Just looking at it made me feel sick.

The Martian chuckled. "That's Apprentice. Cause trouble and he might just give you a little kiss."

Apprentice said nothing. His breath hissed through a narrow grille in the front of his mask. He was wearing a long coat even though it was hot. The coat had round metal buttons as wide as golf balls stitched all over it. It hung heavily from his shoulders and swung ponderously when he moved.

The Martian shoved me again.

"Found this one sneaking about," he said to Frog-face in a low voice. "Thought he might be more comfortable with his family. Little lost duckling."

I glared at him, and he chuckled again, his eyes fixed on a point several inches above my head. For some reason, the fact he wouldn't look me in the eyes bothered me almost as much as the metal mask that had ruined Apprentice's face.

"Where's Frederick Winchester?" Frog-face asked. "And don't pretend he's not here. We know he is."

"He decided to take a walk," I said loudly, hoping Freddie would hear me through the door. "He said he had a headache."

"Keep your voice down," the Martian said, jabbing me with his knife. I winced as it cut into my skin again.

"Leave him alone!" Papa said.

Frog-face took a step and smacked Papa across the face with the back of his hand. Papa's head rocked back, and his glasses went flying.

"What do we do?" the Martian asked. "Wait for Winchester to show up?"

"No," Frog-face said. "We can't afford to wait. We've got enough hostages, and Winchester is an idiot. He'll be no danger. Apprentice." He nodded at the third man. "You look for Winchester. When you find him, kill him. Then come back and cover this lot."

This time, Apprentice did speak, but I couldn't work out what he was saying. Instead of words, the mask let out a series of loud clicks. Immediately, the buttons on his coat split and lifted away in a whir of metallic wings. In moments, a cloud of clockwork beetles surrounded him, their sharp pincers glittering in the gaslight. Jane screamed. Mama clutched Papa's hand in a white-knuckled grip.

Apprentice strode to the drawing room door, and the clockwork beetles rushed ahead of him. I bit my lip as he pulled the door open, but the corridor was empty. Apprentice and his swarm slipped out. I hoped Freddie had found somewhere good to hide.

"You and you." Frog-face pointed to Papa and Mama. "You come with us. In front." He tugged Jane through the door.

"Where are you going?" I demanded.

The Martian cuffed me across the back of the head. "Shut up." He shoved me toward the nearest chaise longue. "Sit there."

I collapsed onto it, between Olivia and Putty. My legs were shaking.

"Now," the Martian said, "if any of you three brats so much as move, I'm going to slit you from ear to ear. Hear me?" He fingered the back of his head and winced. "Especially you." He jabbed his knife at Putty. She glared, and I laid a restraining hand on her leg.

After a couple of minutes, the faint gurgle of Papa's water abacus came from the basement.

I fixed the Martian with a cold gaze. "You're not going to get away with this."

Papa had sent his note to the magistrate last night. Town was ten miles away, but surely the guards would be here soon? I was surprised they weren't already. Maybe the magistrate had told them to wait until after the garden party.

The Martian's eyebrows rose. "Really? Who's going to stop us?"

I didn't answer.

He grinned. "You weren't expecting rescue, were you?"

He reached into his waistcoat pocket, pulled out a folded letter, and threw it to the floor. I recognized Papa's seal on the letter. It had been sliced open and read.

"No one is coming," our captor said. "No one will rescue you."

Footsteps sounded in the corridor outside.

The Martian crossed silently to stand next to our chaise longue, his knife held out of sight behind his back. A moment later, the footsteps stopped. The door swung open, and Freddie sauntered in.

"There you are!" he called. His ever-present walking stick swung jauntily from his hand. "Thought I'd wandered into the wrong house again. Ha-ha. Did I tell you about the time when old Tuffy and I got completely . . ." He seemed to notice the Martian for the first time. "I say, have we met?" He took a couple of steps toward the Martian, shifting his stick to his left hand and holding out his right. "Jolly good to meet you. Frederick Winchester."

The Martian stepped past me. In a single, fluid move, his knife darted out, stabbing toward Freddie's throat.

He didn't get a chance to finish his move. Freddie's walking stick whistled up faster than I could follow and struck the Martian on the hand. The knife spun away.

The Martian shoulder-charged Freddie. He was larger and heavier, and Freddie had no time to dodge. The impact knocked him back. They tumbled to the floor, but even as they fell, Freddie twisted in the air. They landed with a crash that shook the floorboards. The force of the landing stunned them both for a second.

I dived from the chaise longue, sprawling toward the fallen knife. My fingertips hit the hilt, sending it spinning away. I scrambled after it.

The Martian was the first to rise. He shook himself free of Freddie's grasp, drew back his fist, and thundered it toward Freddie's chin.

Freddie jerked his head aside. The fist smacked the floor. The Martian roared in pain.

The knife had come to rest not three feet from the fight. I lunged, but too slowly. The Martian saw me and kicked my legs away. I fell. He shoved me aside and reached for the knife. Triumphantly, he snatched it up.

Just as Freddie's walking stick whipped down on the back of his head.

The Martian collapsed on the floor.

The next second, Putty was at my elbow, helping me up. Olivia sat like a statue on the chaise longue, gaping at Freddie.

Freddie knelt beside the fallen Martian and, with one swift tug, tore the man's shirt from his back. He ripped the shirt into strips, then twisted them into ropes and tugged at one. "That should hold him." He lashed the man's wrists together, then his ankles. He pulled the Martian's legs up behind him and tied his ankles to his wrists.

"Aren't you going to gag him?" Putty asked. "What if he calls out?"

"Best not," Freddie said. "Not unless you want him to choke while he's unconscious. Anyway, if he calls out, that might be a distraction we can use. Now." He climbed to his feet and pulled me to one side.

"They sent someone to look for you," I said.

Freddie hefted his walking stick. "He was looking the wrong way. Those beetles are useless without anyone to command them."

"Then I hope you hit him hard."

"Hard enough. What did they do with Jane and your parents?"

"Frog-face took them with him," I said. "They went down to Papa's workshop."

Freddie tipped his head to one side questioningly. "Who?"

"The other intruder," I said.

Freddie nodded. "It's going to be hard to get to them without being seen."

"Impossible," I said. We wouldn't even get close before Frog-face saw us. "Why don't we just let them do it? All they want is to use Papa's water abacus to decode that map. Give them what they want and let them go."

The Martian groaned. Freddie hurried over, knelt beside him, and peeled back an eyelid. The Martian's eye was rolled back, showing the white.

"Still out," Freddie said. He straightened. "The only reason they're keeping your father alive is because they need him to work the abacus. Once they've got their answers, they'll kill him and destroy the machine. They might take one hostage with them—Jane, probably—but the rest of you? They'd be happier if you were dead." He shook his head. "These people aren't playing games, Edward. If the map really does show a hidden dragon tomb, whoever finds it will make a fortune. Every single dragon tomb has contained fantastic technology far beyond anything we could have come up with, as well as terrible weapons. The Emperor Napoleon's agents are all over Mars, sniffing after the secrets of the dragon tombs. There's no limit to how much they would pay. We can't let the emperor get his hands on a new tomb."

I gritted my teeth. "So how do we stop them?"

Freddie scratched at his head. "What's on the other side of the workshop wall, behind the water abacus?"

"The winding room," Putty said, coming up beside us. "You want to destroy the abacus, don't you? Papa isn't going to be happy."

"He can rebuild it," I said.

"You won't break through," Putty said. "The wall's solid brick. Papa reinforced it when he built his workshop."

"If the boiler explodes, it'll rip through that wall," Freddie said. "The abacus will be torn apart."

"And so will anyone in the laboratory," I said. "Papa and Mama and Jane. Forget it, Freddie. We should go for reinforcements. Men with guns. Surround the place and tell the man down there to give himself up. He's on his own. He can't escape."

"Too slow," Freddie said. "Trust me, Edward. We can get your family out before the boiler blows."

I sighed. "Fine. But, Putty"—I looked at my little sister—"I want you to get Livvy out of here, far away from the house. When the boiler explodes, everyone inside will be in danger." I held up my hand as she started to protest. "You need to look after Livvy."

I met Olivia's eyes over Putty's head, and she nodded minutely in understanding.

"Good," Freddie said. "Then I'm going to need you to go down to the winding room. Close all of the valves from the boiler to stop the steam coming out and build up the pressure. You'll need to get the automatic servants shoveling coal into the furnace until the pressure is high enough for it to explode."

"They'll be killed!" Putty said. "You can't do that."

"They're not alive," Freddie said brusquely. "They're machines."

Olivia slipped an arm around Putty's back. "We have to go, Parthenia."

Freddie met my gaze and held it. "When the boiler starts to overheat, just get out of here. Don't wait for me. You won't have much time."

Most of the automatic servants had returned to the winding room, their springs run down by the garden party. They'd backed onto their spindles, and the slow grind of the powerful steam engine vibrated the room. I disengaged the spindles, and the servants jerked forward.

They weren't conscious. Their only thoughts were switches

and gears and fine cogs, and a series of commands stored on punch cards that sent them about their duties. But these servants had been here for most of my life. They'd always been around, doing all the work that we didn't want to do. It seemed wrong to do this to them. But Freddie was right. Without them, the chute that fed coal into the furnace would be too slow. We'd never build up enough pressure.

Reluctantly, I crossed to the brass speaking tube. "Shovel coal into the furnace," I said. "As fast as you can. Don't stop. Ten copies." Inside the machine, cogs whirred and levers pinged, translating my voice into a pattern of holes on cards. The punched cards shot into the tray. I collected them.

A couple of the servants were absent, still working out on the lawn or in the house somewhere. Maybe when the boiler exploded, they'd be all right. The ones down here wouldn't have a chance.

One by one, I fed the punch cards into the servants' command slots. Without a word, they turned from me, picked up shovels, and began to pile coal into the front of the furnace. I felt the heat in the room rise.

I crossed to the boiler and closed the valves that let the steam reach the turbines. Now it had nowhere to go. As more water boiled, the steam would build up, increasing the pressure, until the boiler couldn't hold it anymore. Then it would erupt.

Almost immediately, steam began to whistle from the

safety pressure-release valve. I could try to jam it with a piece of metal or stone, but would that hold it? Before the metal-bellied boiler exploded, the pressure would be enormous.

Our ro-butler was lined up with the other automatic servants, a shovel in his hands, lifting scoop after scoop of coal and tossing it into the furnace. The glow of the fire reflected from his metal body, turning it a deep red. His movements were awkward, though. His worn cogs kept slipping.

I trudged across to the speaking tube.

"Hold the pressure-release valve closed," I said. "Tight. Don't let go. No matter what. One copy."

With a whir, the machine spat out its punch card.

The ro-butler straightened, dropping his shovel, when I fed him the punch card. I had to turn him to point him toward the valve. His body was hot under my hands. I wanted to cry.

His fingers clamped around the valve, shutting off the escaping steam. I imagined the pressure building up, the steam shrieking past his metal fingers. Then the explosion, tearing through him.

The ro-butler had never been alive, but he'd seemed it. He'd felt like part of the family.

"I'm sorry," I said.

The ro-butler didn't reply. He just kept on holding with those strong metal fingers. I turned away.

The thrumming of the boiler grew louder and louder around me. The heat from the furnace became so great I couldn't bear it. I backed away. Steam shrieked through seams and around valves.

"The boiler is going to explode," Freddie shouted down the workshop stairs, mimicking the voice of the native Martian. "Get out of there!"

There was a moment's pause, then, faintly, the other man replied, "Then stop it."

"I can't," Freddie shouted back. "Someone's jammed it. It'll destroy the house."

Frog-face cursed.

Another seam sprang on the boiler. Steam punched out, splitting bricks apart and scattering fragments across the wet floor. I backed away. The automatic servants were grinding to a halt now, their delicate mechanisms overwhelmed, but it was too late. The furnace was roaring too fiercely. No one could stop it.

I turned and ran.

The boiler's shriek increased behind me as I raced up the servants' stairs. I burst into the corridor just as Frog-face came up the stairs leading from the workshop. Freddie grabbed him around the neck with one hand and punched him in the stomach. Frog-face folded over. Mama, Papa, and Jane emerged behind him.

Freddie had done it! He'd freed them. I started to cheer. Then something cold touched my throat. I smelled sweat. A rough hand grabbed my arm.

The native Martian had somehow managed to free himself and had found a weapon. The serrated edge felt like a kitchen knife.

"Edward!" Mama screamed. The native Martian pushed the knife harder against my throat. Papa laid a hand on Mama's arm, his eyes never leaving me.

"Step away!" the Martian shouted at Freddie. "Keep your hands above your head and get against the wall."

Freddie did what he was told.

Frog-face took a long club from his belt. In a single, vicious movement, he drove it into Freddie's stomach. Freddie's breath exploded out. He fell to the floor and curled around his stomach. Jane shrieked. Freddie gasped as he fought for breath.

The Martian dragged me toward the door of the house. Frog-face followed, herding Mama, Papa, and Jane ahead of him.

A sharp crack sounded below. The house seemed to lunge to one side. The movement knocked me forward. I turned the motion into a roll as the Martian shot out his arms for balance. I hit the floor, still moving, came up onto my feet, and ran. Spitting fury, the Martian chased after me.

We came out onto the lawn, into the clear, steam-free air.

I cut suddenly left, and the Martian missed me by an inch. He was taller and faster than me, but he couldn't turn as easily. I dodged under a thrown-out arm. Mama, Papa, and Jane stumbled out of the house, followed by Frog-face. There was no sign of Freddie.

"Leave him!" Frog-face shouted at the Martian. "Look."

The Martian slackened off. I tore away from him.

An airship lifted over the fern-trees. It blotted out the setting sun. Its huge, spring-powered propellers pounded the tops of the canopy, sending the fern-trees into a cacophony of sleepy protest.

The men hurried toward it, still pushing Mama, Papa, and Jane ahead of them. A ladder unrolled down.

Another, much louder crack shook the house. For a moment, it stood frozen. Then, as though a giant had shrugged beneath it, it bucked up. Bricks and timbers separated, and glass splintered from the windows. The house seemed to hang, broken, in the air. Then gravity took hold, and it crashed down, sending bricks, dust, and shards of wood flying.

Freddie sprinted from the collapsing ruin. He flung himself down, covering his head. The dust rolled over him, hiding him from view.

The men reached the airship ladder. The Martian manhandled Jane onto the first rung and forced her up. Mama and Papa followed, and finally Frog-face climbed onto the bottom rung. The airship started to rise.

"No!" I yelled. I raced toward the airship. It was rising

slowly, fighting against gravity, but soon it would be out of reach. I increased my pace.

Almost lazily, Frog-face pulled a device from his pocket and flicked it at me. Another clockwork Martian starblade whirred through the air. I threw myself to one side. The starblade *thunked* into the ground not a yard distant.

Then it was too late. The airship rose and turned. In seconds it was above the fern-trees, swinging away, its propellers driving it up and on.

I stood there and watched until it was gone, out of sight, and Mama, Papa, and Jane with it.

PART TWO

Into the Wilds

The Chase Begins

Dust settled over the red Martian grass.

The sun was going down. Long shadows stretched from the fern-tree forest across the lawn and the ruins of our house. In the distance, the *thwop-thwop* of the airship's propellers faded into silence.

"They're gone," I whispered.

I hadn't been able to stop them. I'd read a thousand stories in *Thrilling Martian Tales* about kidnaps and villains and daring rescues, and I still hadn't known what to do. I'd never felt so useless or so frightened in my life.

"Blast it!" Freddie was limping toward me, leaning on his walking stick. He was covered in so much dust he looked like a ghost. "They got away?"

I nodded. "And took Mama, Papa, and Jane with them."

Freddie swore again. "Our friend with the face mask got away, too. He wasn't where I left him."

Putty and Olivia hurried across from the other side of the lawn. For once, Olivia seemed too shocked to reprimand Freddie for the swearing.

"They had an airship!" Putty said, eyes wide and shining. "Why did they want to kidnap Jane? They should have kidnapped me. I've never flown in an airship."

"It was Sir Titus," I said to Freddie. "After you saw him leave in the airship, he must have circled around and waited for his men to do their job. He must have planned to pick them up the moment they'd finished their work."

"Then straight off to Lunae Planum and the dragon tomb." Freddie shook his head. "That way no one would have a chance of stopping him. I underestimated him."

"I don't understand," Olivia said. "Why is Sir Titus doing this? He's a friend of Mama's."

"Sir Titus Dane isn't a friend of anyone except himself," Freddie said.

"Sir Titus has a map that shows the location of an undiscovered dragon tomb," I said. "But it's in code. He wanted to use Papa's water abacus to decode it and lead him to the tomb. Those men were working for him."

"But you destroyed the abacus," Olivia said, her face pale. "And now he has our family."

"What will Sir Titus do with them?" I asked Freddie.

Freddie looked grim. "He'll take them to Lunae City and

force your father to build a new machine. He may not know exactly where the dragon tomb is, but it won't be far from Lunae City."

I turned to Putty. "So how long will it take Papa to re-build the water abacus?"

Putty thought about it for a moment. "Ten days. It's easy now we know how. An extra day to get the parts, I expect."

"And another day to get to Lunae City in that airship," Freddie said. "Twelve days total."

Twelve days. That wasn't long. My family might be safe until the water abacus was done, but there was no way Sir Titus would just let them go afterward. As soon as he didn't need Papa any longer, they would be finished.

"What if Papa refuses to build it?" Olivia said.

"He won't," I said. "Sir Titus has Mama and Jane. Papa will do as Sir Titus wishes. He'll build the abacus and decode the map." Then Sir Titus would have no further use for any of them. I clenched my fists. I would never let him hurt them. Never. "We have to go to Lunae City," I said. "Right away."

"We?" Freddie said. "Edward, this won't be a carriage ride in the park. It'll be difficult and dangerous, and I don't need—"

"Don't need what?" I said, feeling my cheeks redden.

"Forget it. Look, does your father have an automatic carriage?"

I nodded toward the stable block. Bricks from the explosion had crashed down on it, shattering the roof tiles, but it was still in one piece. "In there. Freddie, I'm not staying. Sir Titus has my family. It's my job to rescue them."

"It's your job to look after Olivia and Putty," Freddie said. "Have you forgotten?"

"The girls can stay," I said. "They'll be safe with the neighbors."

"No." Olivia's voice was quiet but firm. "We're coming. They're our family, too."

"It's too dangerous," I said, knowing that I was using the same argument that Freddie had just used on me.

"If it's too dangerous for us, it's too dangerous for you," Olivia said. "And what would you have us do? Play cards and sing and chatter with our neighbors while your lives hang in the balance? Sit and wait as though nothing were wrong, all the while not knowing if you are alive or dead, whether you have rescued Mama and Papa and Jane or been captured yourself? Do our sewing and embroidery like good little girls while we wait for word from you, word that might never come? No, Edward. We will be coming with you."

"Enough!" Freddie thumped his walking stick on the ground. "We don't have time for this. Very well. We will all go. And God help us, because this is no way to run a rescue mission." He jabbed his walking stick toward the stables. "I will be getting the automatic carriage prepared. Be ready to go in five minutes. If you are not, I *will* leave without you." He stomped off, and Putty scurried after him. I took one last look at our ruined house.

In the late evening light, the glitterswarms were rising from the depths of the Valles Marineris, turning the sky into a sheet of shifting gold. High, wispy clouds reflected red from the sinking sun. Dust and smoke from the collapsed house rose and spread to obscure the sight. I turned away.

My foot caught on a piece of debris. Lying among the splinters of wood and the shards of brick was my copy of *Thrilling Martian Tales*. Its cover was torn and its pages filthy.

I almost left it there, but it was the only thing I still had. Everything else was gone. I shoved it into my jacket pocket. Then I followed Olivia, Putty, and Freddie to the stables, where Papa's automatic carriage awaited, to begin our long journey north in pursuit of Sir Titus and my family.

◆

The drive to Ophir City in Papa's automatic carriage took all night. The sun was rising over the hills as we came through a pass between overhanging claws of rock and saw the city spread below us. I couldn't help but count down the hours. Not twelve days anymore. Eleven and a half. Maybe less. The automatic carriage was so *slow*.

Freddie rolled the power dial back to zero and disengaged the round spring that drove the carriage. He loosened his shoulders, then slumped with an exhausted sigh.

"This is it," he said. "Ophir City. There's been a town here for over two thousand years."

Tall, closely packed wooden buildings in the old Martian style clustered in unplanned confusion, their turrets, spirals, and spires prickling the air like an enormous, crazy hedge-hog. Clockwork Express tracks swept high over the hills to the west in a glittering bronze arc and plunged down to the city. Pillars every couple of hundred yards held the railway above the ground. In the morning light, the tracks shone like thread in the Martian sky.

"You can see the Clockwork Express tracks from the void when you fly from Earth to Mars, you know," Freddie said. "When the Mars-ship sails down into the atmosphere, you can see them like a golden spiderweb laid across the surface of Mars."

Putty sighed.

"That's beautiful," Olivia said.

"Yes," Freddie agreed. "And empty. When you're up there, coming down, you see just how little of Mars we've con-quered. The spider's web looks fragile and it doesn't stretch far. There are places it doesn't even get close to."

"Like Lunae City," I said.

"Yes. Like Lunae City."

Ophir was the last stop on the Express line that ran all the way from Tharsis City, a journey of over two thousand miles. Beyond Ophir, the only way north or east was by air-ship. The morning Express had already arrived. It would have run all night, skirting the Candor and Ophir Valleys in the dark. I could just make out the passengers disembarking. A single, giant airship was tethered to a spindly tower above the station. Its silvery, oblong balloon was over a hundred yards long, and it cast a shadow over a large portion of the city.

Freddie glanced at his pocket watch. "Time to go. The airship departs at ten. If we miss it, we'll have to walk to Lunae City." He flashed a smile as he dropped his watch back in his waistcoat pocket.

"Walk?" Olivia said. "Is it far?"

Freddie waved a hand negligently. "Oh, just hundreds of miles of wilderness and desert. Hardly worth mentioning."

"We're not going to miss the airship," I said. "We've got three hours."

"That's true," Freddie said with a smile. Moving the brake lever forward, he started the automatic carriage rolling down the hill toward the city. "But we have a problem. If we intend to book tickets to Lunae City, we'll need to pay for them. And I don't have a penny to my name."

Olivia dropped her gaze. "Then we are destitute . . . helpless."

"Nonsense!" Freddie said cheerily from the driver's seat. "You have me!"

"Marvelous," I muttered. I was exhausted from the night's drive, feeling my bruises, and worried about Jane and my parents. I wasn't in the mood for Freddie's sense of humor.

The automatic carriage reached the tangle of wooden Martian houses on the outskirts of the city. The tall houses jutted out so far that they nearly touched each other, turning the road into a tunnel.

"Actually," Freddie said, "I do have a solution. We'll sell the carriage."

"No!" Putty said, jerking upright in her seat. "Papa built it himself. There's not another one quite like it anywhere."

"Which is why someone will buy it," Freddie said.

"We haven't got a choice," I said. "We have to be on that airship."

Freddie turned his attention back to the road. This early in the morning, the sunlight didn't really penetrate between the tightly packed native Martian houses, but the street was already full of men pushing barrows, women carrying baskets, and children darting about.

I'd only been to Ophir City once before, when I was five years old. The twelve-hour drive from our house was too far to be comfortable. Usually when we traveled, we took a boat up the Valles Marineris to Candor City on the other side of the Candor Valley, and then continued on the Clockwork Express toward Tharsis and the rest of British Mars. I wasn't used to this city.

The people here were a mixture of native Martians and those of Earth descent, and although they shared the streets, they didn't really mix. The taller native Martians kept their gazes fixed firmly above the heads of the Earth natives.

"They're not very friendly, are they?" I said, remembering the native Martian who'd captured us. We hardly saw any native Martians where we lived, and there were none at all in my school.

"You're wrong," Freddie said. "Native Martians are as friendly and generous as any Englishman. More so than most."

I snorted.

"If they trust you," Freddie added.

"Why wouldn't they?" Olivia said.

Freddie steered the carriage around a man who had set up his stall in the middle of the street. "Mars was their world for thousands of years," he said. "Then we arrived from Earth and swept across it, taking their cities and ransacking the tombs of their kings. Imagine they had done that to Earth. How would we feel? Why should they trust us?"

"We don't all approve of the way they've been treated," Olivia said.

Freddie smiled. "I wish there were more on Mars like you, Cousin Olivia."

Olivia blushed and ducked her head.

"The native Martians think it's rude to meet the gaze of someone who isn't a friend or family," Freddie said. "Just like you would think it was rude to speak to someone you hadn't been introduced to. To them, we're the ones who are being rude."

"If anyone had stolen my planet," Putty said, "*I* wouldn't be polite to them."

Freddie laughed. "You'd make a fine native Martian, Cousin Parthenia." He nosed the carriage through the press of people. "Blast it!" He slapped the seat beside him. "This is taking too long!" He glanced up at the airship that was still visible between the elaborate spires of the houses. His lips twisted into a half smile, and he looked back at Olivia. "Forgive my language."

"We're all tired," Olivia said.

Freddie cleared his throat awkwardly. "The truth is, native Martians have good reason to treat outsiders with suspicion and fear. But prove yourself a friend and you will see how welcoming they truly are."

◄◆►

It took us well over an hour to reach the station. When we got there, the street below the concourse was packed from end to end with a mixture of steam-driven and horse-drawn carriages. Drivers were shouting at each other, but no one seemed to be moving.

"Better get out," Freddie said. "Wait for me in the station."

"Where are you going?" I said.

"To sell the carriage."

"Then we should all come." I looked out the window. "This doesn't look safe."

Freddie shook his head. "I need to get rid of the carriage fast. That means no questions, no delays. I might have to go to someone whose . . . ah . . . morality is not of the highest standard."

"Criminals?" Putty said, perking up for the first time since we'd reached the city. "Can I come?"

"Parthenia!" Olivia said. "No young lady should dream of associating with criminals."

Putty made a face.

"He's right," I said, opening the carriage door. "We should wait in the station. We'll be fine."

I helped Olivia climb down from the carriage onto the crowded walkway. Putty jumped out after us. Olivia stared after the automatic carriage as it pulled away.

"I can't believe he left us here."

"But he is very handsome, isn't he?" Putty said, gazing up at our older sister with wide eyes.

Olivia blushed.

"He'll be fine," I said. "Freddie can look after himself."

"I didn't say I was worried about him!" Olivia said, then turned away with an "Oh!" at Putty's spreading grin.

Even though the Clockwork Express tracks dipped down at the terminus, the platforms were high above the rest of the city. A wide staircase led up to the concourse, and a steam-powered elevator hauled up heavy goods and the passengers who didn't want to climb. We took the stairs.

The ticket counter for the Imperial Martian Airship Company stood on one side of the main station concourse, beneath a large clock. We flopped on a bench opposite and settled in to wait. We were all exhausted. I thought we probably looked more like something nasty that had been washed up on the beach than respectable people waiting to travel high above the surface of Mars in a luxurious airship. None of us had slept much on the journey. We were unwashed and stained with dust from the explosion. My head ached from being whacked about by our captors. I decided to have a bet with myself about whether we'd be arrested as vagrants before Freddie got back.

I watched the hands of the clock creep slowly around its face.

"We should explore," Putty said. "I've never been in a real old Martian city before. There could be anything here."

"Exactly," Olivia said. "That's why we're not going any-where."

Through the steel and glass ceiling over the concourse, I could see the airship tethered high above us. The giant springs that would drive its propellers were being hoisted up and the spent springs lowered down on the other end of pulleys. The passenger gondola had been winched down on its ropes from the long, cigar-shaped balloon to meet the boarding platform. Passengers were already embarking. I drummed my fingers impatiently on the bench.

By half past nine, Freddie still hadn't appeared. The trickle of passengers heading for the airship had almost dried up, and the elevator carrying the luggage now stood empty.

"What if he doesn't come?" Putty said. "What if some-thing's happened to him?"

"Nothing's happened to him!" Olivia said. Her fingers twisted nervously.

The clerk behind the counter sat back in his chair, yawning. The airship would have to leave on time; the Imperial Martian Airship Company *always* left on time. If we weren't on board, it wouldn't wait for us.

"Stop fidgeting, Edward," Olivia whispered. She straightened her back and lifted her chin.

I clenched my fingers and bit my lip.

Twenty-five to ten. Where on Mars was Freddie? I couldn't wait any longer. I jumped to my feet. "I'm going to look for him."

"No!" Olivia said, then dropped her voice, as though she'd surprised herself by speaking so loudly. "You can't just go wandering off. What if *you* get hurt or lost? Who's going to come looking for you? We can't split up."

Across from us, the clerk stood, stretched, and reached for the blind above the counter.

"Here he is!" Putty shouted, bouncing up. She waved wildly, drawing disapproving glances.

Freddie hurried toward us across the concourse, carrying two heavy cases, one in each hand. His walking stick jutted from under his arm.

"Oh, Cousin Freddie!" Olivia ran past us. I stared after her, astonished, as she flung her arms around him. Freddie dropped the cases.

"Cousin Olivia . . . I . . ."

Then Olivia must have remembered how improper this was, because she backed away.

"We were so worried," she said. "What would we have done if you'd been hurt? You shouldn't have left us for so long."

Freddie wilted.

"I . . . ah . . . that is . . . I bought us all some clothes," Freddie stuttered. "I do hope I got the right sizes and styles. Not exactly my specialty, girls' clothes. That is to say . . ."

Olivia's eyes widened. "You are wonderful, Cousin Freddie. I could not have worn these for another hour. The dust has ruined them."

"I'm starting to feel sick," Putty muttered.

"The counter's closing," I said. "We're going to miss the airship."

Freddie blinked, then whirled, snatched up the cases, and rushed across to the counter. Too late. The clerk snapped down the blind. Freddie knocked on the glass. The clerk's head appeared around the edge of the blind, one eyebrow raised disdainfully above his glasses.

"We're closed. Come back tomorrow."

Freddie leaned forward, blocking my view of the window, but I saw enough to notice him reach inside his jacket, pull something out, and flash it briefly to the clerk.

The clerk popped up the blind again.

Whatever Freddie had shown the clerk had been enough to make the man abandon his procedures and reopen his counter. Clerks *never* did that. *Another of Freddie's blasted secrets.* I'd thought we were done with those. I fixed his back with a baleful glare.

"How many?" the clerk said.

"A suite with two cabins," Freddie said. "Four people for Lunae City."

Grumbling, the clerk produced the tickets.

Behind us, heavy footsteps came running up. I turned to see a small man with extravagant eyebrows staggering toward us, pulling two enormous trunks behind him. He was slumped under the weight, his cravat was half undone, and he was sweating like a waterfall.

"I'm not too late, am I?" the man called as he stumbled up to us.

Freddie stepped aside, giving the clerk a wide smile. "I don't believe so."

The clerk shot Freddie a look of disgust, but he didn't protest.

"Thank you," the little man said. "I must reach Lunae City. I believe a particularly interesting strata has been revealed by the shifting sands."

"I beg your pardon?" Freddie said. I couldn't have put it better myself.

"I do apologize," the man said. He let go of one of his trunks. It hit the ground with a solid, heavy clunk. "Dr. Octavius Blood, Martian. I am a geologist."

"Martian?" Putty said. "You don't look like a native Martian."

Olivia winced at Putty's rudeness, but the geologist didn't seem to notice.

"Indeed not, although, in a way, are we not all native Martians now? I do call myself a Martian, because I believe I am a Martian first and foremost. It may be that I was born in the British Martian Territories, but I do not see myself as such. I am no more British Martian than Chinese Martian or Turkish Martian or Patagonian Martian. No, we are all children of the Martian rock, are we not? We crawl upon its surface, and it is to Mars that we belong."

"I'm supposed to be closed," the clerk said, shooting a glance at Freddie.

"Ah, yes, yes," Dr. Blood said. "One, to Lunae City, where my new rocks await! First class, if you please!"

The moment the geologist had his ticket, the clerk slammed his blind back down and stalked away from the window.

"Now," Freddie said, "we'd better run. Time and airships wait for no man. Ha-ha."

We reached the elevator just in time. The final pieces of luggage had been loaded, and the porter stood tapping his finger against the gate as we rushed up.

"All aboard!" Freddie shouted.

The geologist, Dr. Blood, scampered in behind us and let his trunks fall. He gasped, then wiped his brow and looked up at us.

"What on Mars do you have in there?" Freddie asked.

"Looks like you're carrying half a mountain around with you. Reminds me of the time old Huffy—do you know old Huffy?"

"Er, no," Dr. Blood replied, looking confused.

"Don't know old Huffy? Well. I thought everyone knew old Huffy. Anyway, it reminds me of the time we were going to go boating on the—"

"My rock samples," the geologist said, before Freddie could launch into his story, which I was sure he was making up on the spot. "I always carry my rock samples with me. You never know when you might need them. Are you interested in rocks, sir?"

Freddie blinked. "Ah . . . Um . . . Can't say I've exactly *studied* the fellows. Still, never too late to learn, eh?"

"Quite, quite," Dr. Blood said. "I have some particularly fascinating samples of sandstone. I have, in fact, published several monographs on the subject."

"Monographs, you say?" Freddie said. "Well, well." But by now I recognized that look in Freddie's eyes. He didn't believe a word the geologist was saying, and neither did I. Because when Dr. Blood had let his trunks fall, the sound had distinctly been of metal clanking together, not rocks.

— 10 —

Secrets and Spies

The airship gondola hanging beneath the great balloon was made up of two levels and was almost as long as the balloon itself. Walking up the boarding platform to the top level would have felt like walking up the gangplank to an enormous ocean-going ship . . . if the ship had been a hundred yards up in the air with nothing underneath it. I looked down and had to grab the safety rail.

I hadn't forgotten that Freddie was still keeping secrets from me, and I hadn't forgiven him. We were going to be stuck on this airship for a full day. If Freddie thought he could keep me in the dark the whole trip, he was fooling himself. The moment I got him alone, I'd get the truth. I pushed myself off the rail and followed him up the boarding platform, glaring the whole way.

The top level of the gondola was made up of a grand salon

for the passengers to relax in, a drawing room, a large dining room, a kitchen, and a small ballroom, although why anyone would want to spend the trip dancing was beyond me. The back third was closed off. I guessed it must contain the springs that drove the propellers. Each spring was almost as big as a house.

At the front, there was a wide viewing deck with a high rail so that passengers could sit or stroll about. A walkway stretched around both sides of the gondola, all the way to the back, where I could see teardrop-shaped wooden lifeboats the size of big carriages, hanging like chrysalises from the stern rail. Each lifeboat was wrapped in wide canvas wings and had a square entry hatch that stood open on its roof. Rope ladders led over the rail to the hatches.

We followed a white-uniformed steward down to the lower level, where the cabins were located. Freddie sauntered along as though he hadn't a care in the world. My teeth clenched as he twirled his walking stick in the air. Did he think this was all a *joke*?

Our suite of cabins was on the left of the airship—the port side, the steward called it. There was a single door leading into a small private salon for the four of us to share. It had two chaise longues, a couple of high-backed chairs, a low table, a sideboard, and a small cabinet. On either side of the salon, polished wormwood doors led into the bedrooms. Someone had spent far too much time inlaying tiny brass patterns into the wood.

"Well. Here we are," Freddie said. He passed one of the cases to the girls. "There should be something you can wear in there. I'm afraid I was only able to procure secondhand clothes. I know it's not what you are used to, Cousin Olivia. There was no time for a fitting . . ." He cleared his throat. "Edward and I will meet you here when you are done."

I gave them a quick jerk of my head, then stalked into our room.

There were two neatly made beds in the cabin I was sharing with Freddie; a writing desk with quill, ink, and paper laid out; a couple of chests of drawers; and a cupboard. The rugs that lay across the wooden floor were thick enough to lose a foot in. Ignoring Freddie, I crossed to the window and peered down to the city below, my hands clenched on the windowsill. The houses and the people hurrying along the streets looked tiny from up here.

"You're angry with me," Freddie said, throwing himself onto one of the beds.

I didn't bother to reply.

A horn sounded. I braced myself against the window frame as, with a slight jerk, the whole passenger gondola winched up toward the airship's balloon.

Freddie sighed. "We're under way."

I watched out the window, trying to calm myself, as the tether fell away from the nose of the balloon. Springs engaged, and the enormous propellers began to beat. Slowly, the airship turned and pulled away from its tower.

"Are you going to tell me why you're angry?" Freddie asked after a moment.

"What did you show that clerk?" I demanded.

Freddie folded his hands behind his head. "Not sure what you mean, old chap."

"Oh, don't play the fool, Freddie. I saw you." I pushed away from the window.

"Can't hide much from you, can I? I showed him the identification of an Imperial Martian Airship Commissioner."

"You're not a commissioner."

"I got the papers from the men I sold the carriage to. I thought everything might go more easily if I had some official papers."

I shook my head angrily. "I don't believe half of what you're saying. I know you're not an idiot, and your stories don't hold up. What are you really up to?"

He turned a perfectly blank face to me. Normally, I could read every emotion on Freddie's face as easily as I could read my magazines. Right now, I couldn't get a thing.

"You're either going to tell me," I said, "or I'm going to tell Putty and Livvy everything I know and everything I've seen. I'm going to make sure they're as suspicious of you as I am. I'm not going to let you lie to us and put us in danger anymore."

Freddie sighed, then gestured me over. "If I tell you, Edward, you can't tell anyone else. Not even your sisters. Do you understand? It's important."

Reluctantly, I nodded.

He let out a deep breath. "Very well. I'm not a student at Oxford—well, I am a student, but that's just cover. I work for the British-Martian Intelligence Service. I'm a spy."

"You?" I choked out. "A spy?" I felt the color rise in my cheeks, and my throat tightened until it hurt. "You can't be."

Freddie was a spy? Freddie was an idiot! A famous idiot. *I* was the one who wanted to be a spy. It felt like he'd stolen something from me. I'd rather he punched me in the gut.

Freddie shrugged. "I wouldn't be very good at my job if it was easy to believe. You're not *supposed* to suspect me." He leaned forward on the bed, bringing himself closer to me. His voice was scarcely more than a whisper. "When Sir Titus Dane disappeared so suddenly ten years ago, the service thought he must be up to something. They'd been keeping an eye on him, but he managed to slip away. They didn't track him down again until a couple of years ago, when they found him working under the identity of Professor Alfred Westfield at King's College, Oxford." He gave half a grin. "That's where I came in. I'd already been recruited by the Intelligence Service when I turned sixteen. The service often recruits promising candidates young and directs our education and careers."

"That was when you suddenly turned into a blithering idiot," I said.

He smiled. "It was cover. Trust me, when you get to that

age, most people are half expecting you to turn into an idiot, so no one was surprised. People are much more likely to let something slip if they think you're stupid. Anyway, by the time the Intelligence Service uncovered Sir Titus's new identity, my training was complete. I was the right age and from the right background, so I was sent to Oxford to spy on him."

"I'm guessing you found out what he was up to," I said. My voice sounded hollow. "What's it got to do with the map you stole?"

"Copied, not stole. It took me almost two years to find anything, but one day he must have been called away in a hurry. I found the dragon tomb map he was trying to decode, shoved under a pile of papers in a drawer in his office. When Sir Titus disappeared from Mars, he'd been disgraced. He'd led three missions that had discovered and opened dragon tombs, but he'd been stealing their locations from other archaeologists. Society turned against him."

"Mama seemed happy to see him," I said.

Freddie nodded. "Sir Titus Dane was an important man. Most people wouldn't have anything to do with him, but he still had friends and admirers. The Danes are an old family, and his dragon tombs gave British Mars some of its most spectacular inventions. But even before his disgrace, Sir Titus had been frustrated that the profit from his discoveries had gone to British Mars rather than to Sir Titus himself. He had no interest in helping his country, only in increasing his own wealth and fame. What the British Martian government paid him wasn't enough for the likes of Sir Titus Dane."

"So he's been trying to find a dragon tomb on his own?" I said. Despite myself, I was being drawn into the story. "Using this secret map?"

"With the intention of selling the discoveries to whoever would pay the most. Part of my job was watching what he was doing and who he was meeting. He'd started receiving secret visitors late at night. At least one of them was a French agent. You understand what that means? He would've sold the discoveries to the Emperor Napoleon. Neither Earth nor Mars can afford to put more power into that madman's hands."

"But Sir Titus couldn't decode it," I said. "That's the whole point, isn't it?"

"Maybe. But he'd been working on it for years. I didn't know how close he was."

And wasn't *that* convenient? I paced the floor, my footsteps swallowed by the thick rug. "Why didn't you destroy the map?" I said. "Or steal it? Unless you really wanted it for yourself."

"I won't deny that British Mars would like what's in the dragon tomb, but that's not the main reason. Sir Titus would have copies. He's not a stupid man."

"So you made a duplicate," I said. "And then you came to us. You brought those men with you."

Freddie sighed. "I never meant to. I'd heard about your father's water abacus. I thought I could use it to decode the map, and if I could do it before Sir Titus, British Mars would be able to open the tomb. The discoveries would benefit everyone."

"So how's that turning out?" I said.

He ducked his head. "I made a mistake. Somehow, they were onto me."

"A mistake?" I spat. "You got Mama, Papa, and Jane kidnapped. You nearly got Putty and Olivia killed. You destroyed our house and Papa's inventions." I kicked the writing desk. "God, Freddie. Was it really that important?"

"Yes!" He pushed himself off the bed and grabbed my shoulder. "The technology used by the people who built the dragon tombs was far more advanced than anything we have. Those aren't just toys in there. There are terrifying weapons. We can't allow them to fall into French hands. The Emperor Napoleon has turned his eyes toward Mars. If we give him the means, he will invade."

"Then you should have asked!" I snapped, pulling myself free from his grip. "The government should have asked. Papa would have helped."

"Sir Titus still has friends in high places. He still has influence and wealth. We couldn't risk it. If he'd found out—"

"If he'd found out," I said bitterly, "it would've been no worse than the mess you've managed to make."

I stalked back to the window. The tempo of the engines

increased, and the airship picked up speed. I watched as we curved out over the city, avoiding the spreading plumes of smoke and steam from the vast manufactories in the north of the city.

Freddie in the British-Martian Intelligence Service. It was a joke.

"Edward," Freddie said urgently, "you *mustn't* tell anyone of this."

I nodded grimly, still not looking back at him. "I promised, didn't I? I'll keep my word."

"We should change into some clean clothes," Freddie said. "I'm not happy leaving the girls alone for too long."

◆

Freddie had done a good job of picking out clothes for me. The breeches, waistcoat, and jacket fit perfectly. The sleeves of my shirt were a bit long, but I pulled them up under my jacket to hide them. He'd even managed to find a pair of shoes that were my exact size.

He'd done even better with Olivia. When she came out of her cabin half an hour later, she was already blushing. She was wearing a gown exactly the same color as her eyes, and it was far tighter than anything I'd ever seen her wear. Even Freddie seemed surprised. He gaped at her. I had to nudge him to break his trance.

"I, ah, trust you were able to find something that suited? The storekeeper assured me the gowns were the height of fashion in both Tharsis City and London. Um."

Olivia blushed even more deeply.

"Oh, for heaven's sake!" Putty pushed her way past Olivia. "Are we going to stand in the doorway all day long?" Putty was wearing the exact same thing as me. I hid a grin.

"Ah, quite," Freddie managed. He was still staring at Olivia. For once, I thought, he wasn't putting on the impression of imbecility. I was used to men making fools of themselves over Jane, or even Mama, if they were men of a certain age, but I'd never seen it happen with Olivia, and by the looks of it, neither had she. A shy smile spread across her face.

"So," Putty said enthusiastically. "Do we get to see it?"

Freddie blinked. "I beg your pardon?"

"The map," Putty said. "The one you stole from Sir Titus."

"Copied."

"Whatever. Can we see it?"

Freddie glanced around, as though he thought someone might be watching. The door leading to the corridor was firmly closed and latched.

With a nod, he summoned us over. He reached into his sleeve and drew out a rolled sheet of paper. We crowded around the table as he smoothed it out. The map showed a steep valley with several towers of rock. To one side, a symbol had been drawn.

"That symbol on its own always means 'dragon tomb,'" Freddie said, pointing to it. "It's unmistakable."

Across the top of the sheet, Freddie had copied several lines of symbols and pictures in a neat hand.

"What are those?" Olivia asked, her finger trailing across the symbols.

"Ah!" Freddie said. "Well noticed. They're called ideograms."

I squinted. "I've read about them."

Freddie looked up at me. "I'm impressed. Not many people study the Ancient Martian civilization. Where did you read about ideograms?"

I coughed, suddenly remembering and wishing I'd kept my mouth shut. "In *Thrilling Martian Tales*," I mumbled.

"Edward gets everything he knows from *Thrilling Martian Tales*," Putty said.

"Oh, that's not fair!" Olivia said, her lips twitching. "He also reads *Unlikely Adventure Stories*."

"The point is," I said, "they're what the Ancient Martian tyrants used to write their commandments and their, um, death warrants and . . ." Now that I thought about it, *Thrilling Martian Tales* had been a bit thin on the details. "Anyway, they're a language," I finished.

"Almost," Freddie said, smiling. "But it's a little more complicated than that. They're not the kind of writing we're used to. The symbols and pictures are called ideograms because each one stands for a particular *idea.* That stork"—he pointed to a weird drawing of a bird standing on one leg in the middle of the first line—"means balance, or the equal flow of energy in and out. The cloud next to it represents abstract thought. And so on. When you put them together, the ideograms act a little like a sentence."

"But you know what the ideograms mean?" I said. "Why can't you read it?"

"It's not that easy. The ideograms don't mean the same when they're together as when they're on their own. They interact with each other to give information, and you have to know how they interact to find out what has been written."

"And you don't."

"No." Freddie scratched at his temple. "Think of it this way. Just because you know all the letters of the alphabet, that doesn't mean you can understand a word you've never seen before. It's even worse if you don't even know what language it's in. The word might be in English or French or German or Spanish, except when you're dealing with ideograms, it's as if there are ten thousand languages and you have no clue as to which one is being used. That's why you need a key."

"What kind of key?" I asked.

Freddie straightened. "A key is just a set of symbols that give us a hint as to how to read the ideograms."

"And there's no key?"

Freddie slapped his hand on the table. "No. And there's *always* a key! Without one, it's completely meaningless. It would take us a hundred years to try every key we've discovered, and even then it might be written using a key we've never come across before. Someone didn't want us to be able to read this."

"But with Papa's water abacus . . ." Putty said, eyes lighting up.

"Exactly! The abacus is a powerful computational device capable of running hundreds of calculations each minute. It could complete every possible combination using every key."

And in about eleven days, Sir Titus would have a new abacus. Then he wouldn't need our family anymore.

Olivia bent over the map, frowning. "Why do we need to translate anything? Can't we just find a valley that matches what's shown on the map?"

"Unfortunately not," Freddie said. "The Lunae Planum around the Martian Nile is riddled with narrow valleys like that. There are hundreds of them, and the map is almost two thousand years old. Even on the Lunae Planum, where it scarcely rains, the valleys have changed shape. It would be impossible to find the right valley simply from the map."

"I don't know why everyone's making such a fuss," Putty said. "We'll simply rescue Mama and Papa—and Jane, I suppose, if we must. Then we'll find the tomb. There is no need to worry, Cousin Freddie." She patted his arm. "I'm really rather good at this kind of thing."

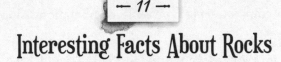

Interesting Facts About Rocks

The airship flew north throughout the day, its powerful propellers pushing hard through the air.

The day was clear, and only a few thin, high clouds broke up the blue sky. Above us, the vast balloon blocked the sunlight. Below, the farmlands around Ophir gave way to wilderness. Trees and undergrowth tangled and pushed up, as though they were fighting to get to the sun. Whip-vines lashed hundreds of yards into the air, trying to snare the shadow of the passing airship. Faint roars, cries, and bellows drifted up, and sometimes whole areas of vegetation shook and bent, as though great battles were being fought out of sight. The wilderness was so big and untamed, it was frightening. Looking at it roll past, mile after mile, was like being hypnotized. I shivered. I was glad to be so high above it all.

In the middle of the afternoon, we passed over the first of a series of crater-shaped, eye-blue lakes, seething with bird-life. Olivia and Freddie joined Putty and me at the rail of the viewing deck.

"I've never traveled so far from civilization," Olivia said, gazing at the deep water far below. "It seems . . . lonely."

"It is," Freddie said. "I spent some time on an expedition into the wilderness. Down there, you might be on a world upon which mankind has never set foot. There's only the wild. But come." He straightened. "The airships are safe, and we'll be in Lunae City by tomorrow." He took Olivia's arm and escorted her to the deck chairs at the rear of the viewing deck. "Perhaps we should have some tea? I'm exhausted."

Putty and I stayed at the rail, watching the landscape slip by beneath us. What would happen when we reached Lunae City? I hadn't paid much attention when my teachers talked about Lunae Planum and the Ancient Martian civilization. History and geography books were boring. My magazines were far more exciting. Now I had no idea what to expect.

We were flying over one of the larger lakes—I guessed it was about a mile wide—when several big, winged shapes launched themselves from the jagged cliffs surrounding it and flapped their way up toward the airship.

Putty leaned out through the railings to peer down at the shapes. "Pterodactyls."

I grabbed the back of her jacket.

"Immature ones," a voice said behind us. I jumped and almost lost my grip on Putty's jacket. Dr. Blood stood at my shoulder. I pulled Putty back through the railings and stepped away. I felt nervous with Dr. Blood standing so close behind me.

"I understand young pterodactyls have taken to following the airships in this part of the world," the small geologist said. "The cooks throw the leftover scraps from meals overboard as we fly, and the pterodactyls snap them up as they fall. You will see it after dinner. It is considered a fine entertainment among the passengers, although, of course, the diet is not good for the beasts themselves. I fear it can only hasten their tragic extinction."

"We'd better get back to my cousin and my sister," I said, gesturing toward Freddie and Olivia, who were talking quietly together. I stepped past Dr. Blood, dragging Putty after me.

There weren't many passengers on the viewing deck. Four men stood by one rail, talking. One of them turned away from his friends to watch Putty and me as we made our way over to Freddie and Olivia. I quickly looked away. I didn't like the way he was staring at us. I'd spent the morning worrying about Sir Titus. What if he'd had someone watching the airship terminal? They could have followed us on board. We were too exposed out here.

"Your cousin," the geologist said, scurrying after us. "Of course. You both showed so much interest in my collection of rocks." He looked around as we reached Freddie and Olivia. "Only, I am not sure I wish to set them out here." He threw a glance at the group of men clustered by the rail. "Some of the rocks are quite valuable, you know. Very rare."

"I really don't think anyone is going to steal your rocks," I said.

Dr. Blood peered up at me through his thick eyebrows, his forehead furrowing. "You are not a collector, I take it, young man. In any case, what if they were to roll off the edge of the deck? It would be most unfortunate if the airship were forced to land to retrieve them. Strange beasts stalk the wildlands, and even the plants are deadly." He shivered. "I would not like to find myself down there."

One of the men by the rail was still watching us.

"You're right," I said. "Let's go inside. The wind's getting a bit chilly, and you'll be able to lay your rocks out on a table."

"An admirable suggestion, young man," Dr. Blood said. "Admirable!"

Freddie offered his hand to Olivia to draw her out of her chair. "Lead the way, cousin!" he said heartily to me. "Always wanted to see a bunch of rocks."

The men by the rail had stopped talking, and every one of them was watching us go.

"Did you see the newspaper this morning, Mr. Winchester?" Dr. Blood said to Freddie as we reached the grand salon. "Terrible news."

"The newspaper?" Freddie said, opening the door and allowing Olivia and Putty through. "Good Lord, no! All that news and whatnot. Can't keep my eyes open through it."

"Look!" Putty said, ignoring both of them. "They have photon emission globes!" Three chandeliers hung from the ceiling of the grand salon, but instead of candles, they each held half a dozen brightly glowing balls the size of my fist. "I saw some of them in a photonic mechanician's shop. They are so amazing!"

"Today's news was not trivial," Dr. Blood said, talking over Putty.

Putty glared at him.

"Tell me later," I said, laying a hand on Putty's shoulder.

We made our way to an unoccupied table opposite the counter. An immaculately dressed automatic waiter moved smoothly through the salon on its well-oiled machinery, taking orders.

"What do you mean?" Freddie said, frowning at Dr. Blood.

"The *Tharsis Times* reports that South America has surrendered to the Emperor Napoleon," Dr. Blood said. "His forces have overwhelmed their brave resistance at last. It will not be long before Britain herself feels the full fury and might of the French Empire. And worse. Bonaparte is building vast shipyards at Pittsburgh in his American colony of Pennsylvania. It will not be long before they are able to turn out ships."

"Does that matter?" I asked. "Napoleon already has a large enough fleet." The British fleet had been shattered at Trafalgar eleven years ago and had never recovered. If the emperor hadn't been fighting in Europe and America, he could have captured Britain right then.

"But those ships are not for Britain," Dr. Blood said. "Pittsburgh is the location of North America's only dragon path terminus. The ships are intended for a future invasion of Mars."

For a moment, there was silence as we all imagined Napoleon's ships appearing in the sky above Mars.

"But do not fear!" Dr. Blood exclaimed. "The *Times* also reports that the Martian governments are constructing gun platforms that will float in the void around the dragon paths. Any ship that attempts to make the passage will be utterly destroyed. The monster may build as many ships as he wishes, but he may send them only one at a time past our guns."

The dragon paths were vast currents of air that twisted through the void between Mars and Earth. While Mars-ships traveled along the currents at great speed, the dragon paths were only wide enough for ships to travel in single file. If the Martian governments were able to deploy gun platforms, every Mars-ship that passed would be subject to withering fire.

"I wouldn't be so sure," Freddie said. "The emperor is no

fool. He has a crafty mind and a genius for strategy. If he's building ships, he's confident that they will reach their destination."

"Poppycock!" Dr. Blood said. "He cannot fly his ships through the void, nor can he create a dragon path where none exists. Mars shall not bow to his ambition!" He sat back, arms folded, looking smug.

Putty leaned across the low table. "Have you traveled by dragon path, Dr. Blood?"

"I?" Dr. Blood looked offended. "Indeed not! The dragon paths are a curse!"

Olivia blinked. "I beg your pardon?"

"The dragon paths have allowed Earth's parasites to come swarming over the bones of the once great Martian civilization, despoiling it and looting its treasures. Now the Emperor Napoleon threatens a new swarm of parasites. We shall not allow it. *I* shall not allow it."

"All our families come from Earth," Freddie said carefully. "Including yours, I suspect."

The small man sniffed. "I have become a true Martian, as we all must. Mars is our mother now."

Freddie settled back, hiding a smile. "I'm sure you are right."

"But we have forgotten our purpose here!" Dr. Blood reached into his overcoat and brought out three small pieces of stone, which he laid on the table in a line. "Sandstone!"

he said triumphantly. "All of them, even though it might seem hard to believe."

As far as I could see, they were all the same.

"Look at the variation in texture. Isn't it astonishing? No, please do not touch." This last bit came as Putty leaned forward, reaching for the rocks. "The grain on the second sample is quite delicate, you see. My personal theory is that it must have been formed when—"

I'd had enough. I couldn't just sit there. If Sir Titus had had someone following us, it would be the perfect opportunity for them to get up to mischief while we were being bored senseless by Dr. Blood.

"Please excuse me," I said, jumping to my feet.

Dr. Blood's eyebrows shot up. "No, no, my dear fellow! You have yet to see the finest piece in my collection. You will be astonished. However, first let me—"

Freddie shot me a quick, considering look, then gave me the briefest of nods. A moment later, he bent forward.

"I say!" he said loudly. "Is that a . . ."

His hand knocked into one of the stones, sending it flying from the table. The geologist let out a wail.

"Do forgive me!" Freddie said. "Knock my own head off next. Ha-ha. Here, allow me." He leaped to his feet, and his knees caught the table, flipping it over and sending the remaining stones spinning away. I took the opportunity and slipped out of the grand salon.

The four men had left the viewing deck and I didn't see them anywhere else in the passageways. Maybe they'd gone back to steerage. A few other passengers were stretching their legs. I exchanged polite nods as I passed.

There was no one in sight on the lower deck, either, and the passageway was quiet. I heard a faint, murmured conversation from behind a cabin door, but otherwise nothing but the beat of the propellers and the thrum of the wind in the ropes that bound the passenger gondola to the balloon.

The door to our suite was closed. I relaxed. The men who'd watched us on the viewing deck had simply been bored. Why would Sir Titus think three children and his idiot student would follow him so far? He wouldn't waste his time setting traps for us.

I laid my hand on the door. It swung open with a creak.

I froze. We'd locked it behind us. I knew we had.

I bent down. The lock had been forced. The wood was splintered around it and the locking mechanism bent. I held my breath and listened.

Nothing. If anyone was in there, they had stopped still the moment the door had opened. I didn't much fancy my chances if I came face-to-face with an intruder. But if I had to go all the way back to the grand salon and return with Freddie, they would be gone.

Letting my breath out silently, I slid into the room.

Chairs had been ripped open, their cushions scattered and disemboweled. Drawers had been pulled out and dumped on the floor. Paintings had been torn from the walls. The table had been overturned. Even the rugs had been pulled up.

I stopped for a moment, my chest tight, trying to take it all in.

There! I heard a slight sound in Olivia and Putty's cabin, as though someone had set something down very gently. I crept over and leaned forward to press my ear against the door.

It crashed open.

I jerked my head back, but not quickly enough.

The last thing I saw was the wood slamming into my face. Then all turned black.

— 12 —

A Suspect

I woke to the touch of a hand on my forehead. My head
hurt. My face hurt. My neck hurt. Even one of my arms
hurt. I forced my eyes open. *Ow!* The light was too bright.

"Oh, good. You're alive."

I squeezed my eyes into focus. Putty was leaning over
me.

"What happened?" I said.

"Well." Putty sat back on her heels. "Dr. Blood kept
going on about his rocks and how one of them had been
chipped when Cousin Freddie knocked them off the table,
and then *I* tried to tell them about how the photon emission
globes worked, because they're really interesting and quite
clever, but no one was listening, and—"

"I mean to me. What happened to me?"

Putty's face fell. "Doesn't *anyone* want to hear about the photon emission globes?" She looked around. "What happened to you?"

"Help me to a chair," I managed.

Putty grabbed my painful arm.

"Other one!"

She released me. "You're a complete mess, Edward."

"I was attacked," I said. I managed to stagger to a chair. My legs were still shaky, but things were slowly coming into focus. "Where's Freddie?"

"That's what I was *trying* to tell you. I was telling everyone about the photon emission globes—except they weren't listening—and then Freddie said he thought you'd been gone too long, and would I go and look for you. Only . . ." She frowned. "I think he might just have been trying to get me to stop talking and go away. He wouldn't do that, would he?"

I tried a smile. "Something *had* happened to me, so he was right. Did you see anyone?"

She shook her head.

"Good." I didn't want Putty running into the people who had done this to me.

Putty put her shoulder under my arm, and together we staggered back to the grand salon. The moment we came through the door, Olivia shot out of her chair with a look that was half relief and half worry. Dr. Blood sat frozen, his hand raised, holding a lump of rock.

"What happened?" Freddie asked.

"I was attacked," I said. "In our cabin." I told them quickly all I knew.

"The ruffians!" Dr. Blood spluttered. "They must have been after your valuables. This is what happens when one allows the passengers in steerage to roam free. Steward! Steward!" He gestured to the steward who was already hurrying over.

"Sir?" the steward said.

"This young man has been robbed and assaulted in his own cabin. Are any of us safe? Are we to be murdered in our beds?" He grabbed his rocks from the table and shook them in two fists at the steward. "Are our valuables no longer to be protected? I am a Martian!" He clutched the rocks to his chest. "I have valuable samples in my cabin. Granite and flint among them!"

He hurried off, only pausing to bow swiftly to Olivia.

"I didn't see my assailants," I said. "I don't think anything was taken."

"They smashed up our rooms," Putty said, sounding happier than she should have. "And they knocked Edward unconscious. It was very dramatic. I thought he was dead!"

Olivia gasped. "Parthenia! Don't say such things."

"You would have, too," Putty protested. "He looked dreadful."

Olivia fixed the steward with a gaze that would have

scared a stone-snake. "And what exactly do you propose to do about it?"

The steward straightened. He ran a nervous finger under his collar. "Ah . . . Your cabin will be restored immediately."

Olivia didn't reply. She just kept her unwavering gaze on the steward.

"And, um, we shall refund your fares. Of course."

He was sweating. Olivia didn't blink.

"You must accept our apologies. Please?"

Olivia held his eyes for another moment, then nodded. The steward slumped in relief and hurried off. I let myself fall back onto a chaise longue.

"You were magnificent, Cousin Olivia!" Freddie said when the steward was gone.

Olivia stared down at her folded hands to hide a blush.

"Edward keeps getting thrashed, doesn't he?" Putty said. She seemed to be enjoying this. "I bet you wouldn't have been knocked out, would you, Cousin Freddie?"

Freddie smiled. "I'm rather more concerned by Dr. Blood. Didn't anyone else think he was very keen to keep us here while our cabins were being searched?"

I frowned. "Perhaps."

"There's something very strange about that man, and it isn't just his rock samples. I think it would be a good thing if we stayed together for the rest of this voyage. I don't want any of you wandering off on your own." He held Putty's gaze until she nodded. "If Edward's attackers were Sir Titus's men, they will try again, and they won't hesitate to hurt us."

The dinner bell rang at six, raising us from our exhausted stupor.

"Ah!" Freddie said. "At last. I believe I could eat a pterodactyl. Whole. And not one of those pint-sized ones that have been following the airship." He helped Olivia to her feet.

"I trust you will leave a wing or two for the rest of us," Olivia murmured.

"Perhaps a claw," Freddie said. "I am very hungry. Come, Cousin Parthenia, arise!"

With a grunt, Putty rolled herself off the chaise longue, rubbing her eyes. "I was asleep."

"And snoring in a most charming manner. But dinner awaits, and that lady who just exited the salon looks like she might polish off the entire lot before we're even seated."

The sun had sunk low in the Martian sky so that it was now below the level of the balloon, and golden sunlight streamed through the windows. We trailed with the other first-class passengers toward the dining room.

"Now," Freddie said quietly, "we'll be safest in company. I don't think Sir Titus's men will be desperate enough to attack us while we're surrounded by other passengers."

"And what happens when night falls?" Olivia said.

"We'll have to retreat to our cabins."

"It's very exciting!" Putty said. "I wonder if we'll be murdered in our beds?"

"Sadly, I don't think it'll come to that," Freddie said. "I'll insist the captain provides guards. I doubt we will be disturbed."

"Oh," Putty said, sounding disappointed. "I'd really hoped to see Edward demonstrate his special fighting techniques again."

I reached out to swat her, but she ducked out of range.

The dining room was nearly full when we got there. Like the grand salon, it was illuminated by photon emission globes. The walls were paneled in dark, polished wormwood, its spiraling patterns carefully set to catch the light. A dozen waiters stood around the room. Half were human, the other half automatic servants. The automatons were Papa's models, but none of them were the latest designs. The truth was, automatic servants were no longer as fashionable as they'd once been.

Freddie accompanied Olivia, her hand on his arm, to the table nearest the doors. Putty and I found a pair of seats on the far side of the dining room.

Across the table sat an older man with red cheeks and great, bushy muttonchops that were so big they looked like a strange, hairy creature that had snuck in from the wilderness and attached itself to his face. He was talking loudly with the young men on either side of him. I leaned forward slightly, trying to listen in without being noticed.

". . . thought we'd break the back of the monster right then and there," the old chap boomed happily, "until those enormous metal beasts of his came rolling over the hill. Smashed us to pieces. Almost lost a leg, you know."

"You fought a monster?" Putty demanded. One of the young men lifted his quizzing glass and peered at her through it.

"Eh? Eh?" the old gentleman said. "A monster, you say? *The* monster, that's who. And it was only then," he confided, leaning over the table himself, to the horrified looks of those around us, "that we heard of the fleet's destruction at Trafalgar. Shocking news."

"Oh, you're talking about the Emperor Napoleon," Putty said, disappointment clear in her voice. "I thought you meant a real monster."

"What a singular child," one of the young men muttered. The other laughed.

Putty reddened. I bit back an angry comment and rested my hand on her shoulder instead.

The old gentleman harrumphed, then turned back to his companions. "Wounded and captured, and by the time I was ransomed back, Britain's part in the war was all but over. And that, gentlemen, is why the name of Colonel Fitzsimmons is not as well known as it should be. But that will change, mark my words. Ah. Look. Here comes the food."

I sat back as the waiters laid out the meats, soups, pies,

fish, vegetables, and sweet puddings that made up the first course. When they were done, the old colonel glanced furtively around and gestured his companions to lean closer. I pretended to be interested in my food.

"You have heard, no doubt, of the dragon tombs of Lunae Planum?" the old colonel said. Beside me, Putty straightened.

"Of course," one of the young men replied. "We are making our Grand Tour of Mars and intend to visit them."

"Ah," the colonel said, his voice dropping further. "But what if I were to tell you that there is an undiscovered dragon tomb and that I—Colonel Daniel Fitzsimmons—know its location?"

I stopped eating, my fork held unmoving before my mouth. An undiscovered dragon tomb? The coincidence was too great. Putty was almost vibrating beside me. If the colonel knew about the dragon tomb, he had to be working with Sir Titus.

"I have a map," the colonel confided to his now rapt audience. "When I reach Lunae City, I intend to hire native guides and uncover the tomb. The name of Colonel Fitzsimmons will be known across Mars and Earth. You may tell your children that you once shook my hand."

With that, he settled back and reached for his glass of wine. I saw a raw scrape across the back of his knuckles. I felt cold. In my mind's eye, I saw him waiting behind our cabin door. Then, when I was right up against it, listening, he had slammed it open, knocking me out and injuring his hand. And here he was, sitting opposite me, enjoying his wine.

The rest of the meal seemed to go on forever. By the time Freddie signaled across the dining room, Putty looked like she was going to explode.

"Freddie," I whispered as we entered the grand salon, "I have to talk to you."

Freddie glanced around and led us to an isolated table. "What is it?"

"I think I've found the man who attacked me. He was sitting opposite me at dinner. His name is Colonel Fitzsimmons."

"How do you know?" Olivia asked. "Didn't you say you hadn't seen him?"

"He has a map!" Putty blurted out. "To the dragon tomb! That must mean he's with Sir Titus and he's trying to kill us. He was talking to two other men. I bet he was trying to recruit them so they could help attack us while we're asleep. We should ambush him. I wanted to stick him with my fork across the table, but he was too far away."

Freddie leaned back with a smile. "It's a good thing you didn't. Half the gentlemen on this airship will have dragon tomb maps."

I stared at him. "I don't understand."

"There's a whole industry making fake dragon tomb maps in Lunae City," Freddie said. "They sell them to gullible men and women like your colonel. You have to understand,

Lunae City is in the middle of the desert. Travel a mile or two away from the Martian Nile and there's nothing. Just sand and rock. If it wasn't for the money people like Colonel Fitzsimmons bring in, it would scarcely survive. The native Martians get almost nothing from the real dragon tombs. Can you blame them for trying to better themselves from the likes of Colonel Fitzsimmons? And I can promise you, the colonel is having a far better time than he has had for many years."

"It's wrong," Olivia said.

"Perhaps," Freddie said. "But I think it's necessary."

I wasn't so ready to give up the idea. *Someone* had gone through our cabin. *Someone* had knocked me stone cold.

"He had a scrape along the back of his hand," I said.

"Which he could have gained in any number of ways," Freddie said. "Is it really likely that an elderly gentleman was the one who attacked you, or that he should discuss dragon tombs and maps opposite you at dinner? You can't go suspecting everyone with a bruise. But I can assure you, we will know the identity of our attackers before the voyage is out. They will not let us land in Lunae City without one last attempt on the map."

⸺◆⸺

The photon emission globes in the chandelier above us glowed brightly, but even so, in the warmth and with a heavy dinner inside me, my eyes drifted closed. We hadn't slept much last night, during the rough automatic-carriage ride, and despite the excitement of the day, I could hardly keep myself awake. Putty had already drifted into a light sleep, and Olivia seemed ready to join her. Only Freddie was managing to keep himself alert.

"Spy training," I half muttered, and snorted a laugh, waking Putty. I rubbed my eyes.

The evening drew on. Freddie told ridiculous stories about Oxford, most of which I was sure he was making up, and Olivia sat ramrod-straight in her attempt to stay conscious.

I shuffled in my seat, trying to find a comfortable position, and something poked me in the ribs. I pulled the folded copy of *Thrilling Martian Tales* out of my jacket. It was battered, covered in dust, torn, and charred on one corner. I brushed the dust from the cover.

There he was. Captain W. A. Masters. Hanging from a dragon's claws far above the ancient Martian landscape, back arched in pain, grimacing. But his hand was reaching for something in his backpack. I opened to the first page.

Putty looked up sleepily at me. "Haven't you read that yet?"

I glared at her. "Are you trying to be funny?"

She smiled and her eyes drifted shut again.

"Do you think they've nearly finished repairing our cabin?" Olivia murmured as the hands of the large clock on the wall dragged past ten.

"If they haven't," Freddie said, "we should demand

another one. We can't stay here all night." He stood. "I'll find the steward. We're going to need rest before we get to Lunae City." He caught sight of an automatic waiter and lifted a hand to summon the mechanism over.

I turned my eyes to the page and read those lines that opened every Captain Masters adventure: *My name is Captain W. A. Masters. I had an accident and woke up on Ancient Mars. . . .*

But I got no further. The salon door burst open and four men rushed in, carrying knives. Their faces were hidden by scarves.

Chairs tumbled as the passengers around the card tables noticed the intruders. Several people screamed or swore. Then, like a flock of birds, they fled for the other exit.

The attackers spread out, moving slowly but confidently toward us.

"Putty," I said. "Get Livvy out of here. Find a steward or one of the crew."

I thought she was going to resist, but when I gave her a push, she scooped up Olivia's hand and dragged her after the rest of the passengers. With all this noise, the crew would soon be alerted. They'd be able to overwhelm the attackers. If we could hold them long enough.

"You should go with the others," Freddie said tightly.

I shook my head. "You can't manage four of them."

He didn't argue.

"This doesn't have to be difficult," one of the attackers

called as they stalked forward. "Give us the map. That's all. No one wants you dead. Give us the map, and we'll be gone."

"No," Freddie said.

"Is it that important?" I hissed at him.

"Listen to your little friend, Mr. Winchester," the attacker said. "He's got sense."

Freddie let a smile spread on his lips. "If you want it, why don't you come and take it?"

The men spread out further. I found myself wishing Dr. Blood were here. At least I could have thrown his rocks at the attackers. Instead, I picked up two of our teacups.

"Edward," Freddie whispered, "when I say 'now,' I want you to cover your eyes."

He stepped away from me. As though this was a signal, the four men charged.

Freddie leaped onto the table, then threw himself upward, stretching for the chandelier. He caught it with his right hand and swung himself higher.

The first of the attackers vaulted a chair and came at Freddie.

Freddie grabbed one of the photon emission globes from the chandelier.

"Now!" he shouted, and threw the globe onto the floor.

I only just managed to cover my eyes in time. The sound of glass shattering was accompanied by a flash of light so bright it seemed to burn through my forearm. I heard screams.

When I uncovered my eyes, it was to see Freddie drop from the chandelier. Broken glass lay on the floor nearby. Our attackers writhed on the carpet, clutching their heads, blinded.

He glanced up at me and smiled when he saw my expression. "You should have listened to your little sister."

"What?" I said.

"The photon emission globes. She was trying to tell us how they worked." He grinned. "I'm afraid I already knew." I must have still looked blank, because he said, "They are mirrors, reflecting inward. When sunlight is trapped within them, it seeps out only slowly to illuminate the surroundings. When the last dragon tomb was opened ten years ago, it was full of devices like these. There were also plans for an arrangement of mirrors and lenses that could focus enormous amounts of sunlight to a single point." He ripped the scarf from one of the attackers. They were the men we had seen watching us on the viewing deck. "The sunlight sealed inside the photon emission globes is incredibly intense. Release it all at once"—he gestured to the broken glass globe—"and it's bright enough to blind. Luckily, only temporarily." He straightened. "We should tie these men up and summon the steward. Then . . ." He looked grim. "Then we will get some answers."

The door at the back of the grand salon burst open. Putty and Olivia came racing in.

"We saw the light!" Putty said. "You used a photon emission globe, didn't you?" Her face was alight with joy. "See! I told you they were marvelous. Oh. You've beaten all of them."

Freddie nodded. "We have. And now I think we can relax. I believe we're safe."

But no sooner had the words left his mouth than a faint mechanical clicking sounded from outside the salon, followed quickly by another, then another, until there were dozens, then hundreds of the sounds, like tiny knives snicking together.

— 13 —

Attack of the Killer Crabs

"Close the door!" Freddie yelled.

I sprinted past my sisters, grabbed the door, then froze. The passageway was full of shiny metal creatures that looked like crabs. They weren't much bigger than my hand, but there were dozens of them. They scampered along on little articulated legs. I heard the whir of cogs and the click of metallic joints. Glittering black eyes stared at me. Each creature held two pairs of razor-sharp claws before it that snapped furiously together.

I heaved the door shut. Too late. Three metal crabs slipped through.

They were fast. The first of them scuttled across the wooden floor and snapped at my foot. Its claws sliced through my shoe, parting the leather as easily as paper.

I flicked my foot. The metal crab lost its grip and spun

away across the floor to crash into the wall. The next moment, it regained its footing and came for me again. I backed away.

The other two crabs stalked Freddie, Putty, and Olivia. Outside the grand salon door, claws scraped across wood. Elsewhere in the airship, someone screamed.

The impact with the wall hadn't damaged the mechanical crab. It darted at me. I leaped back and shoved a chaise longue over. The crab dodged.

From behind me came a sharp crack, and a mechanical crab tumbled past. Freddie lined up the third, holding his walking stick like a cricket bat. He swung as the crab scuttled toward him, and smashed it back through the air. But already the other crabs were coming again. I raced back to the others, and we retreated.

"They're too well armored to damage," Freddie said. "Maybe we can run their springs down. They can't have that much power in such small bodies." He sounded doubtful.

Suddenly, Putty turned and raced away. I grabbed for her, but missed. I chased after her.

Freddie hit one of the crabs, but the next slipped past him and came after me and Putty. Behind me, Olivia screamed and Freddie cursed.

Putty headed for the waiters' counter. Maybe she thought if she climbed on top, she would be safe. She was wrong. I'd seen the pincers on the end of the crabs' legs. They were just like the ones Papa's mechanical spiders used to climb in the conservatory.

Putty scurried around behind the counter. Did she really think she could *hide* from them?

A second later, she reappeared, clasping a large glass jug in one hand. I blinked, and she slipped past me again. The crab snapped at her unprotected legs. Before I could open my mouth, she slammed the jug down, mouth-first, on top of the crab. Inside the jar, the mechanical crab spun angrily, snapping at the glass, unable to get a grip. Putty held the jar firmly over it.

She glanced up at me. "Get some more, Edward!"

I had forgotten the crabs menacing Olivia and Freddie. I grabbed two jugs from behind the counter. Freddie was using his stick to flick away the crabs as they approached, but he couldn't keep it up forever.

"Freddie!" I shouted.

With a sweep, he sent both crabs spinning away. I leaped past and pushed one of the jugs into his hand.

Like the automatic servants, the crabs had no real intelligence. Their minds were no more than tiny levers and switches, following preset commands. They didn't recognize the jugs or what had happened to the first of their number. Instead, they righted themselves and came hurrying back, little metal legs clicking on the floor, razor-sharp claws opening and closing ahead of them. Their metal bodies gleamed in the light of the photon emission globes. My hands were sweaty. The jug felt slippery in them.

I thumped the jug down so hard I thought it would crack.

I almost got it. The crab dodged to one side, and the edge of the jug caught its back leg, pinning it in place. Its claws snapped, inches from Olivia's feet. I held the jug with all my might.

Olivia scrambled away.

"Easy now," Freddie said. He'd trapped his own crab. It rattled around inside its upturned jug, its claws ticking uselessly on the smooth glass.

Slowly, the crab I was holding worked its leg, trying to get free. I twisted to a more steady position. I'd have only one chance. I closed my eyes, took a breath, then opened my eyes and lifted the jug.

The crab shot toward me. I slammed the jug down again.

This time I got it right dead center. The crab hit the inside of the glass jug and skittered around, lost.

"Olivia," Freddie said. "Find something to slide under the jugs. Some metal trays. We need to seal them in."

One at a time, Olivia slid trays under our jugs. We flipped them over, leaving the crabs caught in the bottom of the jugs, with the trays on top. Just to be sure, we placed heavy bottles on top of the trays.

Now that the crabs couldn't escape, Putty peered closely at one of the trapped mechanisms. It tried to grab at her, but the glass foiled it.

"They're not very well made," she said. "Look. The joints are positively shoddy. Very inefficient. Papa would never make anything so badly." She shook her head. "Poor work."

"They're good enough," Freddie said. "And there were more than three of them."

In the silence, I realized the noise of the crabs outside the door had disappeared.

"They can't get in," Olivia said, with a sigh of relief. "We're safe."

"Unless someone lets them in," I said.

Olivia's hand fluttered to her chest. "What do you mean?"

"Someone had to bring them on board," I said. "Someone had to send them after us. That person is still out there. All it would take would be for them to open one of the doors—"

"Quickly," Freddie said. "Find a way to block the doors. Chairs or tables. Anything to hold them closed."

I headed for the door, but before I could reach it, the airship lurched violently to the side. Freddie crossed to a window in three quick strides. Shading the window against the light in the salon, he peered out. I hurried over to join him.

The gas lamps around the walkway were dim. The airship's balloon blocked out the light from the stars and Mars's moons, so it took me a moment to see what was happening.

In the darkness, the crabs were scrambling up the railings onto the thick ropes that held the airship gondola to the balloon. There, they were cutting the ropes with their sharp claws. Even as I watched, another rope parted and the airship lurched again.

"They're cutting the gondola free!" Freddie shouted. "We're going to fall. Get to the lifeboats!" At the same moment, the airship's evacuation siren started, blatting its urgent tone into the night air. Shouts of confusion and panic sounded outside.

I cursed silently. The lifeboats were right at the back of the airship. We'd have to get past the crabs to make it. I looked through the doorway. The passage was clear.

The airship stuttered, slipping to the left before righting itself. The jugs we'd used as traps tumbled over. Glass smashed. The mechanical crabs scrambled free.

I pushed Olivia through the doorway, and the rest of us followed, slamming the door behind us. The outside of the door was scarred by the crabs' claws. At the far end of the passageway, the double doors leading to the dining room stood ajar.

The dining room was deserted and the photon emission globes had been removed from the chandeliers. The only illumination came through the windows from the lamps spaced along the outside of the gondola. We heard the shouts and screams of the other passengers. Silhouettes of men and women raced past the windows, like bats darting in front of the moon. Inside, shadows layered upon shadows, turning the spaces under the tables and sideboards into pools of gloom. Every glitter from a mirror or polished metal made me jerk around, expecting to see the metal crabs come scurrying out of the darkness, claws raised. I clenched my fists, fingernails biting into my palms.

We were passing a sideboard still laden with dishes from the evening meal when the airship gave another lurch. The dishes crashed to the floor. Splintered china spun past us.

This time, when the airship steadied, the floor was sloping to the side. The engines whined as the airship tilted forward.

"The captain's trying to land," Freddie said. "He won't make it. We're too high."

I tried not to think of all that open air beneath us. It was too easy to imagine the gondola sliding free of its cradle of ropes and plunging down into the blackness. It would be smashed to pieces.

The airship bobbed and slipped as we hurried across the slanted floor. The door ahead of us swung and banged as though it was caught in a gale.

"Edward!" Freddie shouted from behind. "Run!"

The door behind us had come open, and silvery crabs were pouring through: three, then four, then a dozen, scuttling toward us. Their claws sounded like hail on the wooden floor.

Freddie turned to face them, raising his walking stick. I grabbed Olivia and Putty and raced for the exit. I heard

Freddie's stick thwack against the first of the crabs, then I had to turn all my attention to running.

A table slid toward us. We dodged as it shed its cutlery in a clatter of metal.

Olivia stopped, pulling on my hand. "We have to help Freddie."

"No," I said. "He doesn't need us getting in the way." I hauled her onward.

We reached the exit and I grabbed the door to stop it swinging. A wide passageway ran crossways from one side of the gondola to the other. The door leading to the kitchens was wide open. Pans and knives lay scattered across the floor. Water dripped from an overturned kettle.

I pulled Putty then Olivia into the passageway and turned to watch Freddie. He was backing toward us, left arm thrown out for balance. With his right hand, he wielded his walking stick like a sword, jabbing and swiping at the crabs as they came toward him, sending them tumbling down the sloping floor. But as soon as they fetched up against the walls or the furniture, they came again.

Outside, something exploded with a crack like a cannon firing.

Slowly, the crabs edged their way around Freddie, out of reach of his stick.

Freddie glanced over his shoulder. "Shut the door, Edward!"

I shook my head. Even if the airship hadn't been about to

crash, I wouldn't have closed Freddie in there with the crabs. Just inside the kitchen, I saw an oar-shaped bread paddle that had fallen away from the stove.

"Get the girls out of here!" Freddie shouted.

I let go of the door and half fell across the passageway. I grabbed the kitchen doorway and swung myself in.

"Putty," I said. "Head for the lifeboats. I'll catch up."

Another rope sprang free outside. The airship protested and settled further. I heard planks snap. Pans slid across the kitchen floor. Hot coals tumbled from the stove and scattered like red stars. A pair of bellows bounced past. I flinched back, then stretched for the bread paddle as it slipped toward me. The end of the paddle caught on a flagstone and it flipped, spinning through the air. It smacked into my fingers. I let out a shout of pain. Then my fingers closed around it.

"Edward!" Putty shouted.

Putty and Olivia were halfway down the passage, but above them, a crab had appeared. It levered itself around the doorjamb. I pulled myself out of the kitchen and swung the paddle. The crab dropped into the passage. The end of my paddle smacked it back.

I stumbled across the passage and took up position in the doorway. Freddie was still a dozen yards away, his progress slowed almost to a standstill by the crabs that had gotten behind him. A couple more were heading for the open doorway. I braced myself and swept the paddle at them. The first was flicked cleanly away, but the second clamped its claws around the end of the paddle. I smacked the paddle into the floor, trying to dislodge it.

"Freddie!" I shouted. "Come on!"

He glanced back at me, then spun and leaped over the crabs behind him. I swung my paddle again, crab still attached, clearing the way.

Freddie landed awkwardly and stumbled. He crashed down on one knee. The crabs scuttled toward him. He pushed himself up, wincing, but the crabs had cut him off once again. I couldn't reach them from where I was.

I flung my paddle. It spun into the crabs and smacked them out of the way. Freddie lunged for the door, and I pulled him through.

I slammed the door. It wouldn't latch. It had swung too violently and twisted its hinges, and now it wouldn't close. I hung on to the handle as the crabs scraped at the far side. Their little claws dug around the edge of the door, cutting away the thick wood.

Freddie closed his hand over mine.

"Go," he said. "I'll hold it." He reached into his sleeve and pulled out the map. "Take this. Keep it safe. If I don't make it, take the map to the British-Martian Intelligence Service and tell them what happened. We can't let Sir Titus get away with this. Go!"

"We're not going to leave you," I said.

Freddie met my eyes. "You'll do what you have to, to keep the others safe. Understand?"

Reluctantly, I nodded. Freddie took the door handle.

"Follow us," I said. "We can hold them at the next door."

The girls had reached the end of the passage and were waiting by the outside door.

"If I can," Freddie said.

I released my hold and let myself slip down the steeply sloping passage. Putty and Olivia caught me. I glanced back at Freddie. He was holding grimly on to the door. Glittering crab claws reached through, snapping at him.

The outside walkway was illuminated by the glow of gas lamps. Hanging on the ropes above the railings were the silvery bodies of crabs. One sliced through a rope as I watched. The rope parted with a vicious twang. The crab was thrown into the night.

Carefully, I lowered Putty and Olivia onto the walkway. I dropped through and braced myself against the railing.

"Now!" I called to Freddie.

He released his hold on the dining room door and threw himself down the passage. Behind him, the door burst open, and crabs surged through.

Freddie's headlong momentum was too great. He couldn't stop himself. He reached for the door frame, but he was traveling too fast. I seized his arm, and his weight threw us both over the railing, into the night.

We grabbed the rail as we went over. It creaked as we swung over the black void. Then Olivia hauled us back, and Putty slammed the door shut behind us. Crabs rattled against it.

Shakily, I got to my feet.

The engines were still whining desperately, but the airship had developed a spin, and the captain didn't seem to be able to control it. We didn't have long. I took the lead again, and we rushed along the walkway, clutching at the railing that was now nearly beneath us. Freddie brought up the rear, his walking stick ready to fend off any crabs that came too close.

Most of the lifeboats were gone, but one still hung beneath the rear of the airship, swinging wildly as the airship spun. We sprinted toward it.

From our left, a tide of silvery crabs came tripping and sliding down the walkway at us. They were like a wave ready to break over and engulf us.

Then Freddie was there. He leaped up beside us, sweeping at them with his walking stick, dancing around them, flicking them over the railings into the dark. I dragged Putty and Olivia to the lifeboat. They dropped through the hatch, and I followed. Freddie was still fighting the crabs, but they were all around him. He spun and kicked and slashed, but he couldn't get free.

One rope popped, then another and another and another. Now they didn't need the crabs to cut them. The weight of the gondola on the remaining ropes was too great. The fibers parted. Like a baby slipping from a torn sling, the gondola slid slowly from its cradle of ropes.

"Go!" Freddie shouted. "Get out of here!"

Crabs scuttled toward us. There was no way he could pass them.

I swung into the lifeboat, throwing the end of the rope ladder out, and slamming the hatch behind us.

"No!" Olivia screamed.

"Strap yourselves in," I ordered.

I pushed myself into the pilot's chair and pulled the release lever. Our lifeboat dropped from the airship. Angry pterodactyls swooped away from our falling craft. Through the viewing window above our heads, I saw the great airship gondola fall, finally free of the balloon that held it. Then, with a snap, the vast canvas wings unfurled on either side of the lifeboat and we were sailing away through the dark night air. Behind us, the gondola plummeted to the ground.

— 14 —

Slime

"No!" Olivia shrieked again.

I clenched my fists on the steering levers, feeling the wooden body of the lifeboat shudder through my palms.

Freddie was dead. We'd left him behind and now he was dead. He'd been trapped in the gondola when it had crashed thousands of feet to the ground.

My throat felt so tight I couldn't speak or even sob. He'd sacrificed himself so that we could get away. I hadn't trusted him. I'd thought he only cared about his dragon tomb, and now . . .

I was holding the steering levers too tight. The lifeboat fought against me as it tried to lower us gently to the ground, but I couldn't make myself loosen my hold. If I did, I might just fall to bits. I was having a hard time focusing through the viewport, looking for obstacles. My eyes kept clouding.

"We have to go back." In the dim fluorescence of the emergency lamp, Olivia had straightened in her seat. She gripped Putty's hand so tight her knuckles turned white. Her hair was a mess, spilling and jutting from her hairpins. Her eyes looked wild.

"Back?" I said.

"Freddie might have . . . He might have . . ." Her voice trailed away. Her head dipped and she stared into her lap.

"He couldn't," I said, trying not to choke. "There's no way he could have survived that drop."

"We have to know!" Olivia said.

I didn't have the strength to argue. I pulled on the left-hand lever, and the lifeboat slipped into a wide curve. Now that we were low enough, the light from Mars's moons and the stars showed the vague shape of the land. I saw the outlines of hills and a steep, sharp valley, but that was all. It was impossible to make out details on the ground. I couldn't see any sign of the fallen airship. I didn't even know where to look.

I swooped around again, but it was hopeless.

"There's nothing," I said.

I should've gone back and helped Freddie. I should've gotten him free of the crabs and to the lifeboat before the gondola fell. But I hadn't. I'd just left him. My hands started to shake, and the lifeboat shuddered.

I forced my hands to be steady and tried not to listen to Olivia crying and Putty trying to comfort her while fighting to hold back her own tears.

Putty had worshipped Freddie. Suddenly, I was furious at him. He'd made Olivia fall in love with him and Putty think of him as a hero. Then he'd gotten himself killed and left them like this. The stupid idiot! I wanted to punch him, but I couldn't. He was lying dead in the wreckage of the airship somewhere in the Martian wilderness. I realized I was crying.

I pulled on the left lever again, dipping us down. I just wanted to get out of this horrible, suffocating lifeboat. I couldn't see the other lifeboats in the darkness, and I didn't care. I didn't want to meet any of the other survivors. I didn't want to talk to anyone.

The ground rushed toward us. I caught glimpses of strange night birds flapping clumsily from the trees, like black rags thrown in the wind. All I could see below was a mess of tree-tops, bushes, and sharp rises and falls that told of uneven ground beneath.

I tugged the lifeboat around to the right, sweeping across the darkened terrain. It dropped away beneath us. For a few seconds, we were soaring through the air again on wide canvas wings. Then the ground reared up in front of us. I tugged both levers back. The wings dipped, scooped air, lifted us, slowed us.

And we dropped.

"Hold on!" I said.

Something snatched at the left wing. Our lifeboat jerked around. The other wing lost its lift. The lifeboat tipped to the right and we crunched to a halt. If we hadn't been strapped in, we would have been thrown against the wall. Blood spun dizzyingly in my head.

From the left wing came a ripping sound. Olivia screamed. The lifeboat fell.

Twigs and branches scratched across the hull. We crashed into something, shaking me in my seat. My teeth rattled, and I bit the inside of my cheek.

We thumped down, then finally the lifeboat came to a rest again, swaying.

Cautiously, I released my straps. We hadn't reached the ground yet.

"Don't move," I said. "I don't know how stable this is." The lifeboat might fall at any moment.

I tested a step. The lifeboat rocked slightly, but it held firm.

"We need to climb out," I whispered. "One at a time. We need to get onto a tree and make our way down."

Olivia's face was streaked with tears and she was shivering. Putty didn't look much better.

"You go first, Putty," I said. "When you're safely out, help Livvy. I'll come after."

Putty levered herself from her seat and reached for the square hatch above her. The lifeboat swung in the branches. I kept my teeth clenched and held my breath.

She pushed at the hatch. It didn't move. "It's stuck."

"Harder," I said.

Putty put both hands beneath the hatch and shoved. The lifeboat rocked, but the hatch didn't move. I took a step to help. The movement sent the lifeboat sliding forward. I froze in place. The lifeboat came to a stop.

"Try again," I said.

Putty put her shoulder to it and, with a yell, heaved. The hatch popped open, banging back on its hinges. A shower of leaves fell around her. She shook her head free.

"I can see the stars," Putty said. "We're up near the canopy."

"Can you get out?"

She pushed her head through the hatchway. A moment later, she withdrew it. "We're up against the trunk of a tree. If we're careful, we should be able to get at it. But the branches are pretty thin up here."

I nodded. "Try it."

Putty pulled herself up and disappeared through the hatch. I heard her light footsteps on the roof of the lifeboat. I met Olivia's eyes and held them as we heard Putty reach the edge. My heart was thumping. Then Putty's weight lifted from the lifeboat.

My little sister didn't weigh much, but she was heavy enough to shift the lifeboat again. Branches scraped beneath the floor as the lifeboat juddered down another couple of feet.

"Your turn," I told Livvy. "Putty will help you off the lifeboat, but first you'll have to climb out yourself."

And what would happen when Olivia, who weighed more than Putty, stepped off?

"Don't look," she hissed as she reached up to the hatch.

I blinked. "What?"

"Don't look. You'll see my undergarments."

"Oh, good grief," I muttered.

I heard Livvy give an unladylike grunt, then flop heavily onto the roof of the lifeboat. Branches creaked in protest. I bit my lip and held on to the back of my chair. Livvy's dress brushed gently over the lifeboat as she crawled across the planks.

"You'll have to stand," I heard Putty say. "I can't reach you there."

The lifeboat must have slipped away from the tree trunk. I heard Olivia's feet scrape, and felt a jolt as she jumped.

Putty shouted, "Got you!" Then the lifeboat tipped. The balance shifted and it slipped. I crossed the lifeboat in four quick steps, leaped up to grab the edges of the open hatchway, and pulled myself out.

A branch snapped. The lifeboat fell beneath me.

I was too far from the tree trunk. I just had time to see the crisscrossing branches around me before I threw myself outward, arms stretched.

My fingertips caught on bark and slipped. The branch slid away from me. Then another came up from below, whipping back from the falling lifeboat, and I grabbed hold.

I heard a sickening crunch as the lifeboat hit the ground, but I was safe. Eventually, I even opened my eyes.

⟐

We spent the night in the wreckage of the lifeboat. The fall from the treetops had splintered the planks and staved in the right side of the craft, but it still provided shelter from the dripping branches, and I was glad to have something solid between me and the noises of the wilderness night. Strange, yipping voices echoed through the bush. Something large leaped from branch to branch above us, pattering berries, leaves, and twigs on the lifeboat. From all around came the sounds of breathing and scurrying. Once, something shrieked like a baby, so loud and so close that I almost screamed, too.

The interior of the lifeboat was a mess. Bits of broken wood and scattered provisions covered what was now the floor. We did our best to clear space, but in the dark, we couldn't really see what we were doing. Putty and Olivia huddled together in the back of the cabin, pressed against the mostly undamaged planks. I could just make out their pale faces and hands in the fading light.

I wedged myself into the pilot's chair, even though the impact had cracked the post that rooted it in the floor and the lifeboat tilted at a horrible angle. From there, I could see through the wide strip of thickened glass that formed the lifeboat's viewport. The glass had fractured, but it hadn't broken. I hoped that if anything approached the lifeboat,

I might see it before it was too late, but it wasn't likely. Beneath the trees and thick undergrowth, it was as black as a cellar. There was no luminescent Martian grass to provide the steady nighttime glow I was used to, and anyway, my eyes kept drifting shut, until some sharp, sudden noise jerked me alert again.

Nobody said anything. I don't know. Maybe we just didn't know what to say. In the end, Olivia and Putty fell asleep. I'd meant to stay awake to keep watch, but I hadn't slept properly for the last two nights, and it was too much. The next thing I knew, sunlight was shining through the viewport right into my eyes. I sat up and almost fell out of my chair. My head was spinning. I'd slept hanging half out of the chair.

Olivia and Putty were still asleep. They were lying close together, arms around each other. They looked peaceful. I would let them sleep for a bit longer while I worked out what to do. Anyway, I didn't think I could deal with talking about Freddie yet. The longer they slept, the longer I could put it off. Just thinking about it made my throat hurt.

When our airship didn't make it to Lunae City, people would notice. They would send out a rescue ship. We'd have to make sure they spotted us. In the meantime, I needed to see what supplies had survived. I swung awkwardly out of my chair.

A trail of slime twice as wide as my hand came over the broken planks, then down into the lifeboat. Whatever had left the trail had crawled around and slid all the way up to where Putty was sleeping. Then it had turned around and slid back out. I'd slept right through it. I shivered. What if it had been something dangerous? I should have *made* myself stay awake. I was lucky all it had done was rip open the supplies and slime them.

I pulled myself through the open hatch and peered into the morning mist. We hadn't actually crashed in a forest. The trees that had caught our lifeboat and made it crash were a soaring spike of wood and branches that jutted high into the air above thick bushes and tall grasses. Around them, the land was as folded and rumpled as one of my blankets after a bad night's sleep.

I couldn't see any sign of the crashed airship or the other lifeboats. The ground was too broken up and hilly. The wreckage could be over the next ridge, or it could be miles away. I didn't even know what direction it was in. The lifeboat had curved and turned so much as we came down that I had no idea where we'd ended up. When the rescue craft came looking for us, we'd stand a better chance of being spotted if we were near the wreckage. But anything could be out in the wilderness between us and it.

"Edward?" Livvy's sleepy voice drifted up from the lifeboat. I squinted into the shadows. Livvy was disentangling her arms from the still-sleeping Putty. "What . . . ?" she started, then gasped. A hand shot to her mouth. "Freddie."

I lowered myself through the hatchway and dropped

down. "He's gone," I said, feeling my stomach tighten at the words. "He saved us, and now he's gone." I wanted to just start crying, but I forced my face to stay blank. Right now, someone needed to keep us alive and get us out of here. I could cry about Freddie later.

Tears started in Livvy's eyes. She wiped them away. "Are we . . . ?"

"We're safe," I said. "Rescuers will be coming. We just have to wait for them."

I looked over at Putty. She'd rolled onto her side when Livvy had sat up. Her head was twisted around against the hard wood. I winced. If she stayed like that much longer, she'd feel like she'd slept in a bathtub full of saucepans.

I shifted her around so her head was resting on a rolled-up blanket. She flopped loosely to the side again. That was weird. She was still breathing normally, but moving her hadn't even changed the rhythm of her breath. She wasn't normally this deep a sleeper. I knew she must be exhausted from the last couple of days, but still . . .

I laid my hand on her shoulder. "Putty?"

She didn't respond. I shook her harder. "Putty. Wake up."

Nothing.

"What's wrong?" Olivia asked.

"Wake up!" I yelled. "Putty. Come on." I tried to pull her up by her shoulder, but her head just drooped back. Her breathing didn't change at all.

"I can't wake her," I said. I could hear myself starting to panic. "I can't wake her!"

"Why not?" Olivia demanded. "What's happened? What did you do to her?"

I lowered Putty gently to the floor again. My breath was coming in deep, sharp gulps that made my head swim.

I'd been wrong. Whatever had come in during the night hadn't just crawled up to Putty. The sticky trail ran over her arm. There were two small holes in the sleeve of her jacket. I pulled the sleeve back, and the holes were in her skin, too, little puncture marks like thorns.

"Something got to her," I said. "Something came in the night and got her."

— 15 —

Lost in the Wilderness

Putty's breath was steady and her pulse was strong, but when I pulled up her eyelids, her eyeballs had rolled back. All I could see were the whites of her eyes. Her muscles were limp. I clenched my fists. First Freddie, now this. I couldn't bear it.

Olivia grabbed my arm. "You have to get help."

I stared at her. "Where?" We were hundreds of miles from anywhere.

"The airship. That's where people will gather. There might be a doctor." She looked directly into my eyes. "Don't even think about arguing. Parthenia could die out here. I can look after her while you're gone."

"On your own?"

She raised her chin. "If I have to. I'm *not* going to lose my other sister."

"Livvy, this isn't—"

She cut me off with one hand, then picked up a bottle of water that had survived the crash, wiped it on her dress, and passed it to me. "You'll need this."

I gazed at her, uneasy. How was she going to survive? What if something came out of the wild? We might be able to fight it off together. On her own, she wouldn't have a chance.

As if reading my thoughts, she picked up a broken branch. "If that thing comes back, it'll regret it."

I hesitated.

"You don't have a choice, Edward," Olivia said. "Neither of us do."

She was right. We'd run out of choices. I tucked the bottle of water inside my jacket and pulled myself out of the lifeboat.

Under the hot sun, the mist was lifting quickly, revealing hills rolling further and further into the distance. I jumped to the leafy ground and started to hike uphill. I tried not to think of Olivia sitting alone in the wreck of the lifeboat with only Putty's unconscious body for company.

Adventures had never felt like this in *Thrilling Martian Tales*.

◆

I spotted the finger-trail of smoke on the horizon pretty quickly, but getting there was even tougher than I'd thought it would be. The land was broken into jagged ridges that looked like long knife blades as tall as houses coming up through the soil. The red rock was sharp and fragile. At one moment, it was breaking off in my hands; the next it was trying to cut them open. I sweated and cursed my way over them. To think, some people did this kind of thing for fun!

In between the ridges, the undergrowth was more tangled than Putty's hair after a morning in Papa's laboratory. Animal trails ran through the undergrowth, but it was so thick it sometimes grew over the top, turning them into tunnels. Clouds of tongue-bugs swarmed from the bushes, trying to lick the sweat from my skin, and tendrils shivered across the earth, snatching at my feet and legs. Once, an arrow-hawk plunged lightning-fast to spear some prey less than a hundred yards from me. Whatever had been attacked bellowed and writhed in agony, kicking down bushes and uprooting trees, before it finally fell still.

Here and there, great spikes of trees, like the one we'd crashed into, rose out of the undergrowth, looking like airship towers made out of wood and leaves.

It took me almost all morning, but eventually I got close to the smoke. The thick undergrowth had changed to finger-thick grass as high as my head. I struggled uphill toward the smoke. I'd almost reached it when I heard angry voices.

I dropped to my stomach and wriggled my way to where the grass ended. Just past where I was lying, the ground dropped steeply down. I'd come to the edge of a deep valley. It was full of great chunks of split red rock that looked like they'd been strewn across it by a giant in a really bad mood. On the opposite slope was the wreck of the airship gondola. Smashed wood and twisted metal had been thrown over hundreds of yards of rock. What was left of one of the great spring-powered propellers jutted into the air. The spring itself had unwound violently, scattering the pieces of broken airship and cutting a track through the ground. Smoke still rose in places from the smoldering wreckage. Just looking at it made me shudder. It must have hit with an almighty crash. I tried not to think about Freddie being caught in there when it smashed down. At least it would have been quick.

A group of men stood nearby, arguing. I recognized one of them straightaway. Dr. Blood's face was red, and he was gesturing at the airship. He was probably worrying about his rock samples. I stilled my breathing and listened.

Dr. Blood's voice drifted up to me from the valley. "I want his body found. If it's not in the wreckage, you'll search until you find it. Understand?"

I goggled at him. What was he talking about?

One of the other men mumbled something in reply. Dr. Blood's hand whipped out, cracking across the other man's face. The other man was far bigger than Dr. Blood, but he stumbled away, then dropped his gaze to the ground.

I pushed myself back behind the ridge. Why was Dr. Blood bossing those men about? Was he looking for Freddie's body? That would mean that he'd been behind the attack on the airship. Wouldn't it? Did that mean he was working for Sir Titus?

Sir Titus! I hissed under my breath as my brain reminded me, *Ten days. Ten days until Sir Titus is done with your family.*

He'd wanted to stop us from rescuing our family, so he'd crashed the airship in the middle of the wilderness. He hadn't even cared that innocent people might be killed. Now we'd never even get close to the rescue airship with Dr. Blood waiting. How were we going to reach Lunae City?

The sun was burning hot, and my bottle was almost empty. I only had a single mouthful left. I'd crossed a small, dirty stream about an hour back and I'd filled the bottle there, but it was almost gone again. I swirled the water in the bottle. God, I was thirsty, but if I drank it now, I'd have nothing left.

As his men trudged across to the wreckage, Dr. Blood wiped his brow and walked over to a stand of umbrella trees a hundred yards away, and lowered himself into the shade.

"Good," I muttered. I might be able to spot other survivors before Dr. Blood spotted me. Maybe one of them would be a doctor.

It was getting hotter. How was that even possible? I'd been in ovens that were cooler than this. My brain felt as if it was frying like an egg in the heat. And not even a nice egg. A pigeon-cat egg flavored with marsh-pepper. I fumbled for my bottle and drank the last of the water.

Yech! It was disgusting. How could water taste so vile? I licked at the rim of the bottle. If I didn't get more water soon, I'd end up like one of those preserved Egyptian mummies. All I'd have to do was find some bandages.

Maybe I'd been wrong. Maybe the other survivors would stay in their own lifeboats and wait for the rescue airships to fly over. Signal them with fire and smoke. Maybe they were too far away or they hadn't been able to get to the airship. Maybe they were all dead.

I shouldn't be lying here. I should be out looking for them.

Dr. Blood seemed to have plenty of water. There he was, sitting under his great big tree, swigging away. If I could just crawl around behind him, maybe I could grab some . . .

A shadow swept over me.

If it was a cloud, maybe it would rain on me. I flopped onto my back and stared up, my mouth open.

There, in the sky above me, flying low, was an airship.

Rescuers! Rescuers had come and they'd found us. I could bring them to Putty. We could *fly* there. I staggered to my feet and waved.

The airship slipped over and past. They hadn't seen me. How could they not see me? They must be looking at the wreckage. It didn't matter. I would reach them there.

Wait! My brain might be more cooked than one of our ro-butler's pancakes, but some part of it was still working.

We'd crashed last night. We hadn't been due to reach Lunae City until later today. There had been no time for us to be missed and rescue craft dispatched.

Maybe this was the daily airship heading the other direction, from Lunae City to Ophir. Maybe they had seen the wreckage below and come down to investigate. Except this airship was too small and it didn't have the mark of the Imperial Martian Airship Company.

So maybe it was a private airship. Lots of rich people had their own private airships. Just like the one Sir Titus had used to kidnap Mama, Papa, and Jane.

My brain gave me another kick. *Sir Titus!* He'd planned the attack on our airship. He'd crashed it. Now his airship had come to make sure we hadn't survived. And here I was, standing in full view on top of the ridge, waving like an idiot. I dropped back, hitting the earth hard enough to make me wince.

The airship circled around. Its propellers tilted to push it down. Dr. Blood came out from under his tree and waved at it. I slid back down the slope, dislodging pebbles.

Maybe I could get around to the high, jagged red rocks to the east of the valley. Then I'd be able to watch the whole thing. If they were real rescuers, I could reveal myself, but if they weren't, I could get away.

If only I had some water.

I stumbled away, cutting a wide arc to stay hidden.

By the time I reached the rocks, the airship was down and

tethered, its engines stopped. A group of men were gathered beneath its belly, at the bottom of a lowered set of steps. Dr. Blood stood in front of them, talking to a man I would have recognized anywhere.

"Apprentice," I whispered. I'd been right. Dr. Blood was working with Sir Titus. Now he had reinforcements. I dragged my eyes away from Apprentice's horribly mutilated face with its tight metal mask.

Dr. Blood snapped an order. Apprentice bowed, and the men with him hurried over to lower the luggage platform from the bottom of the airship. Three large crates sat on it. I squinted. Why were they unloading luggage here? There wasn't exactly a hotel around.

Apprentice turned to survey the surrounding terrain. I sank lower.

Men gathered around the crates with crowbars and quickly popped off the lids. Apprentice leaned into each and seemed to fiddle with something inside. I couldn't see what he was working on. All I could hear were the inhuman clicks coming from the grille in his mask.

The men stepped back, clearing the area around the crates. Then, at a command from Dr. Blood, they all stopped absolutely still. What *was* going on?

Glinting metal shapes climbed out of the crates and strode into the Martian sunlight.

The shapes were far taller than a man. If I'd been standing under them, I'd have had to jump to touch their bodies.

They had three long legs, each with too many knees. Their bodies were squat and shaped like two plates, one turned upside down and put on top of the other. Three long, snake-like arms dangled from each body, ending in claws as wide and sharp as swords.

Apprentice said something again in his horrible clicking, and suddenly the tripods spread out, moving faster than a horse could run, racing up the slope.

— 16 —

Hunted

I stumbled, and my foot caught on a stone. The stone rolled away.

The machines snapped around. In a second, all three came angling toward me. Their long legs shot across the ground. Their bodies spun as they ran, their long, loose arms whipping around them. Their claws flashed in the sunlight.

I kicked back, scrambling down the slope away from them. But not fast enough. They'd be on me in seconds.

A hand closed over my face. An arm grabbed me and tugged me back. I hit the ground with a muffled grunt, and whoever had seized me landed on top. I bucked up, trying to throw him off, but the man was too heavy. I bit his hand.

Breath hissed past my ear, but the man didn't shout out and he didn't let go.

"Stay still!"

I stiffened with shock. Then I twisted around violently and stared up into the face of the man holding me. "Freddie?" I managed past his still-clamped hand.

Freddie shook his head. "Don't move," he mouthed. "Don't make a sound."

He'd been on the airship when it had fallen. I'd *seen* him. There hadn't been any lifeboats left. He couldn't have survived. But here he was. He looked a mess. His jacket was torn, and he had a long scrape across his left brow. But he was alive. It was impossible.

He held my gaze. Slowly, I relaxed. I had a hundred questions. But not now.

Freddie took his hand off my mouth.

Above us, only a few yards away, the first of the metal creatures appeared, silhouetted against the sky. I froze. It was so close. Its long arms snapped like whips just above my head. Its body turned slowly, like it was peering around. Why hadn't it seen us?

A moment later, the other two tripods clambered onto the broken rocks. I was almost too scared to breathe. Their arms snapped out, cutting the air. What were they doing? Listening? *Smelling?* I could've stretched out my hand and touched their legs. Freddie was as still as a rock.

Sweat dripped down my dirty skin. My breath puffed up tiny clouds of dust. They must see us. All they had to do was look down. Suddenly, the machines burst into motion. I almost screamed. It took every bit of my willpower not to flinch. Metal feet smacked into the rock beside me. Then the machines raced away over the Martian rock.

I stayed there, unmoving, until Freddie relaxed.

"They're gone," he whispered. He offered me a hand and pulled me up. I wanted to ask him a million things—How had he *survived*? Where had he been?—but he held a finger up to his lips. Silently, I followed him away from the ridge. When we were out of sight, Freddie pulled me behind a boulder and slumped down.

"That was a near thing," he said. "I saw the hunter tripods come out of the airship, but I didn't see you until almost too late."

"They saw me on the ridge," I said, "but then . . ."

"They're blind," Freddie said. "They track their prey through sounds and vibrations. They can feel a footstep hundreds of yards away, and they're deadly accurate, but if you keep quiet and still, they won't find you. If you know they're there. If you don't panic." He smiled wryly. "I know you've got lots of questions, but we're not safe yet, and I don't want to have to explain myself all over again to your sisters." He frowned. "Where are they? Are they well?"

"Olivia's fine," I said. "But Putty's hurt. Something bit her, and she's unconscious."

Freddie looked worried. "That's not good. We're a long way from civilization."

"We need to find someone to help."

Freddie shook his head. "We can't. Sir Titus will have men on any rescue ship."

I scowled at him. "We can't just let her die!"

"I didn't say that. We need to work out what bit her. She might recover by herself. If not, we'll have to find help elsewhere."

"Right," I said bitterly. "Because the wilderness is just full of helpful physicians."

Freddie turned on me. "What do you expect of me, Edward?"

I bit my lip. What *did* I expect of him? A few days ago, I'd thought he was an idiot. Now I expected him to deal with something like this. He wasn't Captain W. A. Masters. He was just Freddie.

"I don't know. I'm out of my depth."

"That's nothing to be embarrassed about," Freddie said, relaxing. "You've done really well."

Really well? Was that supposed to be a joke? I snorted.

"I'm not lying," Freddie said.

"My parents and Jane have been kidnapped. Putty's injured. Olivia's alone and helpless. You call that doing well? I'm supposed to protect them."

Freddie squatted in front of me. I tried to look away, but he wouldn't let me.

"You're twelve years old, Edward. I know why you think you have to look after your family. I know they're absentminded and chaotic. But have you thought that they might surprise you if don't try to do everything yourself?"

"You don't know them like I do."

"Really?" Freddie said. "Shall we test that?"

I shrugged. "If you have to."

He smiled. "Very well. Your father is a genius, and you see your little sister taking after him. Jane has her beauty and her swarms of admirers. Olivia uses propriety to mask her bravery and her quiet, vast compassion, which few of you notice. Your family is extraordinary and you're afraid there's nothing that makes you special. You think your father doesn't respect you and your mother wants you to be something you're not, so you've decided to be the protector of your family. There are things you want to be and things you want to do, but you're ignoring them so you can fill this role. You've chosen it as a way of standing out. You hope your father will notice and be proud of you, and it hurts you that he doesn't. You're angry with me because you think I'm trying to take over your role. How am I doing so far?"

"How does Mama fit into this neat little scheme of yours?" I asked. I tried to make it sound like I was laughing, but it sounded more like choking.

"Ah," Freddie said. "I think you're most like your mother. No, don't protest. You think your mother is vain, selfish, and self-deluding, and you're right. She's all of those things. But she wasn't always. She was the shining star of Tharsis society, not just because her father was a viscount and she was beautiful, but because she was an accomplished intellectual in her own right. She hosted a salon that was the envy of British Mars. In fact, I believe that's where she met your father, when she invited him to discuss his work at the salon. She hoped to host similar salons in Europe, but you know what happened. Her father gambled away their fortune, and she lost it all. Why do you think she shuns any form of intellectual discussion now? It's because it hurts her to remember what she used to have. She decided to live her dreams through Jane instead, but your family doesn't have the status that hers had, and her dreams haunt her. Now that Sir Titus has stepped back into her life, the ghosts of her dreams have stirred. Sir Titus will use them against her. He's a cruel man."

"And you think I'm like that?" I could barely get the words out.

"Not yet. But if you let your own dreams get buried under the responsibility you've given yourself, you'll see them die, too, and you'll grow bitter and lost. That's what your mother did, you know. She married your father because he promised to pay off her father's debts. She gave up her dreams for her family."

I glowered at him.

"Oh, don't look like that. She's grown to love him, that's obvious, just as she loves all of you. But her ghosts don't allow her to show it as you might wish." He smiled crookedly. "I'm a spy, Edward. It's a spy's job to see what other people want to keep hidden."

"You're wrong," I said. "Wrong about me and wrong about my family."

Freddie stood. "I don't think I am."

◄◆►

The sun was already low in the afternoon sky when we finally reached the spike of trees rising from the underbrush. I was exhausted, hungry, and thirsty, and I'd had to lean on Freddie's arm for the last mile.

The lifeboat had broken its back when it had fallen, and it slumped below the stand of trees like a pliosaur washed up on a beach. All was quiet as we approached. Birds called from the branches and small creatures chirped and rustled in the undergrowth. I couldn't hear any voices. My chest tightened. We'd been gone too long. I should never have left them.

Freddie laid his hand on my shoulder. Reluctantly, I let him go first. He hopped onto the body of the lifeboat and snuck up to the hatch. He lowered himself to his stomach and peered inside. A moment later, he jerked back violently. A splintered plank skidded past, almost taking his head from his shoulders. He swore. I scrambled up beside him.

Olivia crouched just below the hatchway, another plank in her hands. As I cut off the light from the hatch, she started to swing at me.

"Livvy!" I said. "It's me."

She lowered the plank. "Oh." She shaded her eyes and blinked at me. "I thought . . ."

"I'm fine. Can we come down?"

"You brought help?"

"Kind of." I dropped into the cabin. "Look who I found."

Olivia stared openmouthed as Freddie followed me in.

"Freddie?" she whispered. Then she threw herself onto him. "Freddie! You're alive!"

He staggered. "I . . ." Awkwardly, he embraced her. "I . . ."

"Are you hurt?" Olivia said, releasing him.

"No. No, not at all. I had feared . . ." He shook his head. "If anything had happened . . ."

I pushed past them. Putty was lying on the floor of the cabin, covered in a blanket. She wasn't moving. Somehow, I'd hoped . . . I'd fantasized . . . that she'd be up and well and causing chaos when I got back, ready to laugh at me for worrying so much and explain why *anyone* who knew *anything* would know *exactly* why it was all fine. But she wasn't. She was as still as a sack of grain.

Freddie stepped past and knelt beside her. He took her wrist, then looked up.

"Her pulse is still strong. What happened to her?"

"Something came in during the night," I said. I pointed to the trail of slime that had now dried and cracked on the floor. "It bit her. There are puncture marks on her skin. Two of them."

"Did you see it?"

"We were asleep. But its trail goes up the tree trunk."

Freddie sat back on his heels. "She's been bitten by a spider-slug. It's a nasty creature, maybe the length of my arm. There're lots of them out here in the wilderness. They live in the tallest trees and they rarely travel far. If you'd crashed out in the open . . ."

"What's going to happen?" Olivia whispered. "Is she going to die?"

Freddie looked serious. "I won't lie to you. The bite of a spider-slug isn't poisonous as such. It merely sends its victims to sleep. The creature wants to keep them unmoving until it's hungry again. It saw Cousin Parthenia as food to save for later. In time, the bite will wear off. But . . ." He shrugged. "There's nothing we can do to wake her. She won't be able to drink or eat while she's unconscious." He reached out and took Olivia's hands. "Parthenia is in a great deal of danger. She could die before the bite wears off."

"Oh." Olivia's head drooped.

"We mustn't stay here," Freddie said. "The spider-slug could return again tonight. I doubt we'd see it unless we built a fire, and I'm afraid we can't risk the light."

"Why not?" Olivia said. "How are we going to signal our rescuers?"

Freddie met my eyes. I sighed.

"We're not going to be rescued," I said. "Dr. Blood set

the crabs on us and crashed the airship. He and his men are looking for us. Sir Titus will have other men on the rescue airships. We have to avoid them."

"Then . . . ?"

"We'll have to find our own way back to civilization," I said. "And we're going to have to carry Putty with us."

<hr />

As the afternoon turned to evening, we rigged up a stretcher for Putty. We gathered planks and spare blankets from the lifeboat, bark from the smaller trees, and vines.

"You haven't told us how you escaped," I said to Freddie as I deposited the last of the supplies next to the frame of the stretcher. "You were trapped. The lifeboats were all gone." I couldn't imagine how frightening it must have been to be stranded there in the dark as the crabs closed in. He must have known he was finished. "We saw the airship fall."

Freddie selected a strip of bark, flexed it, and started to tie one of the planks to the frame. "I won't deny it. When your lifeboat launched, I thought I was dead. Even if I could have fought off the crabs, I had nowhere go." He tightened the bark. "Try that."

I tested the knot. It was neat and firm. "It'll hold," I said.

"You must have been scared," Olivia said, leaning toward him and reaching out with one hand that didn't quite touch his arm.

"I didn't have time to be scared. You saw how quickly the gondola fell. All I knew was that I didn't want to die in the wreckage. I jumped off the side. I thought if I was going to die, at least I'd die falling free." He rubbed his hands on his trousers. "Pass me a blanket, Edward."

What if I'd been the one up there? I didn't know if I'd have been brave enough to do what he'd done. I passed him the blanket, and he tied it across the planks.

"Thank you." He looked critically at the stretcher. "This isn't going to be comfortable." He reached for another blanket.

"What happened?" Olivia said.

Freddie grinned. "Someone told me that a good storyteller always leaves his audience wanting more."

"A good storyteller is going to get a punch on the nose if he doesn't get on with it," I muttered.

Freddie laughed. "All right, all right! The moment I jumped from the gondola, I plunged through the flock of pterodactyls that had been following the airship. One of them must have mistaken me for a scrap thrown overboard by the cooks. It tried to snap me up, and I managed to grab its legs."

"You grabbed a pterodactyl?" I demanded.

He shrugged. "I was desperate. What would you have done? Anyway, I was falling fast, and it was a young pterodactyl. I pretty much knocked it out of the sky." He grinned again. "Can you imagine how embarrassing it would have been to be found dead in the embrace of a pterodactyl? My poor mama would have expired from the humiliation."

"Don't joke about it," Olivia said. She wrapped her arms about her shoulders.

Freddie's grin faded. "Forgive me. This must have been awful for all of you. But don't worry. The pterodactyl was far better at flying than I was. It managed to catch itself, and I ended up dangling from its legs while it flapped along. I started to wonder if I'd ever get down. Pterodactyls can glide for hundreds of miles. Help me with this."

We held curved branches in place as Freddie lashed them above the stretcher to form the ribs of a canopy to shade Putty from the sun.

"Luckily, a pterodactyl isn't used to carrying such a heavy weight," Freddie said. "It tried to shake me off, of course, and once, it attacked me with its beak." Freddie touched the long scrape across the left of his brow. "But it couldn't fly and attack me at the same time. Eventually, it had to land, and I set off to search for you. I was lucky to find Edward at the crash site. This is a big wilderness, and you didn't have the decency to come down anywhere sensible." He stepped back from the stretcher. "There. We're done. This should carry Parthenia." His expression grew serious. "We have to get her to safety quickly. I don't know how long she's got left."

◆

Our trek through the wilderness was sweaty, exhausting, and painful, filled with biting insects, thorns, and dry earth that kept crumbling beneath our feet. I'd never walked so far and for so long in my life, and I had blisters within hours. If Freddie hadn't known how to find water in the wind-carved rocks, we'd have run out within hours.

At the beginning of the third day of the trek, we finally came over a rocky ridge covered in twisted bushes and half-trees. Beyond it, red grasslands replaced the thick undergrowth. Heat haze shimmered above the grass. No matter how hard I peered, I couldn't see how far the grasslands stretched.

Freddie stopped beside me and lowered Putty's stretcher. We'd developed a routine over the last two days. Two of us would carry the stretcher, Freddie taking the front end and Olivia and I taking turns at the back, while the other found the easiest route through the brush and kept an eye on our back trail in case anyone was following. Three times, we'd had to huddle motionless while the hunter tripods strode past.

We hadn't spotted anyone since yesterday evening, and I was starting to think we were safe. Putty hadn't woken, though. She just lay on her stretcher looking like she was asleep. She couldn't eat, and I'd managed to get only a few sips of water down her throat. Every time I looked at her, I started to panic. She looked so small and helpless, and the wilderness went on and on.

"It's going to be hotter down there," Freddie said.

"Hotter?" Olivia said. "Is that even possible?" She was sweating heavily. On the first day, she'd done her best to wipe the sweat away with a silk handkerchief, but by the middle of the afternoon, she'd let out the kind of curse I'd never guessed she knew and torn away part of her long gown, revealing her legs up to her knees. She'd fixed a shocked-looking Freddie with such a challenging gaze that I'd been surprised he hadn't turned tail and run. After that, she'd stopped worrying about the sweat and had even removed her petticoat.

"I'm afraid so," Freddie said. "The Lunae Planum starts on the far side of the grasslands. It's the true desert. There are hundreds of miles of sand and rocks between here and the Martian Nile."

"That's unfortunate," Olivia said. "There's not much more clothing I can take off."

Freddie immediately blushed, and if I hadn't known better, I would have sworn a smile twitched Olivia's lips.

"How are we going to cross the desert?" I asked.

"There are ways across," Freddie said. "Ways with shelter and water. Not everyone can afford airship fares. The native Martians have their own routes."

"Do you know where they are?" I asked.

Freddie gave a one-sided grin. "Not a clue, old boy."

⊰◆⊱

We were a couple of miles into the grasslands, pushing through the stiff, shoulder-high grass, when Putty's breathing changed. She gave a dry gasp and shifted on the stretcher.

I set her down and touched her face. "Putty?"

She didn't respond. Freddie took her wrist. After a moment, he shook his head.

"Her pulse is getting weaker."

"What does that mean?" Olivia said.

"It means she's dying," Freddie said. "She's running out of strength. Without water, out here in the wilderness . . . She doesn't have long."

I pulled out one of my water bottles and tried to get some past her cracked lips. After a few drops, she coughed weakly. I wasn't sure any of the water got down her throat.

"We need to keep moving," Freddie said. "We have to get her help and out of the sun."

"We should signal an airship if one passes over," I said. "We have to risk it."

Freddie rubbed his eyes. He looked exhausted. "Fine. If we see one, we'll try to get its attention. But in the meantime, we keep moving."

I grabbed the back of the stretcher and we hurried on, pushing through the grass. Even though he'd carried the stretcher through each day and taken half of the night watches, Freddie didn't slow. The stretcher's poles were rubbing my hands raw. My arms felt like they were slowly burning from the inside out. My feet dragged and I tripped over loose stones hidden in the grass.

"There's something ahead," Olivia called back. She had pushed on past us. "The land dips and the grass is getting shorter. And . . . Oh."

"What is it?" Freddie said.

"It's the desert," Olivia said. "I can see the desert."

The last of the strength drained from my arms. Freddie, too, seemed to despair. For the first time, he stumbled and had to catch himself to keep from losing his grip on Putty's stretcher.

Beyond the grasslands, great, scree-laden red mesas rose like giant walls, and the jagged valleys were filled with drifts of fine Martian sand.

I'd imagined the desert would be all sand, enormous dunes of it stretching away to the horizon, but this was worse. We'd never make it across all those miles of rock, stones, and sand.

I just couldn't take it anymore. "Why?" I said in despair. "Why is Sir Titus doing all this? Why put in all this effort and hurt so many people for a stupid old tomb? How can money be so important?"

"It's not the money," Freddie said heavily. "I mean, the money is important to him. Sir Titus isn't the kind of man who would tolerate being poor. But it's more than that. It's about his pride. Imagine. People thought he was a hero. He'd found three dragon tombs, and he was still a young man. No one else had ever done that. The whole of good Society looked up to him. Then the truth came out. He'd stolen the locations of the tombs. He was disgraced. When he visited people, doors were shut in his face. There was even a warrant out for his arrest. He *needs* this tomb to restore his reputation and his pride. He'll do anything for it."

It was just too much. We had nowhere else left to go and no way to escape the desert, and all because Sir Titus had hurt his *pride*. I didn't know what to do.

Something brushed against my face. I frowned, then shook my head. The heat was getting to me. I was imagining things.

"Edward?" Olivia said. "What's wrong?"

There it was again. The air against my dry face had felt damp.

My stomach leaped inside me. "There's water ahead," I said. I was sure I was right.

"Water?" Olivia said. She threw a worried glance at Freddie. "Edward . . ."

"Yes," I said. "Can't you feel it?" Now that I knew it was there, it was easy to feel.

Freddie broke into a grin. "A canal!"

"A canal?" Olivia said. "In the desert?"

"Of course! I was hoping we'd find one. The Ancient Martian Empire built canals across the planet, joining their cities. The native Martians still use them to cross the desert. If we can build some kind of craft, we can sail to one of their supply posts. We'll have plenty of water."

I looked down at Putty. She was pale and thin on the stretcher. I didn't think she would last long enough to reach help, but what choice did we have? There was nothing else out here.

We hurried down the slope, toward the hidden canal. But we'd only gone a dozen paces when Freddie looked back and his face dropped.

"We're too late," he whispered.

I followed his gaze. The hunter tripods had appeared at the top of the slope. They were only fifty yards away, and they'd heard us. They sprang into motion, charging down the incline, their long arms cutting through the air.

"Run!" Freddie shouted.

We plunged through the grass. Thick stalks whipped against my arms and face. I ducked my head and kept running. Grass crunched as the machines' metal legs cut the distance. Hot, dusty air burned in my throat. All the coolness I'd felt a moment ago had gone. My legs were weak. My knees wanted to give way. The only thing that stopped me from simply falling was knowing that Putty would drop to the earth, helpless.

The ground dipped again, and I spotted the canal. It divided the grasslands from the desert beyond. It curved into sight from the left, emerging from behind a jutting ridge of rock.

It was too far away. The hunter tripods were too close. Their metal feet thumped the hard ground, and I heard the stalks of grass being smashed aside. We half ran, half tumbled down the slope toward the canal. Putty bounced violently on her stretcher. If she hadn't been strapped on, she'd have been thrown to the ground.

Olivia raced ahead of the rest of us. She scrambled and leaped down the slope. Her elegant boots, which had become torn and ragged during the hike, spun from her feet. But these last few days had changed my sister. She kept running, her soft feet scraping on the rough earth.

Dislodged stones rattled down onto me from behind. I ducked. A metal arm snapped past my head. I lost my footing and the stretcher knocked into Freddie. He tripped and lunged face forward down the slope.

My back hit the ground. I fought to keep the stretcher up. I skidded down the slope on my unprotected back, while Freddie stumbled and slid on his knees and hip and side.

Above us, the tripod tottered, thrown off balance by the sudden slope and its lunge for me. Gyroscopes whirred inside it. Then its leading foot hit a loose rock and it toppled.

I got my heels under me and kicked forward. The great metal machine hit the ground behind me with a crash that peppered my shoulders and back with stones. One of its flailing arms smacked into a rock to my left, splitting it. Dirt and broken stalks of grass choked the air. The metal body rolled down, kicking its legs to find its feet again.

Olivia reached the edge of the canal.

"Jump in!" Freddie yelled.

The second tripod raced toward us. Claws snapped eagerly. There was nothing I could do to avoid it.

"Over here!" Olivia shouted. She jumped around on the canal bank, her feet thudding into the ground, waving and shouting, trying to attract the machine's attention.

It veered toward her. With quick strides, it closed the distance between them. Livvy kept stamping and shouting.

Where was the third tripod? I couldn't see it. The grass and the dust and our plunging fall hid it from me.

The second machine reached Livvy. Its arms lashed toward her. But before they could catch her, she turned and dived gracefully beneath them, into the canal.

We hit the bottom of the slope. Somehow, Freddie regained his feet and staggered on. I clung to the stretcher and was pulled up. The canal was only ten paces away, but the tripod that had chased Livvy was already turning toward us. Smacking footsteps on the slope behind told me at last where the final hunting machine was.

Freddie put his head down and sprinted. I followed, my hands death-tight around the poles of the stretcher. Whatever happened, I couldn't drop Putty now. Even if one of the machines got me, I could use my momentum and the last of my strength to throw the stretcher toward the canal. We were close enough that it might make it.

The machine ahead of us swung on Freddie, its claws coming down. He danced aside, ducking under the backswing.

A claw cut at me from behind. It snagged the back of my

shirt. I was jerked to such a sudden stop that I almost dropped the stretcher. Then the claw closed with a snip. My shirt parted, and the blade sliced through my skin. I cried out in pain. But I was free. I staggered on.

Freddie plunged into the canal, dragging the stretcher behind. I heaved my end in after him, and Putty's limp body splashed with it into the water. I threw myself after her.

Water rushed up my nose and down my throat. I spluttered and surfaced, just in time to feel a vicious splash not a foot away from me. One of the machines had reached from the bank and slashed at me. I dived and kicked away.

I came up next to Putty's half-submerged stretcher. Freddie was holding her head above the water and trying to paddle further out. I grabbed hold and helped him.

Water was in my eyes. I could scarcely see. I blinked and squinted back.

The three hunter tripods stood in a line on the bank, their arms twisting through the air and cutting at the water, but we were out of range.

"They won't come in," Freddie spluttered. "The water would stop their mechanisms."

Not taking our eyes from the hunter tripods, we kicked our way out toward where Olivia was treading water. We were safe. We had escaped the monsters.

I was so relieved and so exhausted that I scarcely heard Olivia's shout of warning.

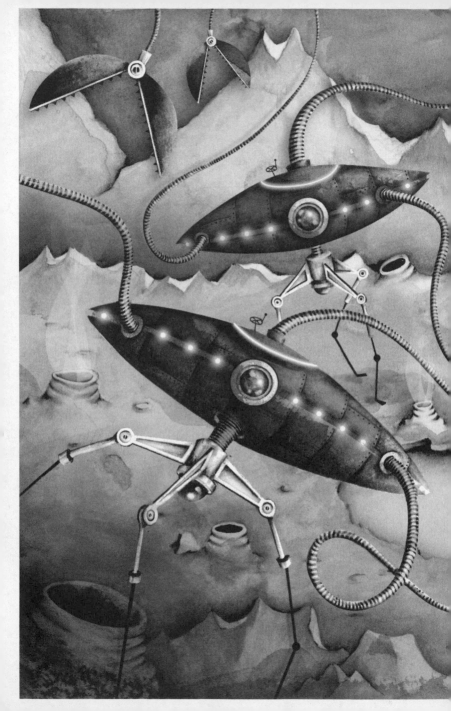

"Freddie!" she screamed. "Edward! Look out!"

I flipped myself around just in time to see a large boat loom up in the water beside me.

It knocked me sideways and thrust me under the surface. I lost my grip on Putty's stretcher. Wood scraped over me, tumbling me about. I breathed in water. My limbs flapped helplessly. All I could see was a wide, flat shape above me. I was under the boat's hull. It rolled across me, spinning me, pummeling me, and knocking the breath from my body. I kicked away, pushing myself further down into the water, away from the hull that could batter me unconscious.

I didn't have enough breath. I couldn't get out from beneath the boat. I rose toward it again. I had to have air, but there wasn't any. Something was roaring in my ears. Everything started to go black.

Then an arm closed around my chest, powerful legs kicked beneath me, and I was pulled toward the daylight.

PART THREE

The Dragon Tombs
of Mars

— 17 —

Lunae City

I didn't remember much after that. Someone grabbed me and hauled me out. I felt a wooden deck under my back, and hands on my chest. Then all was darkness.

When I awoke, the only light I could see was a single candle. Its flickering yellow flame showed me a tall, narrow cabin with what looked like carpets on the walls and glass spheres dangling from the ceiling. The ceiling itself was covered with strange, swirling patterns painted in strong, bright colors. I wondered if I was dreaming. Then a figure I hadn't noticed sat up from a low chair.

"Edward! You're awake!"

Olivia bent over me. She seemed to have borrowed a shapeless, long robe, but otherwise she looked as much of a mess as when we'd been hiking through the wilderness.

"Where are we?" I croaked. Even though I'd swallowed half the canal, my throat felt as dry as the desert.

"On a boat. Freddie was right. The native Martians use the canal for travel. They pulled us out of the water."

I tried to sit up and immediately started coughing. Olivia pushed me down easily.

"You mustn't move. Freddie said you have to rest. You almost drowned."

"What about Putty?" I'd lost hold of her stretcher in the canal.

"They pulled her out, too, but she's still unconscious. The captain and his men have some experience of this bite. They put a tube between Parthenia's lips and they've been feeding her sugared water. But they say we have to wait." She took a deep breath. "There's nothing more they can do."

I rested my hand on Olivia's arm. It was hard to speak. "She'll get better. Freddie said it's just a matter of time, and if they're feeding her . . ."

"I know," Olivia said, sounding choked. "But it's too much. First Mama, Papa, and Jane were kidnapped by Sir Titus, now Parthenia won't wake up, and I thought you were drowned." She shook her head. "I couldn't bear to lose all of you."

Sir Titus! He still had Jane and my parents. We were supposed to be rescuing them.

"How long have I been asleep?"

"Six hours. It's night."

My brain felt like it was being drowned in thick oil. I could hardly think. I forced myself to count back. Sir Titus had kidnapped them five days ago.

"We've only got seven days left!" I blurted. "How are we going to get to Lunae City in just seven days?"

I tried to sit up again, but I couldn't. My eyelids were too heavy, and my body was exhausted. My head fell back.

"Hush," Olivia said. "Go back to sleep."

So I did.

◆

The next thing I knew, sunlight was streaming through a thin cloth that had been carefully fixed over a delicate wooden screen. I lay there for a while, feeling bruised and battered, following the carved patterns on the wooden screen. They seemed to flow and twist away from my eyes, but I thought I could make out a river and a great dragon and fish. Or maybe they were people working in a field. My eyes couldn't settle on them for long enough to be sure what I was seeing.

I dragged myself off the bed. I was weak, but at least I could stand. I found my shoes and slipped them on. They were still wet from the canal. I pulled a face. They were disgusting. On the deck up above, I heard the creak of sails, the gentle padding of feet, and strange, high singing. Water splashed against the hull.

Putty! Olivia had said she was still unconscious. I shouldn't have slept. Anything could have happened. I should have been with her.

I slid open the door. There was a darkened corridor ahead of me, then a set of rough steps and a hatchway above. I climbed out onto the deck. Boxes and bales were stacked everywhere and covered in tarpaulins. A tall native Martian was coiling a rope a few feet away. When he saw me, he called something in his language, grinned at me, and returned to his work. It took me a moment to realize that he'd looked me in the eyes. I didn't have time to think about it, though, because Freddie appeared around the mounds of cargo.

"There you are," he said. "I thought you'd sleep all day. You must be starving."

"Where's Putty?" I demanded. "What's happened to her?"

Freddie nodded. "This way."

He led me to a shack-like cabin standing on the raised aft deck. I bit my lip. What if she was still unconscious? What if she hadn't made it?

The shack doors were folded back, and there on a low chair sat Putty. She sprang to her feet, with a slight wobble.

"Putty?"

"I can't believe you let me sleep through all the excitement!" she said. "Freddie says we were chased by hunter tripods, and I missed them. What were they like? Freddie's useless at describing them. Were they clockwork? Of course, they must have been, or they wouldn't have been so fast. But how were they stabilized? How did they triangulate the sounds they followed? Really, I don't know how you managed to survive without me."

I took two steps and engulfed her in a hug that lifted her off the deck.

"I was so worried," I said. "I thought you'd . . . you . . ."

"Get off!" Putty wriggled free and looked around, flustered. "You must have hit your head too hard. I'm hardly about to die over something so stupid. I'm not that missish. Oh!" She collapsed back into her chair.

I glanced across at Olivia, who was standing nearby, and she gave me a little nod.

"Well, good," I said, and cleared my throat.

"You haven't completely recovered your strength, Cousin Parthenia," Freddie said. "You must rest. There'll be plenty of time for details. We'll be on this boat for several days."

Putty let out a grunt of dissatisfaction, but she didn't argue.

"How many days?" I demanded. "We have to get to Lunae City."

"I don't know," Freddie said. "It depends on the winds. There's nothing any of us can do to hurry it up. We all need to rest and recover."

Grinding my teeth, I lowered myself into a chair next to Putty. Just walking from the cabin to the deck had left me shaky. I toed off my damp shoes and rested my feet on the warm wood. At least my clothes were dry. Someone must have undressed me, dried my clothes, and then redressed me. I'd slept through it all. But if they'd removed my jacket . . . My hand shot to the pocket.

"The map!" I said. "It's gone."

Freddie grimaced. "I know. It didn't survive the water. The paper was sodden and the ink had run. There was nothing I could do."

"It's ruined?" I said.

Freddie nodded.

I buried my face in my hands. After everything we'd been through—our house demolished, my family kidnapped, the airship crash, and the hell of that wilderness—Sir Titus Dane had gotten what he wanted after all. The map was destroyed. Now he was the only one who could find the tomb.

"There was this, too," Putty said.

She passed me a sagging mass of wet pulp. It was disgusting. It felt like snail-bird slime.

"What is it?"

Putty looked pained. "Your *Thrilling Martian Tales*."

I stared down at it. The magazine was a mess. I tried to pull it open, but it tore. I let it fall to the deck.

Freddie cleared his throat. "Your sisters have helped me reproduce what we can."

"Excuse me?" I blinked up from the seeping remains of my magazine.

"The map."

"Right," I said. "Right."

"I've stared at the ideograms so many times that I think

I've got them," Freddie said, "but the map feels wrong. If you could take a look and see what you remember?"

He pulled a piece of paper from his sleeve and unfolded it. In the line of symbols at the top, there was a bird standing on one leg and a cloud, and something that might have been a coiled snake, but those were the only ideograms that seemed familiar. I couldn't have sworn that even those were accurate. The map, though . . . It showed a valley and the lines were roughly the right shape, but there was something wrong that I couldn't put my finger on.

"It's not quite right," I said, "but . . ." I shrugged.

"I agree," Freddie said. "We'll just have to hope that the ideograms themselves give enough clues when they're decoded. Either that or we'll have to get Sir Titus's original map."

"After we've rescued my family," I said.

"We will rescue them," Freddie said. "This canal will take us all the way to the Martian Nile. From there, the captain plans to sail to Lunae City to deliver his goods. We will come up on Sir Titus, unexpected and beneath his notice."

"We've got less than seven days," I said.

"I know," Freddie said. "But we'll get there." His eyes hardened. "And when we do, I will deliver justice to that man for what he has done."

◆

It took us seven days to reach Lunae City by boat, and I knew it was too long. Every day was another day closer to

Papa finishing the water abacus and my family becoming expendable. I knew I should be resting and preparing, but I could hardly sit still.

For the first four days, we sailed along the canal with a steady breeze behind us. Occasionally, we passed other native Martian boats heading in the other direction, tacking backward and forward across the wide canal against the wind.

The canal was amazing. It went straight through the hills and mesas without changing direction. It looked like someone had picked up a giant axe and sliced through even the hardest rock. Where the land dipped down into valleys, great embankments had been raised to support the canal, and while these had crumbled in places, the canal had survived. It had been built thousands of years ago, but it was still there. I couldn't imagine that anything we'd built on Mars would still be around two thousand years later.

I'd never spent any time with a native Martian before. Whenever I'd seen them, they'd only been passing by. Sometimes the Martians on the boat would stop for no apparent reason to sit together on the deck and sing strange, quiet songs. At others, they would work nine or ten hours straight through without even breaking for food. I couldn't figure out why. It certainly wasn't because of anything Captain Sadalius Kol, the owner of the boat, said, but he seemed happy enough to join in even if it meant the boat drifted to a stop or if everyone went hungry. The captain spoke only a few words of English, and I didn't speak any native Martian at all, so I couldn't ask him what was going on.

For some reason, the native Martians didn't use any technology from the dragon tombs, either, even the things that were so cheap they must have been able to afford them. They did everything by hand, although it took twice as long.

"How are we going to pay for this?" I asked Freddie one evening when we were alone. We'd lost most of our money in the airship crash.

"We're not," Freddie said. "No native Martian would dream of charging us. I said they were generous."

"If they trust us, you said."

"Well, wouldn't you trust someone you pulled drowning out of a canal?" Freddie laughed. "Anyway, I'm good at this." He winked. "Spy training, don't you know?"

"You must be," I said, "if they're feeding and carrying us for free."

"You still don't get it, do you?" Freddie said. "They're grateful to us. Native Martians believe it's a privilege to offer someone hospitality. You shouldn't expect everyone to think and act like an Englishman. We're their guests for as long as we want." He stretched his back painfully. He was still covered in bruises from the airship crash and the hunter tripod attack.

"It's interesting, isn't it?" he said. "That the poorest people tend to be more generous than the richest. Imagine what would happen if a group of lost, bedraggled native Martians appeared on your family's doorstep."

I didn't need to imagine. Mama would turn the automatic servants on them. If they came back, she would have them arrested. I'd have been so worried about protecting my family, I might have done the same. It made me feel guilty.

The sailors had set up a canopy across part of the deck so that we could rest in the low, slung-back native Martian chairs and recover. Within a couple of days, Putty had picked up enough native Martian to chat away happily with the sailors. I was still trying to figure out the difference between "yes," "no," "thank you," and "please may I have a bucket for my head."

When I'd first seen the desert, I'd thought we were going to die there. I'd been shocked and scared by just how big, bleak, and threatening it was. Now that we were sitting comfortably beneath a cool canopy, I realized the desert was also beautiful, particularly at nightfall and sunrise.

Great red and yellow sand dunes stretched like the backs of mile-long whales, but there were so many of them they looked like ripples on a lake. Putty wanted to stop and search for the sandfish she'd once been obsessed with, but the captain just laughed and kept on sailing.

Between the dunes, there were a thousand different colors of rocks, delicately layered and bent into vast curves. Putty told me the native Martians thought that once, millions of years ago, this had all been beneath the sea and it had been pushed up by the working of unimaginable forces. It was a strange superstition. I agreed with Olivia that it was really evidence of the hand of a Creator.

◆

It took me a few days to realize that some of the sailors were women, but Putty certainly didn't miss it. By the time we reached the end of the canal, she'd decided to become a sailor. I'd expected Olivia to be horrified when she found out, but she simply said, "Their lives are so different from our own," and spent the next hour staring in silence at the horizon.

The canal joined the Martian Nile at an ancient, heavy lock that looked like it'd been repaired a hundred times. It was large enough to carry several boats, and a couple were waiting when we arrived, so we descended through the lock together.

Once on the Martian Nile, we sped up. The strong current helped us, and although the crew had to watch out for sandbanks, we were making much better time. I still didn't know if it would be enough. We had less than three days left, and the Martian Nile was a long river.

Within a day, we caught sight of the first ruins of the Ancient Martian civilization. A single giant column rose from the middle of a lush green field. Pictures and ideograms were carved all the way up it, although we were too far away to make them out properly. At the top, the column twisted and became the head of a vast dragon, leering out in the direction of the river. Olivia let out a gasp of horror when she saw it.

"Did they really keep tame dragons?" she said.

"It was a great empire," Freddie said. "Even if we don't know much about it." He laid a reassuring hand on Olivia's arm. "The dragons are long gone, and it's possible they weren't as fierce as their statues make them look."

Soon we were passing more ruins, each more elaborate than the last. Massive stone walls jutted from the ground, still speckled here and there by fragments of red, gold, or green paint. Whole temples or palaces—Putty said historians were still arguing about which they were—sprawled over enormous areas, bigger than some towns. Strangely, none of the native Martians who lived and farmed along the banks of the river seemed to build their villages close to the ruins. Superstition, I supposed, or maybe they just realized how far they'd fallen from the glory of their ancestors.

◆

We came into sight of Lunae City at midday, seven days after we'd started our trip on the boat. I should have been relieved, but if Putty and Freddie were right, Papa would already have finished the new water abacus. We were out of time, and we still had no idea where in the city Sir Titus was. We couldn't even be certain he *was* in Lunae City. What if he'd gone somewhere else?

We'd passed an increasing number of boats in the last day, ranging from cargo boats as large as ours, down through smaller versions used by visitors to sail between the ruins of temples and palaces, to tiny paddleboats ferrying the locals back and forth. The city docks stretched for nearly a mile along the river. Stone wharves stood high above the water, and the boats formed a gay confusion of brightly colored sails, flashing oars, and shouting sailors. At least Sir Titus wouldn't be able to spot us here. There were too many boats and too many people. He'd need a hundred men to watch everything.

Lunae City loomed over the river. Native Martian architecture, developed in the low gravity of Mars, looked completely different from that of Earth. The buildings were tall, narrow, and elaborate, often twisting in spirals or overhanging so far they looked like they'd topple over. Delicate spires competed for height above the buildings. Here and there among the Martian buildings were a few squat, bulky buildings of Earth design: a grand white hotel with neat lawns, a Turkish mosque, a long building in the Chinese style.

"We'll need to be careful in Lunae City," Freddie said as we prepared to climb off the boat. "It's not part of British Mars and it doesn't have the same laws. The council likes to play countries off against each other. It's how they keep control. If we get in trouble, we can't rely on the British-Martian ambassador to help. We'll be on our own."

"It is enormous," Olivia said quietly. "I hadn't guessed it would be so big."

"It's been a city for thousands of years," Freddie said with a smile. "It's the oldest city on the planet, and in the time of the Ancient Martian Empire, it was the most important. Then, when the dragon tombs were discovered, people flocked here and it expanded again. Now it's full of glory hunters like Colonel Fitzsimmons, and a good proportion of British Martian society maintain houses here. If you're interested in Ancient Martian artifacts, you'll spend time here. Add to that the tourists, and you've got a city almost as big as Tharsis."

Even though I was desperate to look for my family, I hadn't realized how sad I'd be to leave the boat. We'd been scared and in such danger until the crew had rescued us, and they'd been so kind and friendly, I couldn't stop a few tears from springing up.

Freddie booked us into the Grand Hotel, the enormous white building we'd seen from the boat, giving false names at the desk.

"Isn't this a bit—I don't know—obvious?" I said when we'd settled into our luxurious suite of rooms and I had him alone. "I mean, we're not exactly hiding."

"Sir Titus has his hands full trying to decode the map," Freddie said. "Don't forget that when he disappeared he was in disgrace. He won't want to be recognized. He'll have gone to ground, and his men won't come to a place like this.

Sometimes the worst thing you can do is try to hide. People notice someone trying to hide."

"Freddie, we've run out of time," I said. "Sir Titus must have his water abacus by now."

"Unless your father delayed him."

I shook my head. "Papa would never risk it." I glanced around and dropped my voice. "Can't you get help from the British-Martian Intelligence Service?"

"Intelligence services are banned in Lunae City," Freddie said. "The council doesn't like them. They're here, of course, but in deep cover. I'll have to meet with the British-Martian ambassador, but it'll take time for him to check my identity."

"We don't *have* time," I said.

"I know."

Right this moment, Papa's abacus would be whirring and clicking and gurgling as it deciphered the ideograms. Every second we delayed, Sir Titus got closer, and Papa's miracle machine was supposed to be *fast*.

The door opened behind Freddie, and Putty walked in, followed by Olivia.

"Where are you off to?" Putty said.

"Don't you ever knock?" I demanded.

"No. So, where are you going? You're obviously going somewhere. I can tell."

Olivia had washed her face and arms and fixed her hair. She was still dressed in the loose, slightly transparent gown the sailors had given her, but she'd found a belt for her waist.

"Freddie's going to make inquiries," I said.

"I want to go," Putty said.

"Oh, yes," Olivia said. "I wouldn't feel safe left here alone."

I scowled. "You'd hardly be alone," I said. "I'd be here."

"What if those men came back?" Olivia said. "Or those hunter tripods?"

Putty sighed. "I'd love to see the hunter tripods. Perhaps we should stay here, Livvy."

"They think we're lost in the wilderness," I said, "or dead. There's no reason for them to come here."

"I still wouldn't feel safe," Olivia said, widening her eyes.

Freddie looked around desperately. "Well . . ."

Good grief. Freddie was supposed to be smart now, wasn't he? Couldn't he see she was playing him?

"Excellent!" Putty said. She grabbed Freddie's hand. "So, where are we going first?"

Freddie's shoulders sagged. "Ah . . . I suppose Cousin Olivia needs something to wear. She can't appear in public in that outfit." He paused for a moment, staring at Olivia's oddly belted contraption, until I cleared my throat. "Um. First some new gowns and boots. And while you're doing that, I have to visit the British-Martian ambassador. It'll be horribly boring, I'm afraid, but when we're all done, there's a museum of Ancient Martian antiquities nearby. It's got the largest collection of items recovered from the dragon tombs anywhere on the planet, and the curators are some of the greatest living experts on dragon tombs and ideographic writing. If Sir Titus went to them for help, we may be able to pick up some clues as to where he is."

"And if not?" Olivia said.

"If not, we'll find him some other way. We're not going to give up, I promise you."

I could tell Freddie meant it, and that he was determined. I just hoped it would be enough.

I just hoped we would be in time.

The Museum of Martian Antiquities

The Museum of Martian Antiquities was a vast red-stone building set apart from the narrow streets of Lunae City by a wide paved square. The entire front of the building was made from the wall of an Ancient Martian temple. Ideograms and stylized pictures covered most of the surface, and worn carvings of men, dragons, and strange Martian beasts jutted like gargoyles from ledges and columns. Iron-studded oak doors had been set in the entrance, and as Olivia, Putty, and I approached, Freddie stepped from the shadow of a pillar.

"There you are," he said. "I was starting to get worried. Oh . . ." His voice trailed off as Olivia stepped in front of him.

"Forgive us," she said. "It took a while to find just the right gown and have it fitted."

A while? It had felt like about a million years. How did it take so long to choose a dress and put in a few stitches?

"Do you like it?" Olivia said. When she'd chosen the gown, I'd thought I was hallucinating. Olivia always wore sensible, practical gowns that hid as much of her as possible. But this was very different. Even Jane would have thought twice before wearing something this revealing.

"Good gracious," Freddie managed.

I inserted myself between them before they could start staring into each other's eyes. "Should we really be standing around out here? What if one of Sir Titus's men sees us?"

Olivia shot me a look of annoyance.

Freddie blinked, then shook himself. "Of course. You're right." He put out an arm to herd us toward the doors. "Come on. I've arranged for a brief tour of the museum, then we've got an appointment with a Professor Michel Fournier."

"A Frenchman?" I said.

"I told you," Freddie said, "this isn't British Mars. You'll find as many Frenchmen as Englishmen here. Anyway, Professor Fournier is the leading expert on ideograms. If Sir Titus went to anyone, it would have been to him."

We didn't have long to wait, because a small, dusty man hurried toward us across the entrance hall as soon as we entered.

"Gentlemen. Young lady," he said, bobbing his head like a bird pecking for worms. "I am Dr. Filipo Guzman, junior-under-curator for Third Age antiquities. The senior-assistant-curator has asked me to give you the tour. Shall we get going? You must forgive us our disorder today. We have received a new consignment of pottery from the region around the mouth of the Martian Nile. We are all atwitter." He blinked, as though expecting a response.

Freddie raised an eyebrow. "Well, well. Jolly exciting. Er, pots and that."

"You are an aficionado?" the junior-under-curator said. "Capital! I have always maintained that Third Age pottery is the most refined of antiquity, would you not agree? Sadly, not all of my colleagues, particularly those specializing in the Second Age"—he sniffed—"have such discernment."

"As you say," Freddie said cheerfully. "Third Age is the thing!"

"Well, we cannot stand around talking all day." Dr. Guzman laid his hand on his dusty beard. "Although . . . I have an idea. The tour usually takes us through the mechanisms found in the dragon tombs, but perhaps . . ." He smiled. "I think we could take in the exhibit of Third Age pottery I have been assembling instead. It is not open to the public. The curators"—he sniffed again—"think there would be no interest, but we might take a private tour, do you not think?"

Putty made a choking sound.

The junior-under-curator for Third Age antiquities squinted down at her. "I say. Is something wrong with your brother?"

Freddie grinned at Putty, who was dressed once again in boy's clothes. "I can't think of anything I'd like more than to stare at old pottery for days on end, but we promised my, ah, brother he could see the mechanisms. You know how boys are."

The junior-under-curator looked down with an expression of distaste. "Boys. Yes." He rubbed his fingers together, as though he was trying to wipe something off them. "Well, if you have given your word. You will find the mechanisms, young man, of significantly less interest than the pottery. But if that is to be the way, it is the way."

Olivia took Freddie's arm. "I am sure my older brother would wish to return to examine the pottery in more detail another day. In fact, I've heard him talk about how much he'd love to spend several days at the museum admiring Third Age pottery."

Freddie blinked stupidly at her.

"Well then," the junior-under-curator said, brightening. "It is settled. Well, well. This has quite made my day. Come. Follow. Let us begin."

He led us through a door at the side of the entrance hall. "These are the mechanisms from the first dragon tomb, which was uncovered over a hundred years ago. We believe it was the tomb of an emperor called Har-no-Sek, or possibly Hro-en-Sak. It's not always easy to translate the ideograms of names into something we can pronounce."

The center of the room held an enormous gold

sarcophagus, inlaid with gems and silver thread in the swirling, twisting patterns that seemed to dominate Ancient Martian design. Around the sarcophagus were arranged the fantastic discoveries that had launched mankind into its golden age of technology. I recognized some of them. A large steam boiler, attached to pistons and wheels, of the type that could still be found in old-fashioned steam carriages, occupied a large, roped-off area. In the neighboring glass case stood a suit of some rubbery material with a glass helmet attached and a hose protruding from it. A diving suit of some type, I guessed. There were other strange contraptions of metal, glass, and wood that I didn't recognize. Behind each stood a section of rock face, covered in ideograms.

"You have noticed the ideograms, I see," the junior-under-curator said. "They contain instructions as to the operation of the artifacts. Much of the work when a new dragon tomb is discovered comes in attempting to decipher the ideograms. Some, sadly, are never decoded, and only close examination of the artifacts in question allows their use to be deduced. Indeed, it took the first explorers more than fifty years to understand enough of the ideograms found in the then-ruined Lunae City to enable them to find the first dragon tomb."

"Why are they called dragon tombs," Olivia asked, "if they're the tombs of the Ancient Martian emperors?"

The junior-under-curator smiled. "A romantic idea, I fear. At the beginning of the First Age, the Ancient Martians tamed the great dragons of Mars. It launched their civilization, because the dragons were fierce and unstoppable in battle. Dragons became symbols of status. Each emperor had his own dragon, to prove his worth. It became the Ancient Martians' habit to slay the dragons when their masters died and entomb them with the emperors, much in the way the pagans of Earth might slay horses or slaves and lay them in the tombs of their masters."

"That's horrible," Olivia said.

"Not at all. The dragons were no more than savage beasts, and it was a more savage age. One must not judge the actions of more primitive men by our own standards. In any case, when the first dragon tombs were discovered, the explorers were overawed by the bodies of the dragons and named the resting places dragon tombs."

"Can we see the remains of the dragons?" Putty said.

"Always the dragons," the junior-under-curator muttered, as though he'd bitten into a lemon. "Always the beasts, not the glorious civilization that tamed them."

"But they died out at the end of the Fourth Age?" I said.

"We call that period the Time of Many Emperors," Dr. Guzman said. "Most of the dragon tombs come from a space of no more than ten years. It appears that the empire fragmented, because in that time, dozens of emperors—although perhaps we shouldn't call them emperors; they were too far fallen—were buried, and with each was the body of a dragon. The population of dragons, which was never great, was too decimated to recover. The civilization fell, and the dragons did not survive it."

"That's sad," Olivia said.

"I must disagree. Such beasts have no place in the civilized world. The Ancient Martians were barbarians. This is a new, brighter age."

"And yet all our achievements have their origin in the mechanisms and artifacts of that empire," Freddie said.

The junior-under-curator shrugged. "All knowledge begins somewhere. In only a hundred years, we have improved upon them beyond recognition. Now, let us move to the next room."

The junior-under-curator led us through a series of spectacular rooms, packed with incredible artifacts. We saw the first steam-powered automatic servant, its head laid open to show the tiny levers and fine cogs within that allowed it to interpret instructions. We saw several cannons attached to the steam engines used to pressurize the air that would shoot out the cannon balls, and in the room holding artifacts from the most recent dragon tomb, discovered ten years ago by Sir Titus Dane himself, the device that could focus sunlight into photon emission globes. The wall behind that was densely illustrated and covered in miniature ideograms. We even saw an early version of the cycle-copter that Freddie had nearly crashed into me. Putty raced around, letting out excited squeaks.

Finally, the junior-under-curator of Third Age antiquities

drew us together. "There is but one room remaining," he said. "We always save it for last. I am told it is for reasons of drama, although, for myself, I do not see it, finding far more drama and interest in a fragment of beautifully crafted pottery. Nonetheless . . ."

He strode to the double doors at the end of the room and threw them open.

There, in the largest hall we had yet seen, was a dragon.

I had known that dragons were big, but I'd never really realized just how enormous they were. The sheer bulk of the dragon was overwhelming. It stretched nearly forty yards from end to end. I'd seen a whale, once, breaching the waters of the Valles Marineris, but this creature was even bigger. Its tail looped and curved around its feet, and its vast wings were folded against its chest. Its scaled body rose above us, far higher than our heads, like a wall. I had to crane my neck to see the smooth curve of its back. Long, surprisingly delicate claws jutted from its four feet. From the highest point of the room, where a glass skylight ran the length of the ceiling, the dragon's thin head peered down at us, its eyes glittering like black diamonds.

Putty sighed. "Oh. You have a preserved one."

The junior-under-curator chuckled. "Indeed. At the end of the Fourth Age, the ancient Martians discovered a technique to preserve the bodies of their beasts. Perhaps they had some pagan superstition that the beasts would protect them in their afterlife. It is a shame that their civilization did not last more than a few years after the discovery, or we might have many more complete specimens like this one. Some of my colleagues would like the opportunity to dissect a preserved dragon. Go on. You may touch it."

Slowly, I approached the body of the dragon. It was covered in a slightly cloudy resin. Even so, and even with the dead stillness of the dragon, my hand shook as I reached out to touch it. The creature looked alive beneath its coating.

The dragon was cold to the touch. The layer that covered it was surprisingly giving. Putty came up beside me. Her eyes sparkled with excitement as she laid both hands on the resin. Her breath came fast.

"A dragon, Edward," she whispered. "Imagine. It must have lain like that for thousands of years in its tomb beneath the sands, untouched and still complete."

"Eighteen hundred years," the junior-under-curator said. "That is how long ago their civilization collapsed, and it is from then that the preserved dragons date."

"How did it die?" Putty asked. "I don't see any wounds."

"Sadly, we do not know. That resin that covers it is immensely tough. You could stab it with a knife and you wouldn't get through. Only with the sharpest of tools are we able to penetrate it, but when the resin is pierced, the body within begins to decay, and within mere weeks, it crumbles. Several of the beasts were opened when they were first discovered, but there are too few of the specimens to risk losing more. It is hoped that one day we will discover techniques that will allow us to open the resin without losing the beasts within. However, for the moment, the dragons are safe, and we expend our efforts on more profitable inquiries."

"Such as pottery, eh?" Freddie said. "Ha-ha."

"Quite! I see you are a true enthusiast, sir. I look forward to your next visit. We shall have a fine discussion! Perhaps I may expect you tomorrow?"

"Ah," Freddie said.

"Excellent. Then it is settled. I shall expect you before noon."

"It looks sad, don't you think?" Olivia said. She was standing beneath the dragon's head, peering up.

"Sad?" the junior-under-curator said. "It is a beast. Beasts do not experience emotions. They are more akin to mechanisms than to humans. Why, you might as well suggest a dog could feel happy or a duck feel afraid." He laughed. "No, do not assign human emotions to beasts. They have no intelligence or feelings. Any educated man will tell you as much."

Putty glared at him. I put a restraining hand on her shoulder, but I knew exactly what she was thinking. This man was supposed to be one of Mars's greatest experts? I hoped Professor Fournier was less of an idiot.

I took Putty's hand and led her around the dragon. Now that I knew it was covered in resin, it was easier to see through to the dragon's skin. It was covered in thousands of fine scales, arranged in multicolored swirls, like the patterns we'd seen carved into the Ancient Martian structures. It must have been amazing when it was flying. I bet its scales had glittered in sunlight.

We climbed beneath the dragon's belly, stepped over its tail, and trailed our fingers over the resin-covered claws. Even though the dragon had been dead for so many hundreds of years and all that held it intact was the tough resin, I couldn't help but feel afraid as we walked so close and dared lay our hands on it.

"And now," the junior-under-curator called, "I believe it is time for your appointment with Professor Fournier. If you will follow me?"

Reluctantly, we left the dragon and followed the junior-under-curator.

"If you don't mind," he said as he led us through the museum, "why did you wish to see the professor?"

Freddie smiled easily. "Oh, nothing of real significance. I merely wanted his advice on reading some ideograms. Simple to a man of his intellect, of course, but not to someone like me." He shrugged. "Have trouble reading English sometimes, let alone ideograms. Ha-ha."

"Like the other gentlemen, then," the junior-under-curator said. "Professor Fournier certainly is popular today."

"Other gentlemen?" I said. "What other gentlemen?"

"Professor Fournier's other visitors," the junior-under-curator said. "They, too, had ideograms they wanted interpreted. Quite an exciting day for the old fellow, really. Two sets of visitors. I had just finished showing them in when you arrived. An unusual pair. Not the type one would normally expect in the museum. Quite uncouth and rough looking, I thought."

I met Freddie's eyes.

"Stand aside," Freddie said, pushing past the junior-under-curator. The man let out a squawk of protest. Freddie ignored him and sprinted down the corridor. The rest of us followed.

Freddie stopped outside a polished wooden door that bore a brass plate with the professor's name. Gently, he eased the door open.

"Stay back!" he snapped.

But it was too late. I'd already seen what was within.

The professor lay sprawled on the floor, and he was clearly dead.

— 19 —

Prisoners

"What's happening?" Putty said from behind. "I can't see. Edward, get out of the way."

I held her back with one outstretched arm. "Don't look," I said, although I couldn't turn my own eyes away. The professor was lying on his back, and he'd been stabbed. His white shirt was dark with blood.

"Is he dead?" Putty said. "I've never seen a dead body before."

"And you're not going to start now," Olivia said, her voice sharp. "Come away. You too, Edward. Leave the poor man some dignity."

I tore my gaze away and helped Olivia pull Putty back into the corridor. She protested all the way. It was only when I was out of sight of the professor's body that I suddenly started shaking. My skin felt cold. How could they have done that to that poor old man? Surely the professor had never done harm to anyone.

The junior-under-curator came tottering up behind us. He shouldered his way into the room and stopped with a gasp.

"Professor?" He turned to Freddie. "What . . . ?"

"The professor has been murdered," Freddie said. "You showed some men in just before us. Who were they?"

"Murdered? Who would do that? Why? It is true that we did not all agree with his theories regarding the preservation of artifacts, but—"

"Describe the men, please," Freddie said.

"I . . ." The junior-under-curator backed out of the room. "There were two of them. One . . . One was a native Martian. They all look alike to me. The other was a short man. An ugly fellow, with a squashed face, like a frog. But he seemed to appreciate pottery. How could he murder someone?"

"Where did they go?"

The junior-under-curator gaped.

"You said you showed them in just before us. We didn't pass them. Which way would they have gone?"

The junior-under-curator rubbed at his forehead, as though trying to rub away a headache. "Down there . . . I . . . Why . . . ?"

Freddie turned to me. "They may still be here. Edward, get your sisters out—"

"No," I said. "I'm coming with you."

Freddie didn't argue. He took off at a sprint, and I followed. We raced down the corridors, past closed offices and cavernous storerooms. Surprised faces stared out at us, but we were gone before anyone could say anything. I tried to peer into the storerooms as we passed, but Freddie kept going, head down, pulling away from me with each stride.

We skidded around a corner, and there, ahead of us, a door hung open. Bright desert sunlight spilled through, outlining two familiar figures: Frog-face and the native Martian.

Freddie threw himself forward. The native Martian tried to slam the door, but Freddie barged into it, smacking it open. Frog-face lunged at him with a knife, and Freddie danced out of the way. I forced an extra burst of speed into my legs.

I stumbled into the burning sunlight just as the native Martian swung at Freddie with a heavy blackjack. I crashed into the native Martian, and we went down in a pile.

Freddie jabbed at Frog-face with his walking stick, fending off the knife and forcing the man back. The Martian came to his feet, lifting me off the ground. I clung on and sank my teeth into his arm. He gave a shout and dropped the blackjack. With a roar of anger, he thumped me into the wall. The impact knocked me to the ground. I tried to get up, but my legs wouldn't cooperate. The Martian drew a small dagger.

Freddie drove Frog-face back. A ringing blow sent the man's knife flying.

"Freddie!" I managed as the Martian raised his dagger.

Freddie crossed the gap between us with two quick steps. He whipped his walking stick across the Martian's head. The man slumped, his eyes rolling back.

Freddie spun just as Frog-face thrust. Freddie tried to dodge, but he didn't have time. The knife slid across his ribs. He grunted. His legs gave way and he fell to his knees.

Frog-face stood over him. The man's face was twisted with hatred. Freddie's blood dripped from his knife as he brought it forward.

Then a whistle sounded, and someone shouted, "Militia!"

Frog-face hesitated for a second. Then he turned on his heel and was gone.

◆

We didn't have time to run. By the time I'd helped Freddie back to his feet, the open area behind the museum was full of militiamen.

The three of us—me, Freddie, and the Martian—were marched through city streets. Freddie tried to talk to the militia leader, both in English and native Martian, but they shoved him back and didn't answer.

How had this happened? Surely Dr. Guzman had told them we had nothing to do with the professor's murder? I didn't understand why we were being arrested.

The militiamen took us to an underground cell in a squat,

fort-like building. The only light in the cell came from a small grille above us. The floor was covered in damp straw. A long stone block served as a bed. We were pushed in, along with the Martian, and the cell door closed behind us with a clang. They even took away Freddie's walking stick.

I slumped against the wall and rested my head in my hands. My sisters were out there on their own, unprotected. Sir Titus still had Mama, Papa, and Jane, and now he knew we were here. And Freddie and I were trapped, helpless, with one of Sir Titus's chief henchmen.

How could it all have gone so wrong?

❖

No one came to see us that evening, nor the next day. Somewhere out there, Sir Titus had his abacus and Papa was translating the map. Surely it couldn't take much longer. He might have done it already. I banged against the bars, but it was pointless. The militiamen ignored us.

Freddie's wound was still seeping blood. I'd have liked to clean it properly with wine or spirits and to stitch it. At least there was water in the cell. I washed the wound, then bandaged it with strips torn from Freddie's shirt.

A guard pushed food under the door once the next day, along with more water, then disappeared without speaking. The bread was stale, but I was starving. The hours seemed to drag on endlessly in the dark cell.

Near the evening of the second day, guards came down and led us up to an office. I was tired and grimy. Freddie stumbled as he climbed the stairs and had to lean on a guard's shoulder.

The militia captain was sitting behind his desk as we entered. There was an auto-scribe beside him, but its brass speaking tube was turned down, unused.

"So," the militia captain said. "A respected professor dead, murdered in his office. The museum staff say that you three and the man who fled were the professor's only visitors that day. Then my men catch you fighting in the street." He shook his head. "What do you have to say for yourselves?"

Freddie was bent over his wounded side, his face set in a grimace. A thin layer of sweat covered his face. His shirt was ragged where we'd torn it away for bandages. The bloodstains had turned brown.

"We . . ." I cleared my throat and tried again. "We were just visiting the museum. The professor was dead when we got there." I shot an accusing look at the native Martian.

The captain made a noncommittal sound, then turned to Sir Titus's man. "And you?"

"The professor was alive when my companion and I left," the native Martian said.

The militia captain tilted his head. "Why did your companion run when my men approached?"

"We were attacked by these two. I was knocked unconscious. I'm sure he went to find help."

"You attacked us!" I shot back.

"Enough!" The militia officer slapped his palm on the table. "I could lock the three of you up for a week for fighting in public." He sat back in his seat, sighing. "It appears there were no witnesses. The museum staff didn't see the professor between your visits, and no one was in that part of the building. I can't prove that your stories are lies, but I can't prove they're true, either. *Someone* killed that man."

"Will you release us?" Freddie managed. His voice was strained.

The militiaman shrugged. "Perhaps. But someone must vouch for you. A person of good character." He nodded to the native Martian. "Someone has come forward for you." The captain gestured to one of the guards. "Release this gentleman."

"Wait!" Freddie said. He took a step and stumbled. I caught his arm.

The militia captain turned to Freddie. "Yes?"

Freddie let out a breath. "Nothing. We'd like to see the British-Martian ambassador. He'll vouch for us."

"We'll send for him, but I'm sure he's a busy man. Is there anyone else who could vouch for you? Anyone at all?"

Olivia could, but Sir Titus's men might be watching the prison. She and Putty would be in danger. I shook my head.

"Then I have no choice but to return you to your cell."

The guards led us away again. The moment we were alone, Freddie slumped on the block of stone that passed for a bed. "Blast!" he said. "That's blown it. I was sure they'd release the three of us together. Now there's nothing to stop Sir Titus from finding that tomb and selling the secrets to Napoleon."

And doing away with my family, I thought. But all I said was, "You're not well."

"My injury feels hot," Freddie said. "I think I have a touch of fever. It'll pass."

"Will it?" I asked.

Freddie shrugged painfully. "There's nothing we can do about it here. At least our Martian friend will report back that I'm on my last legs. That'll give us an advantage."

"Not if you *are* on your last legs," I said.

Freddie flashed a grin. "I'm stronger than I look."

"Will the ambassador come?" I asked.

Freddie lay down carefully on the stone bed. "I don't know. Sir Titus has a long history in this city and many important friends. What if the ambassador is one of those?"

"You think he might hand us over to Sir Titus?"

"Nothing so rash," Freddie said. "Sir Titus is a fugitive, and the intelligence service is unforgiving. But he might easily pretend to never have received our message."

"Then what do we do?"

Freddie smiled. "I'm going to sleep. You should rest, too. Wake me if anything happens."

With that, his eyes drifted shut, and I was left there in the cell as the light outside faded.

I must have slept eventually, because the next thing I knew, the cell door banged open.

"Get up," one of the guards said in accented English. "The captain wants to see you."

Freddie seemed a little better when I helped him up, although he was still weak and leaned on my arm.

"The ambassador?" I asked Freddie in a whisper as they led us up the stairs.

"Perhaps. It's early, but if he's verified my identity with the intelligence service . . ."

"He must have."

The guard pushed open the door to the captain's office. I straightened, brushing down my filthy clothes. I knew that I looked awful. If I'd been the ambassador, I would have taken one look and sent us back to the cell.

I'd hardly taken a step inside when something hit me so hard I almost fell. Arms wrapped themselves tightly enough to choke me.

"Putty?" I managed, staring down at my sister.

Olivia was there, too, standing by the captain's desk, her cheeks pink and her fingers clutching nervously at her dress.

"These are your brothers?" the captain said, looking at Livvy.

Olivia nodded. "Oh, yes. We were so worried. My older brother, Viscount Winchester, and my younger brother, the

Honorable Edward Winchester." I tried not to choke. *Viscount Winchester?* Livvy had managed the lie without blinking. "We were in the museum with them. When we discovered the poor dead professor, they went looking for the culprits, and they did not return. We did not know what to do. Had Viscount Winchester been harmed, the scandal . . ." She shook her head. "It is unthinkable." She peered closely at Freddie. "What have you done to him?"

The captain cleared his throat. "We had no idea . . . If only you had said, sir . . ."

Olivia shook her head again. "I don't know what the ambassador will say when he finds out that Viscount Winchester has been abused in your cells. He gave the Prince Regent his *personal* assurances that Viscount Winchester would be safe, and what with Viscount Winchester being a confidant of the Prince Regent himself . . ." She turned sad eyes on the militia captain. "In these uncertain, war-filled times, I shudder to think. I once saw His Majesty's Royal Aeronautical Brigade bombard a city over a matter of honor. It was a frightening sight." She lowered her voice. "It is said the Prince Regent sees allies of the French everywhere."

The captain came out of his chair, his face reddening. "Your ladyship, I assure you—"

"I take it we're free to go?" Freddie interrupted, drawing himself up.

The captain stared, unmoving, for a second. Then he

pulled himself together. "Of course. I will send a detachment of my men to escort you—"

Freddie held up his hand. "That won't be necessary. Now, you have my walking stick, I believe?"

❖

I felt the captain's worried gaze follow us all the way across the prison yard.

The moment we were outside the walls, Olivia turned to Freddie. "You're hurt!"

"It was scarcely skin-deep," Freddie admitted through gritted teeth, "but the cell was full of foul humors. They've seeped in, and we weren't able to clean the wound properly. I'll be well now that we're out of there." He reached out and touched Olivia's arm briefly. "You were wonderful. We didn't think we'd ever be released."

Olivia blushed.

"I've never heard of His Majesty's Royal Aeronautical Brigade," Putty said.

"Neither, I suspect, has His Majesty," Freddie said. "Otherwise Britain might be better placed to see off Napoleon. Your sister made it up."

Olivia's blush deepened.

"You were wonderful," Freddie said again, "but Edward and I have failed you. Sir Titus's man was released before us. We lost him. We have no way to find your family."

Olivia tried to hold back a smile, but she couldn't. "Shall I tell them or will you?" she said to Putty.

"Tell us what?" I said.

"Livvy wanted to get you out straightaway," Putty said, "but I made her wait."

I stared at her. "Why on Mars would you make us wait around in that horrible cell?"

Putty grinned up at me. "Honestly, Edward. I don't know how you manage anything without me. We waited because we knew your Martian would be released sooner or later. When he was, we followed him." Her grin widened. "We have found Sir Titus's house."

20

Into the Desert

"Then we have him!" Freddie slapped his walking stick into the palm of his hand. "He's not going to escape this time."

"He already has," Olivia said. "We found his house, but we were too late."

Freddie stopped. "What do you mean?"

"They were loading his airship. We couldn't stop them. They're gone."

"They've found the dragon tomb," I said.

"Papa must have deciphered the code," Olivia said.

I shook my head numbly.

"He had no choice," Freddie said.

"I can't believe it," I said. My stomach felt hollow. "We were so close." I couldn't bear it. We'd failed. Now Sir Titus would have his new dragon tomb and the fortune that went with it, and my family . . . I'd never see them again. I looked at Olivia and Putty standing there on the narrow Lunae City street. Soon they would be the only family I had. I didn't know how they would survive the loss. I didn't know how I would.

"Still," Putty said brightly. "At least we know where they've gone."

There was a stunned silence. Then Freddie leaned in close. "I beg your pardon?"

"The Lan-Kaltar Valley," Putty said.

Freddie stared at her. "Don't tell me that you've deciphered that blasted map, too? Did you have your own water abacus secreted away all this time? Where have you been keeping it? In your pocket somewhere?" He was going rather red in the face.

"Don't be absurd," Putty said serenely. "It's what Sir Titus's men said."

"Sir . . . They said . . ." Freddie put a hand to his head. "I think I need to sit down. I'm feeling faint."

"Perhaps we should continue this conversation back in the hotel," Olivia said. "You look unwell, Freddie."

With a great effort, Freddie pulled himself upright. "You're right. Come on, then. I want to hear everything." He threw a glance at Putty. "Even if it finishes me off once and for all."

❖

Putty and Olivia had been hard at work while we were locked up. They'd obtained new clothes for me and Freddie, sturdy shoes for all of us, water bottles, a length of rope, a couple of lamps, and even a map.

Freddie blinked at them in astonishment. "How . . . ? You didn't have any money . . ."

"Olivia is very persuasive," Putty said. "You should watch out, Cousin Freddie. When she fixes her mind on something, she's very hard to stop. And you owe money to half the merchants in the city."

"We thought we should be equipped," Olivia said.

"I'm starting to think we should have stayed in our cell," Freddie said to me. "Your sisters appear to have managed rather well without us."

He sank into a low native Martian chair and let out a sigh as he relaxed carefully back. His face was pale beneath the dirt.

"Get him some water," Olivia told Putty. While Putty was fetching it, Olivia peeled away Freddie's jacket and waistcoat. Her face reddened as she removed his shirt, and she kept her eyes firmly fixed on her work. Even though she wetted the bandages, Freddie still grunted as she pulled them free, and thick, tainted blood welled up.

Through gritted teeth, Freddie said, "Tell us what you've been up to."

"It was Parthenia's idea, of course," Olivia said.

"Of course," Freddie murmured.

"We only meant to follow the Martian when he was released. We were going to hurry back and have you released, too. We knew he wouldn't take many precautions, with you and Edward locked up. He'd never suspect two young ladies would follow him."

"The poor, innocent fool."

"I think Cousin Frederick is feverish," Putty said. "He keeps interrupting in a most odd manner."

"No, no. Forgive me," Freddie said. "Please go on. I shall say no more."

"In any case," Olivia continued, sluicing water over the wound, "when we reached Sir Titus's house, we knew we were too late. The airship was almost loaded, and the grounds were full of Sir Titus's men. There was no way we could get back to you, have you released, and return to the estate in time. If we lost Sir Titus, we might never find him again."

Putty bounced out of her chair. "So I rubbed some dirt into my clothes and face—"

"Why does that not surprise me?" Freddie muttered.

"I beg your pardon?" Putty said.

"Nothing! Nothing!"

Putty smiled triumphantly. "Then I shimmied over the wall and mingled with Sir Titus's men."

"That's insane!" I exploded. "Livvy, why did you let her? She could have been recognized. She could have been captured!"

"It's not me who gets captured!" Putty said. "Anyway,

they were hardly going to suspect I would be there, were they? I listened to what Sir Titus's men were saying. I think I might become a burglar. I could have walked off with a fortune."

"And you heard them say 'the Lan-Kaltar Valley'?" Freddie said. "You're sure."

"Of course!" Putty said. "And they were loading some interesting-looking machinery."

I groaned.

"I didn't go and investigate!" Putty protested. "Not much. Anyway, Sir Titus was supervising the loading himself, so I thought I'd better stay away. Even though I was tempted to give him a good kick in the shins."

"The Lan-Kaltar Valley is about fifteen miles northwest of here," Freddie said. "In the desert. I wouldn't have guessed it was the place from the map. There must have been landslides since Sir Titus's map was first drawn."

"Don't worry, Cousin Freddie," Putty said. "We're completely prepared." She pulled a small rock axe from the pile of equipment she and Olivia had gathered. "We're ready to uncover your tomb." She swung the axe. "Or hit Sir Titus."

"I do wish you wouldn't call it my tomb," Freddie said. "It makes me nervous."

"Fifteen miles is a long way in the desert." I looked at Freddie, slumped there in the chair. "I don't know if we'll make it."

"We'll walk at night," Freddie said. "And we won't need to walk the whole way. We can make half the distance on the Martian Nile."

"If we had a boat," I said. "We don't have the funds to hire one."

"Captain Sadalius Kol will help us," Putty said. "He said that if I ever needed anything, I should just ask. He said he would make me a sailor."

Olivia shuddered. "Please don't let Mama hear you say that."

"I expect he was just being polite," I said.

"No," Freddie said. "Parthenia is right. We've traveled with Captain Kol and his men. We've eaten and drunk with them. By native Martian custom, we're part of their family. They'll help us. I'll go to the docks and talk with them."

"You'll do no such thing!" Olivia snapped. "You can hardly walk. Edward will go to the docks. Your wound is infected and you need to rest. Edward, ask the concierge to send up some strong wine for the wound." She fixed Freddie with a stern glare. "This is going to hurt."

"Oh," Freddie said faintly. "Good."

"I'll go with Edward," Putty said, attaching herself to my arm. "He'll need me to translate. I'm sure Cousin Freddie will hurt himself again some other time. I can watch then." She smiled up at me. "Shouldn't you be getting changed, Edward? You smell like a dead fish."

Captain Kol's boat dropped us on the shore of the Martian Nile at midnight. The moons were high and the sky clear. The rocky mesa was a dark shadow against the dark sky.

For the first hour, we followed well-worn paths through the fields and floodplains of the Martian Nile. But soon we had left them behind and entered a narrow valley that cut into the mesa. It was difficult to walk here. Stones and rocks had slipped from the cliffs and lay jumbled across the valley floor. In the darkness, I couldn't make out where I was putting my feet, and I had to feel out each step. We seemed to be moving at a crawl.

I was worried about Freddie. He'd slept most of the afternoon and evening, and he looked better than he had, but he was still pale, and I could tell his wound hurt.

"Do you know how many types of poisonous snakes there are in the desert?" Putty's voice drifted from behind as we trudged along the valley.

"No," Olivia said. "And we don't want to."

"Seventeen. Can you believe it? Seventeen!"

"Well, now we know," Freddie muttered.

"And then there are scuttlebugs, which are even more poisonous," Putty said, "and swarm moths, and—"

"We don't want to know, Putty," I said.

"I'm just trying to be helpful," Putty said. "Some of them are so poisonous that you'd be dead before you could fall over."

I closed my eyes for a second.

"We'll have to hope we don't meet any of them," Freddie said. "Now we should keep quiet. Sound carries a long way in the desert at night, and we don't want any sentries to hear us."

"Maybe they'll be eaten by scuttle moths," Olivia muttered.

"Swarm moths," Putty corrected her. "They're about the size of your fist and they—"

"Hush!" Freddie said.

❖

The first light of dawn caught me by surprise. I'd dropped into a hypnotic routine: put a foot forward, test the ground, step, repeat, over and over again. My body was numb with exhaustion, and my newly healed blisters had burst again. It was only when I noticed I could actually see where I was putting my feet that I realized dawn was arriving. Great red cliffs rose on either side of the valley, still deep in shadow. Ahead, our valley seemed to spread and open, and beyond, another high cliff rose dark and sheer.

I stopped, resting my foot on a large rock. There was more sand in the valley now, spreading like water around the stones. Freddie had fallen behind during the night. Now he came up beside me.

"It's almost light," I said. The sky was turning clear above us, the night retreating like an ink spill washed from cloth.

Freddie nodded. "We're nearly there. That must be the Lan-Kaltar Valley up ahead."

I saw a faint stain of blood on his waistcoat. His wound had reopened during the night. He twitched his jacket across, hiding it.

Putty and Olivia joined us. Olivia looked so exhausted she could scarcely hold herself upright, but her face was determined. Putty looked as fresh as though she'd just awoken.

"Look," she said, pointing. A faint trail of smoke was rising over the western cliff.

"Machinery," Freddie said. "A steam engine of some sort."

"It's Sir Titus, isn't it?" Putty said. "We've found him."

Freddie led us along a narrow path that ran up the side of the valley, among boulders and cracked rocks. I stayed close behind, ready to grab him if he stumbled. Now that we were close, I felt tense. I clenched and unclenched my fists. We'd come so far to rescue my family. We'd almost died. We couldn't be too late. We just couldn't.

"There," Freddie whispered. He sank down behind a boulder.

Sir Titus had set up camp two hundred yards down the valley. His airship was tethered on the ground close to a dozen large tents. Its shadow stretched across the sandy valley floor. Two great metal contraptions, puffing steam and smoke, dug into the side of the valley. Iron blades spun, flinging sand and small rocks behind them. This whole area had been torn and ravaged.

Dozens of men stood nearby, watching. When the tomb was uncovered, the machines would stop and the men would move in, and it would be over.

Freddie eased himself up, grimacing at the pain in his side. "We need to know where they're holding your family. I'm going to scout."

"Wait here," I whispered to my sisters. I took Freddie's arm and led him off several steps. "Freddie, you can't do this. You're too weak."

"Someone has to," Freddie said. "We can't walk into this blind."

"Then let me."

"Edward. You're brave, but this is what I've been trained to do. You have to look after your sisters. Now let me go."

Reluctantly, I released him and watched him hike painfully away into the rocks. I didn't know if he could make it, but what else could I do? I couldn't be everywhere.

The low sun was rising through the thin early-morning mist. Already the air was growing hot. Up here, with only the rocks for shelter, it would quickly grow unbearable. The sky above us was as blue as the Valles Marineris in high summer. I stared up at it, waiting.

Freddie had been gone for about half an hour when Putty, who had been peering around our boulder, stiffened.

"Look!" she whispered.

Moving carefully so as not to draw attention, I came up next to her.

"There." She pointed.

Two figures had emerged from one of the tents and were now heading toward the airship. One of them was a guard. The other was Jane.

— 21 —

Swords on the Sand

"Come on!" I said. "We have to save them." Sir Titus must be holding them in the airship.

"What about Freddie?" Olivia said.

"We can't wait," I said. I hadn't seen Freddie since he'd gone. He might have collapsed out there, but I couldn't go looking for him now. We might not get another chance. "If he's watching, he'll come. We can circle around through the rocks, then come up behind the airship."

The slope below us was rough with tumbled boulders and fractured rock. We angled down, keeping a low, broken ridge between Sir Titus's camp and us. The clank and roar of the digging machines covered the sounds of our progress. Halfway down, the ridge ended. Putty and Olivia scrambled up behind me. Olivia's walking dress was ripped on one side and covered in dust. She'd shed her spencer jacket as the day's heat had risen. Her face was red from the exertion, and her hair had come loose again.

She gave me a tight smile. "Where now?"

Just below us, the slope disintegrated into a chaotic jumble of rocks and boulders the size of houses, which threw deep, long shadows in the early morning sunlight.

I pointed to a gap between two of the larger boulders. "This way."

I waited until the men in the valley moved out of sight, then led my sisters into the rocks. We emerged five minutes later with the bulk of the airship between Sir Titus's camp and us. The passenger gondola rested on the sands, but I saw figures moving beyond it. I wiped the fine line of sweat from my forehead. If they would just move out of sight . . .

The smell of hot oil and coal smoke drifted from the steam engines, turning the clean desert air bitter and sharp.

There! The men near the tents were heading for the excavating machines.

I lifted a hand to alert Putty and Olivia. A few more paces and the men would be gone.

"Four, three, two . . ." I whispered.

"One," a voice said behind me.

❖

Sir Titus's guards were standing a few feet away. They'd crept up behind us, hidden by the noise of the excavation. Two grabbed Putty and Olivia. Putty tensed.

"No," I said, before she could try anything. I raised my hands.

"Sensible boy," a guard said. "Sir Titus said you'd be arriving. We expected you earlier. We were starting to worry something had happened to you. Take them to the cells."

The guards led us across the sands and up into the airship. The interior was dark after the bright sunlight. A corridor cut through the middle of the airship. Our guards pushed us along until we reached a sturdy door with another guard standing outside. He jerked open the door and we were shoved in. Inside the cell, only a tiny, narrow window let in light.

"Edward?" someone said as the door was locked behind us. "Parthenia? Olivia?" It was Jane's voice. "What are you doing here?"

As my eyes adjusted to the dark, I saw Mama and Papa sitting on a bench.

"We're rescuing you!" Putty said. She ran to Papa and threw her arms around him.

"Why on Mars would you need to rescue us, child?" Mama demanded.

"Because Sir Titus is going to kill you!" Putty said.

"Why would he do such a thing?" Mama said. "He has simply been driven mad by jealousy!"

"You know that's not true, Mama," Jane said wearily. Somehow, Jane looked older than she had just two weeks ago. Sir Titus's prison had changed her.

"Why do you say that, child? Do you think your mama no longer capable of driving men mad with jealousy? I was the Crystal Rose of Tharsis. Every man admired me! Sir Titus himself intended to ask for my hand in marriage. When his father sent him away on business, it broke his heart!"

"I am sure that's all true, Mama," Jane said with a sigh. "But you know as well as I do that Sir Titus's only interest is in finding his dragon tomb."

I groaned and rested my head in my hands.

"Do we have to rescue them?" Putty whispered.

I turned to Papa. "I take it Sir Titus forced you to build him a new abacus?"

Papa nodded. "He threatened your sister and mother. I looked that man in his eyes, Edward, and I took him at his word. I did not like his eyes."

"You were right," I said. Sir Titus would have killed both Mama and Jane if he'd thought it would get him what he wanted.

"I did tell him it wouldn't work," Papa added.

I blinked. "What do you mean, 'it wouldn't work'? You're here, aren't you?"

Papa peered at me over the top of his eyeglasses. "The water abacus is a fabulous calculating machine, Edward, and I made some quite sensational improvements in the model I made for Sir Titus. You might easily use it to break any code. But the ideograms are not a code. They are not mathematical puzzles. They are a language. You could run a million combinations through the abacus, and you would still never understand the text. You must know how to combine the ideas within each ideogram to reach meaning. Without knowing the key, you have no hope. Not with a thousand water abacuses. You might as well write sums in the sand."

"But if the water abacus couldn't decode the map . . ."

I sat with a thump on the wooden floor as the realization hit me. Sir Titus had threatened Mama and Jane, so Papa had lied. He'd chosen somewhere at random and claimed it was the location. This was the wrong valley. When Sir Titus found out, his rage would be murderous.

"You made it up," I said. "You bought time, hoping for rescue."

Except the rescue had failed. *I* had failed. Soon, Sir Titus's machines would finish excavating. He would know there was no dragon tomb. He would come and he would kill someone, as a lesson, to prove to Papa that he meant business.

Papa stared at me. "Made it up? Of course not! I deciphered the map."

"But . . ." I spluttered. "You said . . ."

"The water abacus could not decode it," Papa said. "Of course not. I decoded it myself."

"That's impossible," I said wearily. "Sir Titus has been trying for years. Cousin Freddie has been trying for over a month."

"Actually," Papa said, looking a little smug, "it was quite easy"—his voice dropped—"when you realize that the key was not missing at all."

"I don't understand," I said. I'd seen the ideograms on Freddie's map. Putty and Freddie had explained them to me. There had been no key.

"The absence of the key is the key itself!" Papa said. "There is no 'key' symbol because the key is void."

Putty let out a little squeak of excitement that made everyone jump. "Then—"

Papa nodded, although I still had no idea what he was talking about. "The ideograms relate through void."

I frowned. "You mean the ideograms don't relate to each other at all?"

"No, no, no," Papa said. "Think of the void. The space between the worlds. That is the key. At first, I thought it meant there was no distance between the ideograms, nothing to modify the ideas, just as the void itself is empty, so the ideograms should be read individually. But that was too simple."

Simple? I had no idea what he was talking about.

"Then I remembered the dragon paths," Papa continued, excited. "The dragon paths join Mars to Earth, but not in a straightforward way. Mars and Earth are uncounted leagues apart. When ships sail dragon paths through the void, they should take years to arrive. Tens of years. But they don't. They only take weeks. Somehow, the dragon paths compress the void between the worlds. That was the key! It was not that the ideograms had no distance between them. They had less than that. They overlapped. Once I realized that, it was easy."

"Easy," I repeated.

"Yes! All I needed to do was work out how the idea within each ideogram overlapped with its neighbor, and the meaning became clear. But . . ." Papa's brow wrinkled. "The key of void has never been used before. I had never even heard of it. It can only mean one thing. This is a dragon tomb like no other."

He had scarcely spoken the words before the low, constant rumble of the excavating machines cut off. In the silence, a loud cheer sounded.

"They've found it," Putty said. "They've found the dragon tomb."

❖

Sir Titus came for us an hour later.

We'd sat in silence, listening to the shouts of Sir Titus's men and the sound of pickaxes and shovels on stone. I'd wondered how he would do it. Would he shoot us or leave us out on the desert sands with no water and no shade? I couldn't let him. If I jumped him, maybe someone would get away.

Footsteps approached in the corridor outside. I scrambled to my feet. There was nothing I could use as a weapon.

The door slammed open, and I leaped forward. Too late. Sir Titus had already taken a step back and drawn a long sword from his belt. I skidded to a halt.

"Take them," he said. Half a dozen of his men pushed in and seized us. I struggled, but it was no good. They tied our hands behind us.

"What are you doing?" Papa demanded. He was much shorter than Sir Titus. His glasses had been knocked half off and he was unarmed, but he stood glaring at Sir Titus. "You have your dragon tomb. No one will stop you. Let us go."

"Let you go?" Sir Titus raised an eyebrow. "But I had so hoped to hold a family reunion first. Bring them!"

"I do not understand what has happened to you, Sir Titus," Mama said. "You loved me once. I know you did. Why are you doing this?"

A tight laugh escaped Sir Titus's throat. "Loved you? The only thing any of your suitors cared for was your father's fortune. Did you think we enjoyed taking part in your ridiculous salons?" He shook his head. "Didn't you wonder why so many of your suitors suddenly found urgent business elsewhere when your father lost his money?"

Papa lifted his chin. "I, sir, never cared for her lack of fortune. I cared only for the brilliant woman I saw before me."

Mama turned toward Papa, her eyes suddenly wide.

Sir Titus sneered down at Papa. "You? You are only a tradesman."

"And he is a better man than you ever were," Mama said defiantly.

Sir Titus gestured to his men. They dragged us out onto the burning sands. The excavating machines lay nearly silent, emitting only trickles of steam from their stoked boilers. The sharp metal blades gleamed, polished by cutting through the sand and rock. The machines were at least four times the length of a carriage and humped like a sand dune. Dozens of long brass pipes ran up their sides.

Smaller than a dragon, I thought.

A dark hole lay exposed in the side of the valley, not far from the excavators. As we were dragged out, Sir Titus's men came over to stand in an arc behind him.

He lined us up, then drew his sword again. He strode over to Jane and lifted his sword to her throat. She looked pale, but she stared bravely ahead. Was this it? Was this how he was going to do it? I tensed. I didn't think I could reach Jane, but I had to try.

Sir Titus turned and surveyed the tumbled rocks around the valley.

"Frederick Winchester!" he called. "I know you're out there. Show yourself!"

His voice echoed around the valley. There was no answer.

"Show yourself, Mr. Winchester, or I will kill them, one at a time, in front of you."

Papa threw himself forward. The man holding him jerked him back. Mama shrieked. There was still no reply

from the rocks. Where was Freddie? Had his wound over-
come him?

"Are you a coward? Very well." Sir Titus pressed his sword
against Jane's neck

"I am here."

Freddie emerged from the rocks and strode across the
sand, his walking stick swinging from his hand. "Sir Titus
Dane. You are a thief, a traitor, and a murderer. Surrender
yourself."

Sir Titus's men drew weapons and started toward him.

Sir Titus laughed. "Leave him to me. I've waited a long
time for this."

He stepped forward, sword held loosely in his grip. I
suddenly realized just how *big* Sir Titus Dane was. He was
taller than Freddie. His arms were longer and his shoulders
wider.

"Surrender myself to you, Mr. Winchester? Why, you are
not even armed."

With a single motion, Freddie twisted the top of his walking stick. The stick fell away, revealing a slim, gleaming sword.

"Surrender yourself," Freddie said again. "You may receive
mercy."

They circled each other, swords held ready. The low desert sun flashed on the blades.

"You thought yourself so clever," Sir Titus sneered.
"Sneaking around Oxford, pretending to be a student. I had
my suspicions right from the start. I thought you too stupid,

even for a student, but it looks like I was wrong. You really are that stupid. Now I have these people you pretend are your family, and I have you, and I have my dragon tomb."

Freddie only smiled. The smile seemed to drive Sir Titus into a rage. He swung his sword with a great overhand cut for Freddie's head. Freddie slipped to the side, catching Sir Titus's sword on his own and spinning past. Quicker than I could have imagined, Sir Titus regained his balance and turned to face Freddie again. Freddie's hand dropped to the wound on his side before he caught the motion and straightened. But Sir Titus had seen it. He smiled.

"A little kiss from one of my men. Let me give you another."

Something bumped my hands where they were tied behind my back. Putty had edged her way across while her captor was distracted by the fight. She glanced pointedly down. I understood. Very slowly, I bent my knees until my tied hands were level with hers.

Sir Titus lunged, forcing Freddie to twist across his wounded ribs. Sir Titus followed with a fist. The blow caught Freddie on the side of the face. He stumbled back, and Olivia gasped.

Putty's fingers started to pluck at my knots. They were tight, and Putty had to move slowly so as not to draw attention, but she had clever fingers, and I felt the knots begin to loosen.

Freddie turned his stumble into a fall, rolling back over

his shoulder and to his feet. He backed away warily, his sword held before him. Sir Titus followed. Around me, his men rushed forward, following the duel. Freddie's eyes met mine for a second.

"Do you think you can run away?" Sir Titus taunted. "Coward!"

No, you idiot. He's drawing you away. He was relying on me and Putty to free ourselves.

Sir Titus attacked, hammering blows on Freddie from left and right. Freddie defended desperately, staggering back beneath the heavy impacts. His sword seemed too thin to withstand the assault.

A knot loosened, and Putty dug in faster, tugging it apart.

Sweat dripped down Freddie's forehead, matting his hair to his skin. His face creased with pain, and he hunched over his wounded side. I heard his harsh breath over the cheers of Sir Titus's men.

The ropes binding my hands fell away. I found Putty's ropes, still keeping my hands behind my back in case anyone glanced over. It should have been easier. My hands were untied and free. But my fingers kept fumbling.

Freddie slipped on the loose sand. His leg gave way beneath him. Sir Titus's sword slashed in. Freddie threw himself to one side, but too slowly. The tip of Sir Titus's sword cut a thin line across his shoulder.

Freddie kicked out, catching Sir Titus behind the knee.

Sir Titus lurched forward. Then both men were on their feet again, circling each other.

My fingernail caught under one of Putty's knots. I shoved it in further and pulled.

Now Sir Titus's men had begun to chant, shouting his name and calling encouragement in several languages. The chant seemed to lend Sir Titus new energy. He renewed his attack, trying to batter Freddie's defenses down with brute force. And it seemed to be working. Each time, Freddie seemed to find it harder to raise his sword. Both his wounds were bleeding. He looked ready to fall.

"All this way," Sir Titus called, between blows. "All that desperate, pathetic struggle. It comes to this. Cut down on the sands." He laughed and sent a vicious cut at Freddie's head, which Freddie barely parried.

At last. The knot moved. I pulled it loose. A moment later, Putty's hands were free.

"Help Livvy," I whispered, my voice covered by the rising noise of Sir Titus's men.

Now what? If we tried to run, we'd be seen. I hoped Freddie had a plan.

Freddie didn't look like he had a plan. He looked like he was struggling to stay alive as Sir Titus pressed the attack, ever more viciously.

Freddie was a good actor. He'd fooled us into thinking he was a complete idiot. But he wasn't acting that wound to his shoulder, nor the one to his side.

This was going to be down to me, again.

No, not just me. Putty and Olivia, too. Without them, I'd never have made it this far.

Sir Titus swung wildly at Freddie, a sweeping cut that could have sliced Freddie's head from his shoulders. Freddie ducked beneath the stroke and slammed his elbow into Sir Titus's back. Freddie met my eyes, and I nodded minutely, once.

Sir Titus swung around, his sword coming up, and this time Freddie didn't retreat. He surged forward to meet the attack. Metal screeched on metal. For a moment, they were standing face to snarling face, blades locked. Then Sir Titus slammed his head down to head-butt Freddie.

Freddie was quicker. He tucked his chin to his chest, and Sir Titus's nose caught on Freddie's skull. With a roar of pain, Sir Titus staggered back, his hand coming up to his bloody nose, his eyes streaming tears. Blinking, he swung his sword wildly before him.

Freddie stepped in. His narrow blade whipped out, slicing into Sir Titus's arm. The sword sprang from Sir Titus's grip. Freddie rested the point of his sword against Sir Titus's throat.

Around us, the cheering stopped. All I could hear was the gasping breath of the fighters and the low grumble of the stilled excavating machines.

All eyes were fixed on the two men.

"Surrender," Freddie said again. "It's over. You'll never sell these secrets to Napoleon."

Sir Titus glared down at Freddie. "Over? It isn't over. My men have your cousins. They have your aunt and uncle. You will be the one who surrenders, or I will have them killed, one by one." He spat blood onto the sand.

I glanced over at my sisters. Both Putty and Olivia had their hands free.

"Now!" I shouted, and launched myself at the guard in front of me.

I hit him full in the back with my shoulder. Even though he was taller than me, the impact knocked him to the ground. I grabbed his knife and threw myself toward where Mama, Papa, and Jane were being held. The man holding Papa was nearest. He looked around, startled. I collided with him, and we fell to the sand.

Chaos. We needed chaos. We couldn't outfight all these men. I couldn't even beat the man I was struggling with. All we needed was enough confusion for Freddie to use Sir Titus as a hostage to get us away. If we got to the airship, we could escape.

A knife pushed into the back of my neck. I twisted, flailing out. My arm cracked against the hilt, knocking it aside. I kicked free.

There was dust in my eyes. My legs tangled with the man I'd been fighting.

"Enough!" The voice spoke English with a harsh accent.

One of the guards had grabbed Mama by the hair and jerked her head back. His knife lay against her throat, pressing hard enough to leave a white line. She was weeping silently, her lips tight together. Papa had reached Jane and was struggling with her guard, but with his hands tied, he had no hope. I didn't dare move for fear of what might happen to Mama. I couldn't see Putty or Olivia.

Out on the sand, Freddie still held his sword to Sir Titus.

We were stuck. Stalemated.

All around us, men stood, weapons drawn, unsure what to do.

— 22 —

Retreat

The sun beat down on us. Heat radiated from the red sands. No one moved.

Then someone shouted, "Fire!"

Flames darted up the side of one of the tents, catching fast on the canvas and snapping into the air. A moment later, another erupted.

One of the excavators roared into life behind us. Steam shrieked into the air, and the enormous, sharp blades began to spin. I glimpsed Putty's face in the cab. Men scattered, dodging away. The man holding Mama hesitated, his knife still pressed against her throat. Then, as the machine ground its way toward him, he shoved her away and ran. Mama fell, unable to keep her balance with her arms tied, right in front of the excavator.

Putty tried to turn the machine, but it was too close and too unwieldy.

I shoved myself away from the guards and raced toward Mama. Sand, dust, and grit spun through the air, smacking into my bare skin like tiny needles. The machine's roar blotted out everything else. I saw Mama's mouth open in a scream, but I couldn't hear her voice.

I hit the sand, rolled, and came up against her. The machine loomed over us, shadowing the sun. Sharp metal blades plunged down.

I wrapped my arms around Mama and threw myself to one side. We tumbled over the shaking sand. A blade cut the ground not a foot from my head.

I rolled again. Mama's head cracked into my cheek. The sand gave way beneath us, undermined by the excavator. We slid back. I couldn't stop us. There was nothing I could grab.

With a scream, the steam vented from the machine's boiler and the blades stopped turning. I blinked dust from my eyes. Above me, close enough that I could reach up and touch the scarred, hard metal, a blade was poised to cut down.

Sir Titus took advantage of the distraction. His uninjured arm came up, knocking Freddie's sword aside. Before Freddie could react, Sir Titus turned and raced toward his men.

Something swished through the air. I ducked as a cloud of

buzzdarts rushed through the air above me like a squadron of giant, deadly mosquitoes. They rattled off the excavator like metal hail. One of Sir Titus's men prepared to toss another canister of buzzdarts at us.

I struggled to my feet and hauled Mama up after me. Her eyes were wide with shock, her face pale. Jane and Papa hurried toward us, supporting each other as best they could. I snatched up the knife I'd dropped.

All the tents were on fire now, flames jumping between them and racing over the canvas. A couple of men were scooping up sand and tossing it onto the tents, but it did no good.

Olivia burst from the midst of the burning tents. One of Sir Titus's men came chasing after her, gaining on her with each stride. Freddie sprinted toward her. Buzzdarts surged at him, but he rolled under them, came to his feet, and kept running. He reached Olivia just as her pursuer caught her. His punch sent the man flying back.

"This way," I called to Jane and Papa, beckoning them into the shelter of the giant excavator. Quickly, I cut the ropes binding their hands.

"Where now?" Papa panted. His face was flushed, but his mouth was set in a furious line.

"Retreat," I said. "Help Mama."

Mama was close to swooning. Only sheer terror was keeping her upright. I passed her to Papa and Jane, then set myself between them and Sir Titus's men.

Freddie and Olivia ran toward us. A couple of Sir Titus's

men turned to cut them off, but most kept their line, advancing like a ragtag army. Sir Titus urged them on from behind.

We retreated, pressing ourselves against the excavator. The stink of heated metal and oil was almost overwhelming. When Sir Titus's men reached the excavator, our cover would be gone, and we would have nowhere to retreat but the open sand and rock. Nowhere except . . .

The dragon tomb. It was behind us, a dark opening beneath the sand, leading down into the unknown. But it would be a dead end.

A dead end or dead on the sand. Not much of a choice.

The two men reached Freddie and Olivia. The first swung at Freddie. He ducked under the blow and kicked the man's legs away. The second threw himself bodily at Olivia. They went down in a tangle. Freddie brought the handle of his sword down on the man's head. The man slumped, and Olivia shoved him away.

I waved to attract Freddie's attention, then indicated the opening to the dragon tomb.

A door banged open above me. Putty let herself out of the cab of the excavator and lowered herself hand over hand down the rungs on the side of the machine. She dropped to the sand. I hurried to help her up. She was grinning wildly.

"That was so much fun! Except it's very clumsy. Really, they could have a far better gear system. The controls are quite unresponsive."

Papa frowned. "I wonder if we could use some kind of logarithmic feedback on the levers . . ."

"Later!" I shouted. "Putty. Take them to the tomb. Hurry."

One of Sir Titus's men wound a clockwork Martian starblade and sent it whirring toward us. It ricocheted off the excavator. Putty herded our family to the dragon tomb. I backed away, step by step, until the first of Sir Titus's men reached the excavator, then I spun and sprinted for the tomb. Footsteps pounded after me.

The sand was soft beneath my feet. Every stride took twice the normal effort. I barely seemed to be moving. Sweat stung my eyes.

Another starblade whirred past. It twitched the edge of Freddie's coat as he helped Olivia into the opening. He scarcely flinched.

A hand grabbed my shirt. I wrenched free, but my pursuer stumbled into me, knocking me down. I gasped, and sand filled my mouth as I was driven into the ground.

I spat and rolled onto my back, shaking sand from my eyes. There were legs all around me, hands reaching down. I threw myself aside, colliding with legs. Men cursed. One of them aimed a kick at me. I grabbed his foot and wrenched. He tumbled back, bringing another man down with him, but I was surrounded. Weapons lowered, knife blades sharp in the sunlight.

Then Freddie was there, knocking one man down with

his fist and parrying a knife thrust with the sword. I scrambled up, shouldering another man aside. Someone grabbed my arm, and Freddie thrust with his sword. The man let go and jumped back.

"Get them!" Sir Titus screamed, his voice hoarse.

We ran. Freddie reached the dragon tomb a step before me. He dived in and I leaped after him. I hit the floor with a jolt that knocked the air from my lungs. I could scarcely see in the dark. My parents and sisters were pale silhouettes in the black. I could just make out a tunnel, not much more than head high. Putty grabbed my arm and hauled me in.

Someone leaped in behind us. A knife glittered. Then a rock came whistling out of the darkness and caught the man full on the chin. Olivia crouched down and scooped up another rock.

"Back this way," Putty said, pulling on my arm.

We retreated, eyes on the ragged square of sunlight. Heads appeared for a moment, then quickly withdrew, but no one else followed us in.

The tunnel ended in a smooth set of stairs. Papa led us down into the dark. I held my breath. I had no idea what was down here. The tombs in *Thrilling Martian Tales* always had traps.

We'd only descended four steps when light blossomed around us, growing like sunrise in the desert and racing away from us into the chamber beyond. I forced myself not to flinch.

At first we could see only shapes and the vast depth of the chamber. Then, as the light grew stronger, something emerged from the dark. First I saw its eyes, then the head and the great jaws and the long, sinuous neck. A dragon crouched in the center of the chamber, its eyes fixed upon us. Jane shrieked.

"It's dead," I said. "It's preserved like the one in the museum." Its strange, resinous coating glinted.

The light continued to grow, faster now. It spread across the walls and ceiling, tracing a luminous pattern like a million bright veins. Above the dragon, a cluster of globes awoke, as bright as the sun outside. Squinting, I saw dozens of strange machines around the walls of the chamber. Lying between the dragon's feet was a sarcophagus, holding the body of whichever emperor was buried here.

"Oh," Putty exclaimed softly. "Look, Papa. They have photon emission globes that still work after all this time. How can that be?"

Papa frowned. "There must be some means of adjusting the reflectivity of the internal surfaces, in response to some impulse. As we entered the room . . . But that would mean the reflectivity must have been absolutely perfect for all these centuries."

"And the veins of light on the walls . . ."

"Remarkable," Papa said. "Tiny mirrors, perhaps, like threads. I must see them closer."

"No," Freddie said, pushing in front of them. He was

holding a cluster of starblades. He must have grabbed them from Sir Titus's men. "Get to the back of the chamber. I'll cover the entrance." Statues of dragons and men lined the stairs. Freddie positioned himself behind one.

"For how long?" I asked.

Freddie met my eyes. "For as long as I can."

He wouldn't be able to stop them forever. Unless we found another way out or some way of defending ourselves, it would be over. I hurried my family across the chamber, around the body of the dragon. Beneath the cloudy resin, the dragon's bright scales still glittered in the chamber's light. Around us, ancient mechanisms lay dormant. Maybe one of them was a weapon. I squinted at them, but I had no idea what they were.

"Come out of there!" Sir Titus's voice echoed from the entrance. "Come out and you'll be spared. If I have to send my men in, there will be no mercy for any of you."

"That horrible man!" Mama said. "To think that any of you could ever have believed that I had feelings for him. I always said he was no good, even when we were children!"

"Then send in your men," Freddie shouted. "But the first three men through that doorway will die. Which three will it be, Sir Titus? Perhaps you should ask for volunteers." He repeated the same in native Martian, loud enough to be heard by everyone outside.

"Perhaps you should lead your men yourself?" Freddie

shouted. "You've waited ten years for your dragon tomb. Come and get it! Or are you scared to face me again?"

For a moment, there was silence. Then Sir Titus snarled back, "I fear nothing, Mr. Winchester, least of all you. Prepare yourself!"

Something roared outside. It sounded like a great monster clawing at rock. I wondered for a second if the dragon had come to life. Then I realized: It was one of the excavators.

The light globes above us shook. The ground trembled. Freddie took a step back, then another. Stone shattered and metal screeched. Great pistons thumped. With a crunch, rock gave way. The tunnel collapsed, puffing a cloud of dust and sand into the chamber. The excavator ground its way inward. One of the statues on the stairs toppled. Then the excavator emerged. Great blades hammered down, smashing rocks aside and hurling the broken fragments behind it.

Stone ruptured under the machine. A thunderous crack shook the chamber. Shards of rock exploded. Freddie ducked, but too late. A piece of rock caught him on the side of the head. He fell, his body slumping onto the foot of the stairs.

The excavator shouldered its way into the chamber. Its nose hovered for a moment above the stairs, then its tracks found purchase and it lurched forward, shedding rock and sand.

Olivia pulled free of Putty and raced across the chamber, ducking beneath the dragon.

"Come back!" I shouted, but she wasn't listening.

As the excavator crashed down, Olivia reached Freddie and pulled him back. Dust engulfed the pair of them. Mama screamed. I held Putty tight to stop her chasing after our sister.

I saw Sir Titus in the cab of the machine, safe behind thick glass. His face was twisted into a bloodstained sneer. A moment later, Olivia emerged from the dust, dragging the unconscious Freddie behind her. They were matted in red dust, and even from here, I could see the trail of blood on Freddie's forehead.

The blades of Sir Titus's machine crunched through the wall beside the stairs. Where they cut the traceries of light, brightness flared briefly. The veins of light dimmed and faded across that whole wall.

"He's destroying it," Putty wailed.

The excavator lurched down the wide steps, scattering the statues, and blundered into a delicate-looking mechanism made of hundreds of connected brass rods and balls. The mechanism crumpled like paper. Beside me, Papa staggered to his feet, reaching out his hands imploringly.

I didn't care if Sir Titus destroyed everything in the tomb. If it hadn't been for this tomb, none of this would have happened.

But if Sir Titus got the gigantic, steam-powered excavator fully into the chamber, there would be nowhere we could hide. His men would pour in behind him. They would kill us. Freddie was unconscious. There was no one else to stop Sir Titus.

"Stay here!" I yelled above the crashing noise.

I cut to the left, skirting the chamber, hoping the chaos of dust, sand, steam, and smoke would hide me. Strange contraptions of brass loomed over me: twisting pipes, dials, tiny mirrors, spindles, fine wires.

The excavator reached the bottom of the stairs. Its blades shrieked across the floor, then it jolted level again. Its tracks clawed on the stone and it lumbered into the chamber. Olivia was still dragging Freddie toward the dragon. Freddie was starting to come around, but now that the excavator had found a level floor, it sped up. Its heavy tracks ground forward just in front of me. Stone cracked beneath its weight. I leaped for the machine. My hand caught a rung, and I swung myself up, over the grinding tracks.

Sir Titus still hadn't noticed me. He was leaning against the glass, trying to force his machine on faster. I felt the thrum of the boiler, smelled the red-hot metal and over-heated oil—bitter, like burning rubber—and heard the pistons juddering inside.

The cab was enclosed, with a heavy glass windshield at the front, covered in a thick iron grille, and smaller glass windows at the side. I pulled the door open and swung myself in.

The cabin was no more than six feet square. Two seats faced the front windshield. Sir Titus swiveled as I entered. He released a lever and swung a fist at me. I ducked, and the excavator lurched to the side, knocking us both off balance. I fell to the floor. Sir Titus turned quickly back to his controls, straightening the machine. As I scrambled to my feet, he jerked both levers sharply up, locking them in place.

"Now, boy," he said, rising, "it's time to put an end to your interference."

He pulled out a long knife. I grabbed his arm with both hands, wrapping myself around it and pulling. He twisted, then tripped, and came tumbling over his seat.

His shoulder caught the edge of my chest, smashing me into the floor. Something snapped inside. I tried to breathe. It felt like I was sucking in fire. I gasped, and that hurt even more. I kept hold of Sir Titus's arm.

He regained his feet, dragging me with him. He drew his fist back and hammered it right into my face. For a second, everything went black. Then I was falling, back over the seat. My head smacked off the windshield. I slumped, upside down, on the driver's seat. Everything around me was a haze of red. I could hardly see. I scrabbled to pull myself up, but it hurt too much. My arms and legs had lost all their strength.

Sir Titus loomed above me. He raised his knife.

"Your stupid family has been a curse to me ever since your mother lost her inheritance," Sir Titus spat. "I'm going to enjoy this, boy. I'm going to enjoy it very much."

I tried to tumble off the seat, but my legs were still hooked over the back, and I was too weak. There was no escape. I looked around desperately.

"It's time, boy," Sir Titus said. "Do me a favor." He smiled. "Die screaming."

My head rocked back. I didn't want to see it. I couldn't bear to. I had failed everyone. I was supposed to save my family. I couldn't even save myself.

My head smacked into something. I almost closed my eyes, but I wouldn't give in like that. I turned my face.

There was a red handle just below me. I blinked. A pressure release valve for the excavator's steam engine. I pulled the handle.

The steam vented from the boiler with a shriek that ripped through the chamber. The excavator's tracks stopped abruptly and it came to a sudden halt. Sir Titus was thrown forward. He put out a hand to support himself, but it slid off the smooth windshield. He crashed down onto the dashboard above me.

He stiffened with a strange, wet cough. His body went limp and he rolled to the side, slipping to the floor between the seats. I pushed free of the chair and slumped to my knees.

Sir Titus had fallen onto his own knife. The hilt and half

the blade jutted from his chest; the rest was hidden inside him.

"You've killed me, boy," he whispered.

Directly above, staring down at us through the windshield, was the head of the preserved dragon.

— 23 —

The Secret of the Dragon Tomb

The cabin door behind me banged open, and Freddie clambered in. I pushed away from the still-gasping Sir Titus. Freddie looked as bad as I felt. Blood trickled from his forehead, through the thick red Martian dust, all the way to his collar.

"Thank God," he said. "You're alive, Edward."

"And Olivia?" I asked.

"She saved me," Freddie said. "And you saved us all." He cleared his throat. "Your sister's remarkable, isn't she? Olivia, I mean. Not that your other sisters aren't, that is, but . . ."

"She is," I said, and I meant it.

"Thank you," he said, rather oddly. I wondered how badly he'd been hit on the head.

Sir Titus stared at Freddie, his eyes filled with hate. "So, you win. I am dying."

Freddie glanced at him. "Don't be ridiculous. The knife missed your heart. You'll live to face justice." He turned to me. "Edward, could you send Olivia up? I'll need her help to bind Sir Titus's wound. We'll tie him up and leave him here for now. This will make a good cell."

"What about Sir Titus's men?" I said.

"They fled. I don't think they liked how willing Sir Titus was to let them die."

Putty and Olivia were waiting for me outside the excavator. Putty was almost dancing from foot to foot. The moment I reached the ground, she threw herself on me.

I gasped in pain. "My ribs . . ."

Putty let go. "I thought you were killed! Now you've broken your ribs and you won't be good for anything. You're really going to have to let me teach you how to fight."

"Is it over?" Olivia whispered.

"Yes," I said. She nodded, but for some reason, she didn't look pleased about it.

"Freddie wants you up there," I said, and suddenly she looked happy. She hurried past and scrambled up the side of the machine.

"Olivia's acting rather peculiar, don't you think?" I said to Putty.

Putty looked at me with pity. "You are dense, Edward." Then she seemed to remember something. She grabbed my hand. "This way!"

I hobbled after her, completely mystified now. She led me

past the dragon, right to the back of the chamber. Between two machines was a second, much smaller sarcophagus, maybe a yard long. Just large enough for a baby. It wasn't inlaid like the dead emperor's coffin. It appeared to be made of sandstone, with a single cylindrical hole in one end.

"Putty," I said, "I don't think we should . . ." But she was already sliding back the lid.

There wasn't a baby inside. There weren't even bones. Instead, there was a single, large egg, twice the size of my head. It was covered in what looked like scales, but age had dulled them. Once, they might have glistened like water.

"What is it?" I said.

"A dragon's egg!" Putty said. "Maybe when they buried the emperor, they didn't just bury his dragon with him, they buried her egg."

I frowned. "That's . . . cruel."

Putty looked sober for a second, but she couldn't keep it up. "But isn't it exciting? I've never even heard of anyone having a dragon's egg before." Her face fell. "I suppose they'll take it and put it in that museum, even though we found it. That's not fair, is it? Can we keep it?"

I smiled at her. "We'll ask Freddie."

Freddie and Olivia had climbed down from the excavator and were waiting with Mama and Jane at the front of the tomb. Papa stood to one side, peering intently at one of the strange devices and making notes on his shirtsleeve with a piece of charcoal.

"We're saved, Papa," I said.

"Ah . . . what's that?" He reached back and patted my arm. "Um. Good job, Edward." He peered closer at the device.

I sighed. What more did I expect? He never noticed what I did. I tried not to feel disappointed, but I couldn't help myself.

Then, remarkably, Papa turned from the mechanisms and peered at me through his smudged eyeglasses. "I mean it, Edward. You did well. Very well. I'm proud of you."

For some reason, my throat thickened. I had to blink away tears.

"Er . . . I don't suppose you have a pencil, do you?" he asked. "And some paper?"

I cleared my throat. "What will happen now?" I asked Freddie.

"The ambassador will send a team to excavate the tomb," Freddie said. "British Mars will share the rights to whatever's inside, as we were the ones to discover it. The devices will be analyzed. Most of them will be sent to the museum so that inventors like your father will be able to make use of them. Anything dangerous, any weapons, will be kept secret by the British Martian government."

"So many fascinating ideas and inventions," Papa said wistfully.

"I'll put in a word for you," Freddie said. "After all you did to discover the tomb, I'm sure they'll want your help to decipher the functions of the artifacts."

Papa beamed. "I could achieve so much here in Lunae City with a whole new dragon tomb. It is every mechanician's dream." He turned to Mama. "Don't you think, my dear?"

Mama drew herself up. "Lunae City?" she demanded. "How about Jane?"

Papa blinked. "I beg your pardon, my dear?"

"Must Jane find a husband in this . . . this desert? My daughter? Lord Cardale's first and most beautiful grand-daughter?"

I rolled my eyes.

Papa seemed to deflate slightly. "Jane will have her season, I promise you, with all the balls and parties she could wish for."

"Here?" Mama's voice rose several octaves. "A million miles from good society? A season with the urchins and vagabonds of the street, perhaps?"

Papa deflated further. "No, my dear. Um. In Tharsis City?"

Mama's eyes sparkled suddenly. "Ah! Tharsis! You'll love it, Jane. I'll show you the scenes of all my greatest triumphs. They called me the Crystal Rose of Tharsis, you know. Come. We must plan. It will be very grand."

"And very expensive," Olivia murmured.

"Can I keep the dragon's egg?" Putty interjected.

"An egg?" Freddie said. "Well, if it goes to the museum, they'll just cut it open." He smiled at her. "No, I think you can keep it as a souvenir, as long as you don't tell anyone about it."

"And you?" Olivia asked quietly. Her eyes were focused firmly on the floor.

"I . . ." Freddie wet his lips. His face grew determined. "I have to report to the British-Martian Intelligence Service, and take Sir Titus to Tharsis City to face justice. Then I must track down his partners in crime, Dr. Octavius Blood and Apprentice." He straightened. "I may be gone some months."

"Oh," Olivia whispered.

"Some months," Freddie repeated. "It is . . . Dash it all!" He glanced around at the rest of us, then turned back to Olivia. "There is something particular that I want to ask you, but I can't. It wouldn't be fair. I'll be gone too long. I can't expect you to—"

"Yes," Olivia said, and smiled. Even though she was covered in dirt and sand, she looked more beautiful than Jane at her finest.

Freddie blinked through his mask of red dust. "Ah—er—I—That is—*Yes?*"

"Yes," Olivia said. "Of course. Always."

They took each other's hands and grinned like idiots.

"I have no idea what you two are talking about," I said. Just like I had no idea why Mama and Jane burst into tears at that moment, or why Papa clapped Freddie on the shoulder.

I shook my head, while Putty grinned strangely up at me. Sometimes, I don't understand my family at all. But I wouldn't have them any other way.

I turned away from them to face the sunlight streaming

through the shattered entrance to the dragon tomb. So, we would stay here, in Lunae City, while Papa immersed himself in his wondrous discoveries, and Jane and Mama planned Jane's season in Tharsis City, and Putty found no end of trouble surrounded by dragon tombs. But for once, I wasn't worried. My family could look after themselves, far better than I ever would have guessed.

And as for me? Well, maybe there would be something here for me, too, something that wasn't just looking after my family. Somewhere, someone might even have the latest copy of *Thrilling Martian Tales*. It was time to find out.

The End

Acknowledgments

When you publish your first book, there are so many people who have helped you over the years that it's impossible to thank them all. From teachers to critique partners to those who have offered support and encouragement, the list would be absolutely endless. But you know who you are, and thank you! Every one of you has contributed something.

First and foremost I want to thank my wife, Stephanie Burgis, who read this book more times than anyone should ever have to and had something helpful to say every time. I couldn't have done this without you. I'd also like to thank those who critiqued various versions of the book: Tiffany Trent, Eugene Myers, Ari Goelman, Tricia Sullivan, Renee Sweet, and Nadia Williams. This book wouldn't be half as good without the dedication and insights of my agent, Jennifer Laughran, and my editor, Christy Ottaviano. Thanks to both of you. Thank you, too, to designer Eileen Savage, editorial assistant Jessica Anderson, and the rest of the team at Macmillan who work so hard behind the scenes. I am truly grateful for everything you do. Thank you (again!) to

Tiffany Trent, who was so enthusiastic about my first draft that she recommended me to her agent.

I probably learned more about being a writer at the Clarion West workshop than at any time before or since, so I'd like to give special thanks to my instructors Octavia Butler, Nalo Hopkinson, Bradley Denton, Connie Willis, Ellen Datlow, and Jack Womack, and a special shout-out to my incredibly talented classmates.

My high school English teacher, Mrs. Mapes, encouraged me to write when I had lots of enthusiasm but absolutely no talent. There should be more teachers like you.

I owe an enormous debt of gratitude to my parents-in-law, Kathy and Rich Burgis, for vast amounts of baby- and child-sitting when I wrote the second draft of this book. If they hadn't been there, I think I'd still be working on it.

My journey toward being a writer started when my dad, Adrian Samphire, read me *The Lord of the Rings* as a child, and it's been going on ever since. Thank you, Dad, for introducing me to that world, and to my mum, Beth Samphire, for being supportive, interested, and enthusiastic, even though I know these are not your kind of books! Thank you, too, to my brothers, Martin and Ben, for all your support.

And finally, I want to thank my two sons for their smiles and games, and for being so patient when I had to work on this. You inspire me to write books that I hope you will love.

GOFISH

QUESTIONS FOR THE AUTHOR

PATRICK SAMPHIRE

What sparked your imagination for *Secrets of the Dragon Tomb*?

The story came from a whole bunch of different things. Back when I was about fifteen, my dad bought me a book called *The Illustrated Book of Science Fiction Ideas & Dreams* by David Kyle. It was a history of science fiction right from its early days. What I most loved were the wonderful illustrations by Victorian artists, particularly the art by Albert Robida (look him up!). The work of these artists was amazingly inventive, imaginative, and full of fun ideas about the way the world would look in the future and about what alien planets might be like, and those images stayed with me. Much later on, I was watching a lot of Jane Austen adaptations with my wife, and it suddenly occurred to me that it would be incredible to combine Jane Austen's world and character types with the worlds and inventions of Robida and other early science fiction writers and artists. I added in the love I've always had for the Adventures of Tintin comic books, *Doctor Who*, and Indiana Jones. And that's how I came up with the characters and the Martian setting of *Secrets of the Dragon Tomb*.

Which of the Sullivans do you most relate to and why?
All my characters have some parts of me in them. I love Putty's quirkiness and Papa's distracted genius, and, of course, I would really love to be Cousin Freddie. But I think the character I most relate to is my hero, Edward. Other characters are funnier or more brilliant, but Edward *tries* and he's never going to give up no matter how bad things get. Without him, everything would fly apart.

What did you want to be when you grew up?
A writer. Yeah, I know it's a bit predictable. I thought about a bunch of other things—maybe a lawyer, maybe a physicist, maybe a teacher—but I could never actually imagine myself being any of those. Though I did end up as both a physicist and a teacher at various points, these were always pastimes while I was trying to become a writer. I never *loved* them.

When did you realize you wanted to be a writer?
My first attempt at seriously writing a book—one where I thought, *Yeah, I really want to get this published*—was when I was fourteen. I wrote it at school with a friend, and it was terrible. My English teacher, Mrs. Mapes, was incredibly supportive. She even let us sit out from some lessons so we could write, but the book was still terrible. Back then, I don't know if I thought I could be a writer as a career. I'd never met a writer, and I don't even know if I knew it was something you could do as a real job. By the time I was seventeen, though, I was absolutely determined to be a writer. It took me a long time, with quite a long break in the middle, but I got there!

What's your favorite childhood memory?
When I was four years old, my parents moved the family to Zambia (in Africa) where my dad had gotten a job as a teacher.

We spent four years in Zambia, and there were so many things I loved about living there. Not sure about a favorite memory, but I do remember that there was a mango tree on the school grounds, and I remember climbing it to pick fresh, ripe mangos. I don't think we were actually allowed to do that, but I've never had anything that tasted as good since.

As a young person, who did you look up to most?
About the same time I started writing I really got into music (listening, not playing; I have no musical talent at all). My first band-love was the heavy metal band Iron Maiden (they are still my favorite), and the person I most looked up to was bass player and founder Steve Harris. The band is enormously successful, and Harris drove them all the way, but he always came across as modest and approachable, never like a "star." I thought that was exactly the way you should act if you ever became famous. In fact, thinking about it now, he reminds me a lot of Edward in *Secrets of the Dragon Tomb*. Maybe he's who I modeled Edward on.

What was your favorite thing about school?
I liked school. I know a lot of people who hated every moment of school, but I didn't (apart from having to get up in the morning). I think my favorite thing was the role-playing games club that I set up with my friends. At lunchtime, we'd head off to a spare classroom, get out our dice and rule books, and start playing. Mostly we played Dungeons & Dragons, Call of Cthulhu, and Paranoia. Yeah, I was a geek.

What is your favorite word?
Obstreperous, because I've been feeling a bit obstreperous recently. In fact, I recommend that most people are obstreperous from time to time. It's good for you.

If you could live in any fictional world, what would it be?

Most fictional worlds are absolutely terrible! Your chances of being killed, kidnapped, or eaten alive by passing monsters are enormous. I would actually quite like visiting the world of *Secrets of the Dragon Tomb* just to see all the incredible inventions and weird alien creatures that you can find there. But if I had to live somewhere, I think it would be in the Culture of Iain M. Banks's science fiction novels. The Culture is as close to a utopia as it would be possible to reach. *And* there are giant spaceships.

What was your favorite book when you were a kid? Do you have a favorite book now?

My favorites as a kid were the series The Dark Is Rising by Susan Cooper, The Chronicles of Prydain by Lloyd Alexander, and *The Weirdstone of Brisingamen* by Alan Garner. There's something about that kind of fantasy that really grabs me. It did then, and it still does now. These days, my favorite book is *The Dragon with a Chocolate Heart* by Stephanie Burgis. It's a wonderful, warm fantasy story about family, chocolate, and dragons.

Do you ever get writer's block? What do you do to get back on track?

I don't know if I get writer's block as such. There are definitely long periods where I don't manage to write anything, particularly between projects, but it's not so much being blocked as just not having fully formed ideas yet. My books tend to have loads of things going on so I have to pull in lots of strands from all over to make it come together. Sometimes that can take months, and some days it's frustrating that I don't make any progress. The only way to get past it is just to sit down again the next day and keep trying. It always comes in the end. That's why I relate to Edward. Keep on trying, even when it feels like you're failing, and you'll succeed in the end.

What would your readers be most surprised to learn about you?

My family never had a television while I was growing up. Apart from a few movies or shows around Christmas at my grandparents' houses, I never watched anything. When people discussed shows at school, I had to pretend I knew what they were talking about so I wouldn't seem weird. It wasn't all bad, though. I got to read a lot more books than most people!

What can readers look forward to in *The Emperor of Mars*? No spoilers, please!

The Emperor of Mars is even more exciting than *Secrets of the Dragon Tomb*! More deadly danger, more thrilling escapes, more weird inventions, more strange creatures, and more fiendish plotting!

A missing Martian. A sinister plot. A French spy.
If Edward thinks life is going to be easy in
Lunae City, he is very, very wrong.

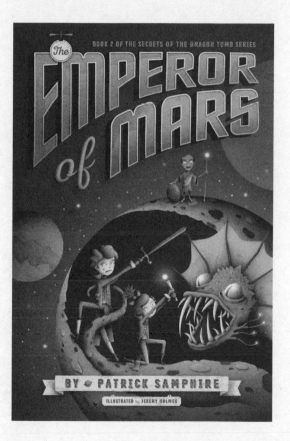

BOOK 2 OF THE SECRETS OF THE DRAGON TOMB SERIES

The EMPEROR of MARS

BY PATRICK SAMPHIRE

ILLUSTRATED by JEREMY HOLMES

Keep reading for
an excerpt.

The Trouble with Vine-Mining

Mars, 1817

I was twenty feet underground, surrounded by glowing blue sandfish crystals, with my head jammed in a beetle-vine warren, when I realized that vine-mining wasn't for me.

I had seen the notice pinned up outside the local office of the Imperial Martian Airship Company:

VOLUNTEERS NEEDED!

ROOT OUT BEETLE-VINES! SAVE LUNAE CITY!

SIGN UP TODAY!

BEFORE IT'S TOO LATE!

Perfect, I'd thought. *What a great idea.*

I had never been so wrong.

You might have thought that living in the middle of Mars's biggest desert would mean that you never got wet. You would have been wrong. Once a year, it rained for a solid month in the wilderness hundreds of miles upstream. The Martian Nile rose, and the river valley turned into a gigantic lake. The Inundation, they called it, and it was very, very wet indeed.

That would be all right if you didn't mind a bit of water. Or it would have been, if not for the beetle-vines. All year they had been burrowing away under Lunae City, sending out satellite clusters through their tunnels. When the Inundation arrived and water rushed into the tunnels, the beetle-vine clusters would erupt like fireworks made of multicolored toffee. The whole city would end up covered in bright, sticky string.

It was a crisis, but I was ready.

We'd been in Lunae City for eight months, and the truth was, I was bored. So when I'd seen the advertisement for vine-miners, I'd thought this was it: something fun to do at last.

I managed to believe that for almost half an hour. Then I found myself wedged upside down, dangling over a particularly ripe beetle-vine cluster, while sweat dripped onto the disgusting-smelling thing.

Water was what made the beetle-vine cluster think the Inundation had arrived, and here I was, dripping on it like a leaking pipe. I wondered what would happen if it exploded right in my face.

Beetle-vines were semidormant at night, so the mining

took place after dark. I'd had to wait until my entire family had gone to bed before I could sneak out. Now I was wishing I'd stayed in bed.

"What the devil are you doing?" a voice snapped out.

I twisted around and saw that a tall, thin man in a long, black coat had emerged from a side tunnel and was peering up at me through thick lenses. My shoulders were still jammed tight, so I indicated the beetle-vine cluster with my head.

"Trying to clear that out."

The man adjusted his lenses with a small lever set into the side of his glasses and squinted up at me again.

"And this is the way you propose to do it?" he demanded. "If you damage it, you'll drive it further underground, and then who will go after it, boy? You?"

"This wasn't exactly my plan," I muttered.

"Amateurs," the man said under his breath. He reached into one of his many bulging pockets and pulled out a small clockwork saw. "Don't move."

"Um, about that . . ." I said.

The man knelt beside the beetle-vine cluster and began cutting one of the tendrils that joined the satellite cluster to the other parts of the vine.

When I'd received my instructions, I'd been told that I would need to slice through every tendril before I touched the beetle-vine cluster itself.

Something crunched where my shoulder pressed into the

tunnel wall. Sand and fragments of sandfish crystal powdered down over my face.

"You might want to hurry," I said.

The man ignored me.

The sand shifted and I felt myself slide an inch down. I still couldn't move my arms. I scrabbled about with my fingers, but there was nothing to grab hold of.

"Seriously," I said.

"Please stop talking," the man said waspishly, without looking up. "I've a good mind to leave you hanging up there all night."

More sand trickled past my ear.

"Somehow I don't see that happening," I said.

The man straightened then moved around to the second tendril. In the pale blue glow of the sandfish crystals, I could see eight or nine tendrils snaking away into little tunnels.

I tried to slow my breathing so as not to dislodge any more sand. My left arm was itching like mad, and I was starting to feel dizzy from the blood going to my head.

Something gave way, and I dropped almost a foot before my arms jammed again.

"Keep still!" the man barked.

I bit back a reply. A knot of sandfish crystals pressed hard against my lips. If I spoke, they'd end up in my mouth.

The man stopped cutting to wind his clockwork saw. I wanted to scream.

"Use a knife!" I hissed through tight lips.

The man didn't bother to answer.

Sand slid against my arms. I pushed them outward to hold myself in place. Hard crystals pressed into my shoulders.

"Oh, God," I mumbled.

The sand crumbled. The sides of the tunnel gave way. With a yell, I dropped like a plunging crash-eagle.

I barely had time to get my arms in front of my face before I hit the beetle-vine cluster with a *splat!*

Sticky, stinking fluid sprayed across me. The smell was like rotting meat. I gagged and spat and clawed the stuff from my eyes.

"You imbecile!" the man screeched. "You useless, careless, dangerous imbecile!"

I pushed myself up just in time to see the vine tendrils whipping away into the tunnels, carrying fragments of the beetle-vine cluster with them. Within hours, each of them would have grown into a new beetle-vine cluster deep beneath the city.

"Get out!" he screamed, waving the clockwork saw at me with a shaking hand. "Get out, and never, ever come back!"

Aching, covered in reeking, gluey beetle-vine goo, I limped out of the tunnels and into the evening streets.

Vine-mining had turned out to be as big a disaster as everything else I'd tried here.

Eight months ago, I'd been caught up in the villainous Sir Titus Dane's scheme to rob a dragon tomb. It had taken an airship full of clockwork crabs, being lost in the Martian wilderness, and a terrifying fight against Sir Titus's minions in the middle of the desert for me to understand something important: most of the time, when they weren't being kidnapped or attacked by deadly hunting machines, my family could look after themselves. It didn't matter how terrible the disasters or how awful the scandals they got into, they could usually find a way out.

Which meant I didn't have to spend my entire life keeping them out of trouble.

On the other hand, I had absolutely no idea what to do with myself anymore. I was like a swarm of Martian slug flies, bouncing off walls and going nowhere.

Out here, surrounded by the tombs of the old Martian emperors and thousands of years of Martian history, it should have been like an adventure out of my favorite magazine, *Thrilling Martian Tales*. I should have been fighting off smugglers and tyrants, and uncovering amazing relics, just like Captain W. A. Masters, British-Martian spy, did in every issue. Instead, I'd been reduced to burrowing after beetle-vines in the middle of the night.

I was seriously thinking about canceling my subscription to *Thrilling Martian Tales*.

The desert chill had seeped into the city, leaving a thin layer of dew on the dusty streets. Years were twice as long on Mars as they were on Earth, and we were now well into the six-month Martian autumn. While the days were still baking hot, the nights often got cold. My clothes were soaked in beetle-vine sap and I was starting to shiver.

"Blasted beetle-vines," I muttered to myself. "Stupid city." Papa might be happy here with all his ancient artifacts to play with, but I'd had enough. More than enough.

I could just make out the sound of the Martian Nile lapping at the docks several streets away as I trudged through the city. Moored boats creaked on the water, and the faint, eerie songs of the native Martian sailors drifted through the night air. Maybe I should just get on one of those boats and go sailing away. I bet sailors never got bored.

The moons were high in the sky, wreathed in a faint mist, but still bright enough to light the cobbled street. I'd been told that Earth's moon was much larger and brighter than either of Mars's moons. That must be weird. I wondered if I'd ever get to see it.

I was still aching from falling into that beetle-vine cluster, and sandfish crystals had gotten into my socks and pantaloons. I glared at the moons, wondering exactly what they had to be so cheerful about.

And that was when I saw the fourth-floor window of Lady Harleston's enormous town house shoot up and a figure dressed all in black emerge, carrying a sack over one shoulder.

I didn't often go wandering about in Lunae City at night, but even I knew that this wasn't usual.

A rope uncoiled and snaked down the wall to end five yards short of the ground. Then the figure swung over the ledge and scrambled down.

I had lived long enough with my little sister, Putty, to see a disaster when it was coming straight at me, and I'd learned not to hesitate.

I launched myself forward just as the figure reached the end of the rope and lost their grip. Feet crashed into my outstretched arms, the sack hit my head, and we both collapsed to the hard road with an explosion of breath. The stranger leaped up and I stumbled after, still half tangled with their arms and legs.

"Are you . . . ?" I started, but I didn't have time to finish.

The figure whipped away the scarf that had been tied around their face and let long, brown hair fall free. I found myself looking up into a girl's dark eyes.

"Oh," I said, letting go quickly and stepping back. At a guess, she was about a year older than me, but she was much taller, and I could see she was part native Martian.

She looked completely furious.

"What do you think you're doing?" she demanded.

"What do I think *I'm* doing?" I spluttered. "What do you think *you're* doing?"

She looked at me like I was an idiot. "I'm escaping. What does it look like?"

I glanced over her shoulder at Lady Harleston's house. "Who are you escaping from?"